DARK HORSE

AN ASPEN FALLS NOVEL

MELISSA PEARL
ANNA CRUISE

http://www.melissapearlauthor.com
https://www.melissapearlauthor.com/page/anna-cruise/

Cover art (copyright) by Melissa Pearl
Photo by Nathan Dumlao on Unsplash

ACKNOWLEDGMENTS

Dark Horse is my favorite Aspen Falls novel so far, and I wouldn't feel that way if I didn't have some vital help from some very important people.

Anna, thank you for helping me get the mystery right. Lenore, thanks for helping me with the Richmond family dynamics.
Rachael, thanks for never missing a detail and being the most supportive assistant anyone could ask for.
Kristin and my amazing proofreading team, thank you for your eagle eyes.
My review team, thank you for loving this book as much as I do and supporting my work.

To my Songbirds & Playmakers, and all of my amazing readers. Thanks for stepping into the world of Aspen Falls. I hope you can find a home there the way Anna and I have.

To my beautiful family. Thank you for the loud, happy conversations around the dinner table.

And, of course, a big thank you to my Lord and savior, who rescued me and watches over me with His perfect love.

xx
Melissa

For my parents

Thanks for always having your priorities straight and giving me the most amazing life.
I love you guys.

PROLOGUE

THE GUN WENT off before Nate could react.

His hand brushed his holster just as the bullet hit him.

Sally screamed.

Her terror punched through his chest and ran straight down his body.

He wanted to reach her.

To protect her.

But he was falling. And there was nothing he could do to stop it.

"Nate!" she screamed once more, but the sound was cut short as his head smacked into something hard.

A bowling ball crashed through his brain, turning out lights until he disappeared into a black numbness.

Sally was gone.

And there was no way he could reach her.

1

5 weeks earlier...

Tuesday, April 24th
6:45pm

THE RICHMOND FAMILY DINNER. Nate's least favorite night of the month.

But it was a ritual that had yet to be broken in his three years with his girlfriend.

Sally came from a tight-knit family and every week, without fail, they got together for a family dinner. Whoever could make it showed up for a night of good-natured banter and interrupted conversation. They talked over each other, shared in-house jokes that had been running for years, and basically showed off, without even realizing it, how close they were.

Nate had agreed to try and make it at least once a month. He managed to find solid excuses to get out of all the other weeks. He would've tried to avoid every single one of them, but Sally's blue-gray eyes made it impossible. She could put on a pair of puppy dog eyes like no one else he knew…and because she didn't use them very often, they got him every single time.

Slowing his Harley Davidson to negotiate the corner, Nate drove them to the Richmond mansion.

It wasn't officially a mansion, but Nate always thought of it that way. It was palatial, with two open living spaces, a kitchen with shiny black countertops that practically sparkled, six bedrooms, and a polished granite-tile entrance that made the place feel more like a museum than a home.

Michael Richmond had accumulated his wealth in construction, starting small with high-end houses that couldn't be matched for quality. His business exploded at a time when the economy was rich and booming, and he soon shifted into property development, with a focus on building subdivisions, luxury apartments, and then branching off into hotels too. He now owned a nationwide real estate development company that made money from coast to coast. The guy could've retired at forty-five, when he moved his family to Aspen Falls, but he wasn't prepared to leave the business completely. Instead he set up a Richmond Construction office in Aspen Falls and left the running of the rest of his company to his trusted directors, whom he kept in close contact with online and through business trips. The move to the peaceful town of Aspen Falls was entirely to do with his family, and so he'd spent the last thirteen years improving the town, not just with homes, but with development projects that ran the gamut. Nate had to give the guy that. He cared about their little town, and most of the projects they'd worked on were for the benefit of the people, not his pockets.

The engine rumbled beneath Nate as he accelerated down the last stretch of road. It was a quiet, tree-lined street, and the Richmonds lived right at the end of the cul-de-sac. It was such a large property it was like their own little world, hidden behind wrought iron gates and a stone wall that protected them. From what, Nate was never sure, but he'd kept his mouth shut. He wasn't the most popular person in their lives, and he didn't want to make things harder for Sally.

Her arms were snaked tight around his torso. He'd never get sick of that feeling. Sally on his Harley was the sexiest thing on the planet. He loved her arms around him, the way she snuggled in and made him feel like the most important man in the world.

Decelerating, he cruised through the open gates and parked between Xavier's Audi and Annabelle's Mini Cooper. Sally's siblings knew how to buy 'em nice.

The most expensive thing he owned was his Harley, which he'd saved years for, finally treating himself on his twenty-fifth birthday. He was pretty sure Annabelle woke up one morning, decided she wanted a Mini Cooper, and so just went out and bought one.

Nate snickered and pulled off his helmet, glancing over his shoulder to catch Sally's smile. She had the world's best smile. It was like moonlight reflecting off a still lake, like fairy lights sparkling against an old barn wall. She fluffed her blonde locks back into place, winking at him as she placed the helmet behind her. He held her arm to steady her as she got off the bike, then leaned in to peck her glossy lips. How could he resist?

She made a sound of appreciation and draped her arms over his shoulders, deepening the kiss like she always did. Desire stirred in his belly, but was quickly tempered by a loud throat clearing from the front door.

"I see you brought your bike," Michael called to him. "Sally's car not good enough for you guys?"

Sally laughed and walked into his embrace. "Oh, please, Daddy. Nate's bike is way cooler than my car. It's a gorgeous, clear day. The weather's warming up. Of course we were bringing the bike."

Michael let the comment slide, but the sharp look he shot Nate over Sally's shoulder said it all. *I hate you driving my precious baby around on that thing!*

Nate looked to the ground, pocketing his keys and rallying himself for a night of silent disapproval. Her family had never really warmed to him. When Sally first brought him into their precious fold, reserved was the mildest way to describe their behavior. Time had only strengthened that feeling, turning it from reserved curiosity to tight-lipped resignation. He didn't know what he'd done to offend or annoy them, but he wasn't about to let Sally go just because they didn't like him.

As long as she was happy for him to stick around, then that's exactly what he'd do.

With his arm protectively around his daughter, Michael Richmond led her inside, Sally chatting about her work week. She'd just come off four back-to-back night shifts at the hospital and always had some decent stories to tell. Her father's pride bloomed to blinding as they left Nate standing in the driveway.

He wondered what that felt like—to have a parent's undivided attention. He hadn't had that feeling since he was five years old, and it was hard to remember.

"Hey, asshole." A firm hand slapped his shoulder before sauntering by.

Nate glared at the back of Xavier's head as Sally's little brother walked through the front door. The twenty-three-year-old, so desperate to be suave and charming like his father, glanced over his shoulder and shot Nate a half grin. He'd never pull it off. He may have owned the Richmond looks—fine, chiseled features, perfectly styled hair and expensive clothing—but the guy had too many clown-like tendencies to ever be as elegant as Michael. He sure as hell wanted to be, though. Nate didn't understand why. He liked Xavier. Out of the Richmond family, he was the most tolerant of Nate. Yes, he called him 'asshole' rather than using his real name, but it kind of felt like acceptance in some weird way.

Nate sighed and followed Xavier into the house. Taking off his boots, he lined them up next to the shoe rack and glanced at the Grant Wood painting on the wall—vibrant greens and rounded trees, which made him feel like he could step right into the countryside. It was an original. Xavier had proudly boasted that fact the day it arrived at the house for Yvonne's birthday two years earlier.

Sally screamed.

Nate jolted to attention, adrenaline coursing

through him as he subconsciously reached for the weapon that wasn't even attached to his belt. Thankfully no one saw his reaction. They were too busy laughing.

Nate padded to the living room archway in time to see Sally jumping into Emmett's arms. Her eldest brother was obviously home on leave. His muscly arms wrapped around Sally as he lifted her off the floor. She giggled against him and kissed his cheek.

"It's so good to see you! When did you get back?" She grinned up at him.

"This morning."

She slapped his arm playfully. "I can't believe you didn't tell me you were coming home!"

"It's only for a few weeks."

The smile on Sally's face dimmed. "You're doing another tour?"

"Not yet, but I'm due back at the base." The tall Marine kissed her forehead, then glanced across the room at Nate.

Nate raised his hand in a half wave, but the gesture wasn't reciprocated. With a resigned sigh, he spun toward the kitchen and found Yvonne Richmond wiping down the counter.

"Hello, Nate." She gave him a polite smile.

It wasn't what he wished for, but it was better than the silent looks of disapproval. Sometimes he wanted to scream in their faces, "What? What have I done wrong?"

But he didn't need to.

He already knew the answer.

To them, he would never be good enough for their precious Sally.

He understood.

She was pure gold. No one would ever be good enough for her, but she'd chosen him and whether it was selfish or not, he wasn't about to let her go.

"So, you're not working today?" Yvonne pulled a beer from the fridge and popped the cap.

He took the cold bottle with a grateful smile. "Nope. All is quiet."

"Well, that's good. Let's hope it stays that way." Her tight expression told him there was more to the comment. She was silently trying to convey something, but he couldn't figure it out.

Did they hate that he was a cop? Was that it?

Did he not work hard enough for their liking?

Gritting his teeth, he looked away and took a swig of beer, unable to help glancing at the clock on the wall. Only three hours to go.

"Hey, baby." Sally's arm glided around his waist. He encircled her shoulders and pulled her close. It was the most natural thing in the world. Resting his lips on the top of her head, he breathed her in and reminded himself why he put up with all of the Richmond bullshit.

Because he loved Sally.

Because she was the best thing that had happened to him since his mother was taken.

As his girlfriend started a speed-talking chat with her mother, Nate thought back to his own beautiful mom. She was like a warm breeze in the summer—both a relief and a comfort. Something to make him smile no matter what mood he was in.

He could remember the way his hand felt nestled inside hers. She'd squeeze it as they walked, singing him silly songs and encouraging him to join in. He'd start to jump over cracks in the pavement, and she would too.

"If you step on a crack, you marry a rat." She'd giggle when he said that, and then turn the phrase into a song.

She was fun and light and laughter.

And then she was dead.

It only took thirty seconds.

They were skipping across the zebra crossing, jumping from one white line to the next when the car came out of nowhere.

She squeezed his hand.

She gasped.

Then he was shoved forward.

He would never forget the sting of the concrete

scraping his hands and knees. The sound of crunching glass.

He spun back, trying to figure out what was going on, and stared in horror as his mother's body flew through the air. She landed like a boneless rag doll, her legs and arms at funny angles.

"Mommy?" He crawled to her, unaware of the people rushing out of stores to help them. "Mommy!"

Her head was covered with blood. It smeared her porcelain skin and soaked into her golden hair. She stared up at the blue sky, refusing to look at him when he cried her name and shook her. Blood trickled down her cheeks—metallic red tears that marred her perfect face. Her skull was dented at the top. As he lifted her head and laid it on his lap, he squinted down the street, trying to see the black car that had taken his mommy away.

But it was gone.

She was gone.

And his life was over.

2

Tuesday, April 24th
7:05pm

NATE HAD that faraway look in his eyes again.

Her lost boy.

Sally squeezed his middle, trying to pull him out of it. His expression made her want to cry.

He never spoke about what he was thinking, but she was pretty sure when he looked like that, his mom's death was running through his mind. Sally had lain next to him when he dreamed. She'd heard his murmured whispers.

Although it had been twenty-six years ago, Nate had never gotten over his mother's death.

Clearing her throat, Sally nudged Nate with her hip until he blinked and looked down at her. She smiled and winked at him, which made his lips twitch the way they always did around her.

She loved their secret smiles and magnetic connection.

She'd felt it the first time she met him. He'd been standing in the ER waiting room, scribbling messy notes on his pad, working a case. Someone had been brought in after a vicious assault, and he was in the process of interviewing the victim's family, trying to solve the case as quickly as possible. It was always his way. He hated injustice more than anything, and finding criminals drove him in a way that even she didn't understand.

He'd been so intense, listening to the traumatized family as they waited for news of their precious son. His voice had been soft and even, applying just the right amount of pressure to get the answers he needed.

Sally had stood transfixed, falling hard before she even knew his name.

Her family never understood it. They'd never fully welcomed Nate into the fold, always wary of the man of few words who wore a frown more than a smile. They didn't get what Sally saw in him, and she'd given up trying to explain. Maybe because it just got too damn hard.

It didn't help that Nate always found work excuses to get out of "family time." It didn't help that Nate found work excuses to get out of everything.

The knot in her chest tightened and she blinked to hide her frustration.

She didn't want her family knowing how lonely the days could be. How she didn't know what to say to Nate to make him understand that she missed him, that she wanted to be more important than his work.

Her parents and siblings didn't need any more reasons not to like her brooding boyfriend.

"Should we go sit in the living room?" Sally tugged on Nate's waist to lead him out of the kitchen.

"I don't know," he murmured. "Will your brother try to kill me with one of his death rays?"

Sally giggled. "Oh, come on. Just ignore him."

It was easier said than done. Emmett was a large, imposing force, which was what made him such a good Marine. The funny thing was, he and Nate were more alike than either of them would admit. They were both quiet, motivated by justice and very protective of the people they loved.

If only they could see it.

Nate reluctantly followed Sally to the living room, giving Emmett and Xavier a tight smile before sitting in the corner of the couch. Annabelle placed a plate of pre-dinner snacks on the coffee table and gave Nate a demure smile before tucking the skirt beneath her legs and sitting down.

Xavier and Emmett were battling it out in a game of verbal banter. Sally shared a grin with Annabelle and sat down to enjoy the show. Threading her fingers through Nate's, she tried to get a word in edgewise but she didn't know enough about *Warcraft* to have any input. That was the one area her brothers played well in—video games.

"Forever boys," Annabelle mouthed and rolled her eyes.

Sally giggled and stole a glance at Nate. He was watching the brothers, scratching the edge of his mouth and looking thoroughly left out. She wanted to nudge him, to encourage him to join in the conversation, but she knew deep down that her brothers would never make room for him.

It freaking hurt, but she didn't know how to fix it.

Besides, Nate wasn't into gaming.

The doorbell rang and Sally shot her sister a quizzical look.

"I don't know." Annabelle shrugged while Xavier groaned and tipped his head back.

Annabelle and Sally let out identical laughs before asking, "What?"

"It's gonna be…"

"Oscar!" Their father's voice was loud and cheerful as he greeted the guest.

"Oscar! What is this, Surprise Sally Night?" She grinned, just as her father walked into the living room with his arm around a good-looking man dressed in a charcoal suit and tie. He was tall, elegant and lean—like a slightly older version of Xavier with dark, styled hair and clean-shaven cheeks.

Oscar Plymouth was one of her dad's favorite employees. He'd been working at the Chicago office for the past two years, and often flew in to visit the Richmonds. Being from England, he had no other family nearby, and her father had taken it upon himself to look out for the guy. It wasn't a hard task. Having been raised in a British boarding school, Oscar had the manners of a prince. He was sweet, charming, intelligent and easy to love.

Which was exactly what the Richmond family had done—loved him, welcomed him, practically turned him into one of their own.

"Hey!" Sally jumped up to give him a hug. "It's so nice to see you. I didn't know you were in town."

Oscar lightly pecked her cheek, then acknowledged Nate with a grin. "Great to see you here."

"Thanks, man." Nate nodded, his lips rising into a half smile. "You in town for the whole week?"

"Actually," Michael patted Oscar's chest and the younger man grinned, "Oscar's moving here. He's going to help oversee the Richmond Apartments project near the college."

The smooth Englishman laughed at Sally's expression and glided a hand down her back. "I thought your father would've told you guys. Xavier knows." He pointed to Sally's younger brother.

Sally glanced across the room. Xavier had been gunning for that project. It had practically been his idea. Richmond Construction had already built one big apartment complex near the community college to provide affordable housing for students, but with AFCC expanding its course offerings, enrollment was up and there was need for more, especially larger units that could accommodate young families or multiple roommates.

Xavier would have assumed the project manager role was his, especially since he had played such a huge part in getting it off the ground. The poor guy had been desperate for any and all kinds of responsibility since leaving high school, but his father kept pushing him aside, blaming immaturity. Last time they'd had a drink together, Xavier had been sure that this would be the year their father would finally give him a more important role in the company.

But no such luck.

"Wow." Annabelle raised her manicured eyebrows. "Big project."

"Oh yes indeed. It's a little overwhelming, but

your father has great faith in me." Oscar slid his hands smoothly into his pockets and winked at Sally before looking to Xavier. "I think Xave and I will make a great team."

"You're on the project?" Sally's voice rose with excitement.

"Yeah." Xavier gave her a tight, plastic smile. "I'm assisting. I guess you could call me Oscar's wingman."

Their father boomed with laughter, no doubt trying to kill any tension, and Sally's mother swooped in to peck Oscar on the cheek and ask him what he'd like to drink.

"Please, take a seat. Annabelle, move over." Sally's mother gave Oscar's arm an excited squeeze. "Why don't you catch them up on where you'll be living? I'm sure we'll all want to stop by and see your little place."

"Of course. You're all welcome." Oscar's gaze glided around the room, including Nate in his invitation.

Sally's chest expanded with relief. Oscar had always been so nice to Nate. Having him in town for a while would be great. Maybe he could lighten up the rest of her family.

Oscar beamed her a smile, unbuttoning his jacket as he took a seat next to Annabelle and asked how her salon business was going.

Sally reached for her wineglass and quietly sipped it while conversation ebbed and flowed around her. She pitched in when appropriate and laughed when the jokes started flying. Even Nate got in on the action, grinning beside her when Oscar started sharing a work mishap that captivated the entire family.

Yes, having Oscar in town for a while was a very good thing.

3

Tuesday, April 24th
8:15pm

HAVING Oscar around definitely eased the tension. Nate grinned as the guy's story bloomed with hilarity, then ended with a good laugh. Almost immediately, he started up another. Nate sat forward and grabbed a slice of cheese off the platter. He didn't usually like reaching for food or drawing attention to himself, but everyone was focused on Oscar and wanting to catch up on the big move from Chicago. He played it down, because that was Oscar's way. He never could acknowledge how accomplished or capable he was. Humility all the way. Nate really liked that about him.

Draping his arm over Sally's shoulders, Nate

pulled her a little closer, loving the way she snuggled in. They fit together like a jigsaw puzzle. It hadn't taken him long to figure out how amazing she was.

That was why he'd kept finding excuses to pop into the hospital whenever he could.

Routine questioning could usually be conducted by police officers, but he would often take the job just so he could bump into her.

They were dating within a few weeks of meeting, and they moved in together before the year's end. Her family had hated him for it, but Sally could be quietly stubborn when she really wanted something. Her family had had no choice but to go along with her decision. But to them, Nate would always be the unapproved outsider—the man who they never quite trusted to take good enough care of their Sally.

He glanced up and caught Emmett's stink eye.

You better be looking after my little sister, you punk.

Nate gave him a tight smile, but refused to remove his arm from around Sally. He wouldn't be put off by the towering Marine. Even if the guy could flatten him in a heartbeat. He was like a freaking WWE wrestler, and the complete opposite of his slight younger brother, Xavier. The family really were chalk and cheese in their appearances. Sally and Emmett had golden blond curls with a slightly rugged edge, whereas Xavier and Annabelle took after their mother—dark eyebrows, chiseled features, dark hair. They looked like supermodels.

Family genes always fascinated Nate. He didn't look much like his younger half-brother, Blaine. The guy had taken after his mother. Nate's insides curdled as he thought of the woman who had infiltrated their home so quickly after his mom had died. She'd brought her son, Silas the Evil, with her as well, and made Nate's life a living hell. She hadn't abused him; she'd just ignored him, acted like he wasn't part of the family. And she'd pulled his depressed, unwitting father right along with her.

It was almost a slap in the face that the year Nate finally got free of her, she actually abandoned Blaine and Dad, taking Silas back to Los Angeles where they'd originally come from.

He'd never seen them again, and he was no poorer for it.

"So, after that, the Chicago office was no doubt happy to see the back of me," Oscar finished.

Everyone cracked up laughing while Michael shook his head. "You're allowed to forget to pay a contractor. It was an innocent mistake."

Oscar cringed. "One I shall never make again."

"Hey, you handled the resolution beautifully." Michael pointed at him. "There aren't many guys out there who can talk big Tommy Filmore out of charging us an extra twenty percent in late fees."

"Yes, well I value my head. I'd quite like to keep it attached to my body if possible."

"I wouldn't have taken it." Michael chuckled. "*This* time..."

Oscar grinned. Xavier watched him, his jaw working back and forth before he downed his wine in one large gulp.

"Thank you for that," Oscar said, his grin still wide. He raised his glass of Chardonnay in the air. "To no more mistakes. And to a new venture, a great boss, and the nicest family in America."

"Cheers." Yvonne laughed and clinked her glass with his. "It's going to be so wonderful having you around."

"Thank you." His smile was bright as he accepted words that Nate had never heard...and would probably never hear, no matter how long he stayed with Sally.

He didn't begrudge Oscar, he just wished he could be included as well.

It riled him.

Not because he needed their approval, but because it hurt Sally. And that sucked.

Why should she have to fight on his behalf? What was it about him that they hated so much?

His insides churned with annoyance. He could feel it growing in his belly and scratching at his throat.

Gritting his teeth, he stood from the couch and excused himself to the bathroom.

People barely noticed. Except Emmett. He noticed everything.

Nate's nostrils flared as he strode away from the family who would never accept him.

Closing the bathroom door, he grimaced into the mirror. He rested his hands on the vanity and stared at himself. Was it his fault? Should he be making more of an effort?

Scratching the short blond scruff on his chin and cheeks, he eyed his worn leather jacket and faded jeans.

Should he be wearing a suit to these occasions? It was bad enough having to wear them to work, but Oscar sure made it look easy.

Should he be waxing eloquent the way the Englishman did? If Nate tried it, it'd no doubt come off as total bullshit.

Sally loved him the way he was. He shouldn't have to shave every freaking day or wear expensive-smelling cologne just to please her family.

With a thick swallow, he thought ahead to Sally's birthday. It was her twenty-fifth, and she'd wanted to throw a big party with her family. The idea had turned his stomach and he'd selfishly convinced her to have an intimate dinner with him instead.

He had to make it special.

And he knew exactly how.

But…

"Knock, knock." Sally tapped on the door and let herself in. Her smile was bright and beautiful as she closed the door behind her and leaned against the wood. "I didn't think you needed to pee."

He cleared his throat and ran a hand through his fine hair.

"Why are you hiding out in here? Is Emmett giving you his dreaded stink eye?"

Nate snorted, capturing Sally against him as soon as she was close enough. He trailed his hands down her familiar curves and gently squeezed her butt. He loved it when she wore her black skinny jeans.

"I can handle your brother's stink eye." He pecked her lips and relished the taste of her strawberry lip gloss.

Leaning back, he licked the flavor off his lips and gazed down at her.

She was so incredibly beautiful—inside and out.

Walking her fingers from his chest to his collarbone, she gave him a playful smile. "You know if you hide out in here too long, my family will think you have gastro issues."

Nate chuckled and raised his eyebrows. "Hey, that'd mean I was sick and you'd have to take me home and nurse me back to health."

"Don't even think about it." She slapped his chest.

"How can my family fall in love with you if you don't spend any time with them?"

"Come on, Sal. They've already made up their minds about me."

"They don't see what I see." She brushed her fingers through his hair, her eyes drinking him in like he was the most important person in the world.

He kissed her—deep and hungry—until she released a moan of pleasure. He loved that sound, and he trailed his lips down her neck to try and coax out another.

She giggled when he hit a ticklish spot and he captured her smile. She tasted delicious, stirring his desire and making his brain jump ahead to when they left. He'd drive like the wind to get her to bed, and then take it slow, peeling off each layer of clothing until she was a naked goddess beneath him, on top of him...whatever way she wanted to be. His blood stirred as he heard her cries of pleasure echoing in the back of his mind.

And then his phone dinged.

He immediately pulled out of the kiss and dug the phone from his pocket.

"Cam," he murmured while reading the message. "Car accident near the college."

"Can't she deal with that?"

He slipped the phone away and shook his head.

"The driver was in possession of heroin. It might link to the case she's been working on."

"Exactly. The case *she's* been working on. This is why the AFPD have two detectives, so that when you're off duty, she's on. You know what I mean? Like she can handle it without you." Her pointed look was kind of cute.

Nate cupped her cheek and smiled. "You know it doesn't work that way, babe."

"It could." She crossed her arms and inched away from him. "You two just like to work together all the time."

His eyes narrowed. Was she jealous?

"We make a good team. A good *work* team, but that's it. You know that, right?"

She looked away, dropping her gaze so she was staring at the floor. She gave a slight nod.

"Sally, baby." He gently lifted her head so he could look into her eyes. "You're the only woman for me."

Her smile was halfhearted as she struggled to hide her disappointment. "I know. I just hate that work always gets in the way."

"It's my job. I've got to catch these bad guys."

"But there will always be more."

"I know." He shrugged. "That's why I work so damn hard."

She pulled in a breath and nodded, the corners of her mouth turning up just a little. Her blue-gray eyes glimmered with pride, then faltered with a look of sadness. She glanced at the floor and whispered, "I guess you better go, then."

He cupped her cheeks, gently forcing her gaze back up to his. "I'll make it up to you. We've got your birthday coming up. It's gonna be a good night. I'm going to make it perfect."

Her smile turned genuine. "You better. I'm forfeiting a party for you."

"Believe me. It'll be worth it."

Oh man, he had to mean that. Twenty-five was a big milestone for the Richmond family. It was the day they scored a chunk of their inheritance. If they'd graduated college and proven a sound work ethic, then Michael and Yvonne would give them a nice sum of money to put toward something big. Annabelle had poured hers into starting up a business. Nate had no idea what Emmett had done with his, but Sally planned on paying off their bungalow in full so they didn't have to worry about a mortgage anymore. They'd also discussed her investing the rest, so she'd have a pretty sweet nest egg when retirement rolled around. She'd be set for life.

Nate kissed her smile and knew exactly what he needed to do to make her birthday the most important one she'd ever had. A nervous excitement fluttered through him as he thought ahead. He'd been toying with the idea for months, and he couldn't even explain what was holding him back. But he'd be a fool to deny it. He wanted to give Sally the perfect birthday present, and he had three days to prepare. He could do it.

His phone dinged again and he checked the screen.

What's your ETA?

He quickly replied, then glanced down at Sally. "You good for a ride home?"

"Yeah, someone will drop me."

"Okay. Can you give my apologies to the family?"

She nodded but didn't say anything.

"Have fun with Prince Oscar, Grumpy Xave and Stink Eye Emmett." He winked, which made her smile as she pushed him out the door.

He wasn't going to bother saying goodbye to anyone—they'd probably be pleased he was leaving, and he didn't want to see the poorly hidden relief on their faces—but then Oscar caught him putting his shoes on.

"Leaving so soon?" He grinned.

Nate looked up from tying his laces. "Yeah, actually. Work's calling."

"Oh dear. Nothing too bad, I hope." Oscar cringed.

"Nah, just a little drug case. Nothing we can't handle." Nate stood tall and dug the keys out of his pocket.

"I'm sorry you have to go early."

"I'm sure no one else is," Nate muttered under his breath, but Oscar heard him anyway.

The guy snickered and shook his head. "Well, I am...and I'm sure Sally is too."

Nate grimaced.

"Hey, don't worry about it." Oscar brushed his hand through the air. "Your work is important, and it's not like you can predict when criminals are going to do something stupid. I understand. And again, I'm sure Sally does too."

Nate gave him a grateful smile and turned for the door, but then quickly spun back around. "Oh hey, man, do you think you could do me a favor?"

"Absolutely."

"Could you give Sally a ride home after dinner?"

Oscar smiled and nodded. "It'd be my pleasure. You go work and don't worry about a thing. I'll get her home safely."

"Thank you." And he really was grateful. If he'd bumped into anyone else while he was trying to sneak out the door, he'd be leaving under a black cloud. But Oscar got it…and he'd take care of Sally for him too.

At least he had one ally in the Richmond world.

He slipped out and ran for his Harley, excited by the thought of work. It was always a thrill. And Oscar was right—his work was important. Catching bad guys made Nate's life worthwhile. If he wasn't a detective, he'd be nothing but useless.

4

Friday, April 27th
5:15pm

THE LITTLE BOY'S wails flooded the emergency room.

"It's okay, Joshie. Everything's going to be okay." His mother's voice trembled, her fear stark on her face as she ran into the emergency room, cradling her son in a towel.

Sally, who happened to be standing at reception, rushed around the counter to examine the child.

"He fell through the window," the mother said. "I don't even know how it happened, but there's blood. It's everywhere. There's glass. There's so much glass."

Sally checked the boy's vitals, peeling away the blanket to check out the wounds while the receptionist alerted the doctor. The cuts were nasty, but superficial. The boy would live.

"Do you have insurance, honey?" The receptionist started clicking away at the keyboard, setting up a patient record.

"Y-yes," the flustered mother stammered. "I have my card in my wallet. I..."

"Let's get you set up in a cubicle first, and then you can come back and fill in the paperwork." Sally smiled kindly and led the panicked duo to the first available cubicle. She directed the mother to place her child down and glanced at Janelle as she walked in with a clipboard and pen. She passed it to the mother and headed back out to reception. The woman held the pen like she'd forgotten how to write.

Sally smiled down at the boy while pulling on a pair of surgical gloves. "What's your name, sweetie?"

His hiccupping sobs made it hard for him to talk, so the mother responded. "Joshua. His name's Josh."

"Hey, Josh." Sally kept her voice light and friendly. "I know you're really scared right now, but everything's going to be okay. The doctor's gonna come and check you out, stitch you up, and you'll be home in time for bed, okay?"

"Really?" The mother sagged with relief, tears spilling over her bottom lashes.

"He's going to be just fine. You don't need to

worry." Sally started prepping the equipment, and the tray of sterilized instruments was ready to go as soon as Dr. Spurgess appeared from behind the curtain.

"So, what do we have here?" he asked in his soft, calm way.

Sally explained what she'd observed but knew he'd be making his own judgment after assessing the child. He asked the mother a list of standard questions as he quietly got to work.

He was an older man who had been looking after the residents of Aspen Falls for the last ten years. The younger doctors looked up to him, and all the nurses adored him because he was such a sweetheart. Quiet-spoken and never flustered, he was perfect for ER.

Sally assisted until each wound had been cleared of glass, properly cleaned and stitched up.

Once the boy had gotten over his fear and knew he wasn't dying, he calmed down and was a brave soldier throughout the process. It took a lot of coaxing to keep him that way, and by the time Sally pulled off her gloves and got cleaned up, she was exhausted.

Glancing at the clock, a relieved smile brushed her lips. Home time.

She didn't bother getting changed before leaving the hospital. Her pale blue scrubs would need soaking, but she'd strip them off as soon as she got home and jumped into a hot shower.

The thought made her pick up her pace.

"Happy birthday, Sal," Robert called across the parking lot as he arrived for his orderly shift.

"Thank you." She waved back.

"Sally Marie Richmond!" someone barked.

Sally spun to see what the problem was and immediately burst into laughter.

One of her best friends, Lena, dashed around cars, waving frantically. "You are not leaving without your birthday hug."

Sally spread her arms wide and caught the girl she'd known since high school. They'd gone to nursing school together and had been tight since ninth grade.

"I love you," Sally murmured into Lena's dark hair.

"*Te amo, mi amiga.*" Lena stepped back and smiled at her. "*Mi hermana.*"

Sally loved it when Lena called her 'sister.' Although Sally came from a close-knit family and already had amazing siblings, she definitely had room in her heart for her three high school besties. They were family too.

Lena was one of her favorite people. They played soccer together on a social team, worked together, had drinks together every week. She never got sick of the spunky Latina woman.

"Now you make sure Nate gives you the night of your life." Lena pointed at Sally. "I don't want to hear some lame story of you watching a movie in your pajamas."

Sally grinned. "He told me to wear something nice."

"Well, that's good." Lena tipped her head to the side, her dark brown eyes glistening. "He better deliver, Sal. You deserve the best, because you are the best."

"I have the best."

Lena's expression told her she wasn't buying it. Sally had obviously moaned too many times about Nate's constant working and the fact that she often felt like an afterthought.

"It's gonna be great," Sally assured her. "You'll see. I'll be back tomorrow with all the juicy details."

"You better. I want to hear every single one of them. Even the dirty ones."

Sally snorted and shook her head. "Goodbye, Lena. Behave yourself tonight."

"You know I won't," she singsonged, tinkling her fingers as she spun and walked away.

Sally giggled and sent up a quick prayer on Lena's behalf. She always did.

Sliding into her car, she started it up and grinned,

already calculating how long it'd take to get home and showered. Nate said to be ready by seven, which wouldn't be a problem. Having to share a bathroom with Annabelle had taught her how to be fast. She could be showered, dressed and polished in twenty minutes if she had to.

Knowing Nate, he'd be a few minutes late, so she'd linger under the hot spray and take her time getting ready.

She'd earned it.

Working in the ER was intense. Some shifts were a little quieter, only dealing with fevers and tummy pains. Others were the adrenaline-pumping kind that made Sally's heart wedge into her throat. On the outside, she remained cool and collected, but her insides felt like chaos. Coming off that high was always draining.

But she wouldn't give up nursing. Not for anything but babies of her own.

She loved helping people, saving lives, comforting the broken or afraid. It gave her such a huge sense of satisfaction.

But another part of her was looking forward to motherhood too. She thought she'd make a good mother—attentive, kind, patient. At least she hoped she'd be all those things. She had a good example to follow. Her own mother had been everything they'd needed, always there to kiss the tears away and bandage up the scrapes.

She wondered how long she'd have to wait to take that next step in life.

She'd been with Nate for three years, but the longer they stayed together, the further she felt from becoming a family. He was obsessed with work, and was it really fair to bring a child into that environment? She'd be raising it alone with a father who was never fully there…in the moment.

Gritting her teeth, she shook the thought from her mind.

It didn't matter.

She wasn't having a baby tomorrow. She didn't even want one that soon. She was just dreaming ahead—a very dangerous thing to do.

Parking her car, she grabbed her bag and headed down the path. Rusty's nails scraped the back of the door when he heard the key go into the lock, and Sally reminded herself that she already had a baby.

"Hey, boy." She laughed as her excited golden retriever bounced in front of her. She dropped to her knees and hugged him, scratching his side. "It's good to see you, buddy."

She always used a high, sweet voice with him. She wasn't sure why; it just seemed natural. He was her baby boy and they adored each other. To Rusty,

Sally was the universe, and whenever she was home, he followed her like a loyal companion.

Unable to resist, she put her shower off for a few minutes and went outside to play. Their backyard was small, but big enough for Rusty to get a little exercise. They played catch and wrestled in the cold grass until Sally's teeth started to chatter.

"Shower time for me, buddy. I've got myself a date." Rusty followed her inside and she kept talking to him, telling him all about her day as she got ready for her birthday dinner.

Excitement flitted through her.

Nate said it would be worth forsaking a party with her friends and family, which meant he had something really special planned.

She couldn't wait to see what it was.

5

Friday, April 27th
6:35pm

THE PHONE on Nate's desk rang, but he ignored it. He had to get out of there before something else came up. It was Sally's special night. He hadn't even had a chance to properly wish her a happy birthday. The few times he'd called her at work, she'd been too busy to talk and when he did finally catch her, their conversation was cut short by an interruption at his end.

Sally had left for work before he'd even woken up that morning. Usually her movements in the house stirred him, but he was shattered after two full days of working Cam's heroin case. The lead she was chasing fell through, but they did arrest the guy who had caused the car accident. He wasn't giving up anything, even though his lawyer was trying to convince him to take a plea bargain.

Stupid criminals.

Nate rolled his eyes and reached for his keys.

Nerves skittered through him.

Would she like his surprise? He'd never mentioned it before, or tested the waters. What if she hated it?

He cringed, berating his lack of confidence.

It was Sally! Of course she'd love it.

Straightening his tie, he put his jacket on and was heading for the door when Jessica appeared, blocking his way. Her dimples and short brown hair gave her a cute pixie look. She was like a dark version of Tinker Bell, and she had the spirit to match. Criminals were often fooled by her sweet smile. She was stronger and faster than she looked, and man, was she tenacious, which was why Nate didn't mind picking her when he needed extra support on a case. If his half-brother Blaine wasn't around, Jessica was the next cop he'd look for.

"I'm kind of in a hurry, Jess."

"Sorry, but whatever you're doing needs to be put on hold."

The spark in her eyes made him pause. "What?"

"Dispatch just called, and you're gonna want in on this one."

"On what one?"

"Human remains were just found buried under the floorboards at the abandoned farmhouse on Fraser Road. Kellan wants you to take the lead."

The words "But I have a more important appointment" should've popped out of his mouth, but there was no way they'd make it.

Human remains?

Under a floorboard?

A homicide?

Those things were rare in Aspen Falls, which was why Nate had specifically requested to take lead whenever one popped up. In his career so far, he'd dealt with two—a bar fight gone wrong and a drug case from earlier in the year.

For reasons Nate couldn't explain, homicides felt like the most important cases he could work on. There was something about catching a killer that meant more to him than anything else.

There was no way Nate could say no.

Glancing at his watch, he quickly worked out how long he could spare. The dinner reservation wasn't until eight. If he didn't shower or spruce up, he could drive past the house on the way and pick Sally up.

Pulling out his phone, he quickly texted to say he was running late but would pick her up at 7:45pm.

If he didn't get an immediate reply, it probably meant Sally was in the shower.

Tucking his phone away, he followed Jessica out to the parking lot.

The young officer walked backward as she spoke to him. "It's 415 Fraser Road."

"Got it."

"See you there, Detective."

He gave her a two-finger salute and ran to the police-issued sedan.

He gunned the engine, anticipation pulsing through him, making his heart rate accelerate. The intrigue of a new case always sent a nervous thrill through him.

Human remains.

Questions were already forming, taking over as he tried to paint a picture of the scene in his mind. Buried under floorboards suggested intentionality, which meant the victim's death might've been covered up. He knew it was jumping the gun to assume it was a homicide, but he couldn't get the thought out of his mind.

He wondered how long the remains had been hidden there.

Who could this mysterious victim be?

6

Friday, April 27th
7:05pm

He arrived on scene twenty minutes later and texted Cam as soon as he cut the engine. She'd want to know. And when she arrived, he could maybe slip away and not be too late for his date with Sally.

Walking onto the property, he scanned the area, taking in every detail as he went.

The farmhouse was an average size, probably three-bedroom, with weathered wood siding. Run-down. The front window, right of the door, was cracked in the bottom left corner. The porch was sagging, the second step caved in. The property looked about a hundred years old and had fallen into major disrepair.

But when?

How long had it been standing empty?

An SUV was parked to the right of the house, next to Lucas McGowan's car and a van that said Polaris Construction on the side.

Nate's eyebrows dipped together. The SUV must belong to Lucas's girlfriend. Nate was pretty sure her name was Alaina. Blaine had told him all about her.

The woman flipped houses. He paused by her vehicle and spotted drop cloths and painting equipment in the back, along with a ladder. Which meant she'd probably bought this place for next to nothing to renovate and turn over for a profit. With Aspen Falls constantly growing, it was probably a sound investment. The property was only ten minutes from a proposed elementary school—construction was due to start in the next few months. Within a couple of years, the area would probably be booming with new families moving in.

There was bound to be someone who'd want a home with a little bit of land, some space to spread out and raise a family instead of squashing into one of those cookie-cutter houses in the newer developments.

Rounding the corner of the house, he spotted one of the squad cars parked in front of a detached garage that looked ready to fall over. It had a definite lean to it. Nate could probably give a decent huff and it'd groan, then crash to the ground.

Officer Bart McGregor stood next to Alaina, his notepad out as he interviewed her. Her petite arms were crossed, her blonde hair neatly tucked up in a ponytail. Lucas stood beside her, rubbing her back as she spoke to the officer.

"Hey, Mick." Nate softly greeted the officer by his nickname. Mick looked relieved to see him. The guy was a brilliant policeman, but useless at interviews. He hated being first on scene.

Nate shared a quick look with Lucas and forced himself to shake hands with the guy. He was Blaine's best friend, but he and Nate never really saw eye-to-eye. Lucas had once been a cop, but he'd quit the force to become a private eye. Nate was aware he'd been injured and taken off active duty, but he always thought it sucked that the guy hadn't taken the desk job he'd been offered. It was a way to still help the community and he'd rejected it, instead branching out on his own to stick his nose into police business from a different angle. Nate found it frustrating, and wasn't shy about hiding his feelings on the matter.

However, this situation wasn't about them. It was about a set of bones that deserved as much investigation as any other mystery.

"It's Alaina, right?" Nate pointed at the petite woman.

"Yes." The blonde nodded. "The guys I hired to help with some demo work found the body about an hour ago. We called it in right away." She pointed to a group of men who were hovering against the side of the house, looking on edge and uncomfortable.

Jessica had just arrived on scene and instantly looked to Nate for direction. He nodded toward the men and she walked across to them immediately, pulling out her notepad for questioning. He had every confidence that she'd get what he needed.

"I've already spoken to the guys," Lucas chipped in. "They found the skeleton under the floorboards in the workshop behind the garage."

"Have you seen it?" Nate's voice took on a tight edge.

"Yes, I looked from the doorway, but haven't disturbed the scene." Lucas's pointed look shut Nate up. "Are forensics on their way?"

"You know they are." Nate looked to Alaina. "How long you been working on this place?"

"The sale went through last week. We just started tearing down the outbuildings that are too far gone to save. Haven't started on renovating the main house yet."

"Your project will have to be put on hold during the investigation."

Her face pinched with annoyance but she nodded. "I'm aware of that."

"Can you show me the remains, please?"

Alaina and Lucas led him around to the back of the garage where a separate workshop had been attached. The shed-like structure had cracked windows and a rickety wooden door with a rusted handle. Nate took mental pictures as he hovered in the frame. Flicking on his flashlight, he stared down at the busted floorboards. Four had been pulled up entirely, neatly stacked as the workers systematically took apart the shed. In the gap that remained was a shallow trench with a blanket-wrapped skeleton inside. The workers must've gotten the fright of their lives when they pulled open the blanket and found the dusty remains.

Nate watched his step as he gingerly entered the shed. Crouching down beside the skeleton, he stared into the empty eye sockets and quietly murmured, "What's your story?"

"Chuck said he didn't know what was in the blanket and that's why it's open. He thought it was just trash," Alaina said.

Nate nodded.

"As soon as he saw the bones, he left the building and called me over. I told the guys not to go near the scene again."

"Good move. Thank you." Nate stood tall and checked his watch, wondering how far away Kelly was. The poor crime tech was in for a long shift. As far as Nate could remember, she'd never had to deal with remains like this before. She'd no doubt have to call in outside help.

Alaina shifted from foot to foot in the doorway, obviously agitated. He glanced up in time to see her sharing a look with Lucas. He gave her a reassuring smile and squeezed the back of her neck before tipping his chin at Nate.

Alaina caught his eyes and sighed. "I guess it would be too much to ask that we try to keep this as quiet as possible?"

Nate gave her an inquisitive look.

"The murder. In the house I'm going to be selling."

Nate held up a pointed finger. "One, we don't know if it was a murder." He held up his thumb. "And two, if it was, we don't know that it happened here."

Alaina rolled her eyes. "You know what I'm saying. There's a body buried under the floorboards. That's no accident. Someone was trying to cover it up. And trying to sell a house where a crime was committed might be near impossible in this town."

"Don't get ahead of yourself," Nate murmured. "We don't know that it's a crime yet."

"But we do know that the dead body is here," she said. "On this property. That I will be selling at some point." She took a deep breath. "So it would be great if we could keep it on the down-low."

"I'm not sure how to help with that. As soon as you called it in, it became public knowledge."

Alaina huffed and closed her eyes like she was only just realizing this.

Lucas winced and kneaded her neck, muttering under his breath, "Jarrett will no doubt be here soon."

Nate's right eyebrow peaked as he gave the guy a stiff nod. "Look, Alaina, I appreciate where you're coming from, and I'll do my best to make sure that the bare minimum is reported in the news. I can't disclose details of an open investigation anyway, so Jarrett's hands will be tied to some degree…especially if we can convince him not to do any snooping of his own."

Lucas scoffed. "That'll be a hard sell. Jarrett's a frickin' bulldog."

"Well, so am I." Alaina straightened, a determined look on her face. "I'll have a word with him when he gets here."

"Yeah, good luck with that." Nate hid his grin by scrubbing a hand over his mouth. "Look, as soon as Jess finishes getting statements, we can send your guys home. The less people hanging around here, the better. Do you have a list of their contact information in case we need to follow up on anything?"

"Yes, I can get that for you."

"Good. I'm also going to need to look at all the records you have on the property. Sales and purchase agreements. That type of thing."

"I'll compile that for you when I get home tonight."

Nate nodded. "Okay, well, you guys can head off when you're ready, then. I'll give you a call if I need anything."

"I'd rather stay," Alaina said.

Nate huffed.

"It's her property. She has every right to stay." Lucas squared his shoulders and glared at him.

Unable to argue with the guy, Nate gave them a tight smile before turning back to look into the workshop.

Tipping his head, he stared down at the blanket with the bones wrapped inside. It looked as though the victim had been rolled up and put to bed.

Had the person been buried alive? Tucked away unconscious? Or already dead?

Was he or she lovingly buried by a family that couldn't afford a funeral? Or was there something more sinister going on?

Nate felt his blood simmer with the questions. The mystery was calling to him, and the fact that it was probably years old only motivated him more. He'd do anything to catch the person who killed his mother. He'd never had that closure, and that's why he fought so hard on every case, but particularly homicides. The two he'd worked had consumed him like nothing else.

Families deserved closure.

He knew firsthand that this was true, because he'd been looking for his own for years.

Nate sensed he wouldn't be able to rest until this case was closed. His mind thrummed with a steadily growing list of things to do.

It was going to be a long night.

7

Friday, April 27th
8:45pm

SALLY TAPPED her finger on her elbow as she paced the wooden floor.

Nate had texted while she was in the shower. His message had been annoying, but not surprising. She hadn't bothered responding, irritation making her throw the phone on the bed and walk out of the room.

It was her birthday. The one day everyone was supposed to treat her like a queen. And her boyfriend couldn't even be on time.

His lateness didn't use to bother her. Nothing about him did. But as the months ticked by and

Sally's faith wavered, the little things had started to annoy her.

Closing her eyes, she fought the sting of tears. Nate was already an hour later than his text had said. She'd worked her way through the standard set of emotions.

Irritation.

Worry that something may have happened to him.

Calm after calling the station and finding out he was working a case. It explained why her call and two text messages had gone unanswered.

She was back to irritation, which was quickly blooming into a desperate rage.

She loved Nate.

In that moment, she wished she didn't.

How much was too much?

How many more years could she go on being pushed aside for his work?

She could've been enjoying a party with friends and family who loved her. It wouldn't have mattered if Nate had had to bail, because she still would've been around people who cared and thought she was important enough to make a priority for one night.

Instead she was pacing her house and fighting off tears.

Her cell phone rang and she walked into her bedroom, Rusty on her heels. She checked the screen before answering. If it'd been Nate, she was going to ignore it. She wasn't in the frame of mind to accept another excuse.

But it was Annabelle.

"Hey, sis." Sally tried to sound upbeat.

"Happy birthday, bee-atch!"

Sally giggled in spite of her wounded spirit.

"Hey, I'm sorry I haven't had a chance to call you today. I was going to stop by after work, but just as I was leaving this poor girl walked in, desperate."

"What happened?" Sally perched on the edge of the bed and Rusty immediately rested his chin on her knees. She nearly stood up so he didn't get her dress furry, but what did it matter? Even if Nate showed up in the next five minutes, she didn't feel like going out anymore.

"She'd tried to bleach her own hair and did the worst job imaginable. Poor kid was only fifteen. I couldn't refuse her."

Sally grinned. Annabelle had set up her own salon right after her twenty-fifth birthday. With her inheritance, she'd purchased the property and turned it from a run-down barber shop into a full-blown beauty parlor. Her specialty was weddings, but she also loved the regular haircutting, dyeing and styling. The year before, she'd purchased the shop next door and expanded into nails, facials, waxing and massage. That's when the brides-to-be had come calling. She'd done incredible marketing, providing wedding day packages that the ladies lapped up. Her business had exploded in a matter of months.

"You're sweet to help her out," Sally said.

"Yeah, well she can now walk out in public without a beanie to hide the big patches of dark brown hair she'd missed." Annabelle cracked up laughing. "Anyway, I know you're out with Nate, so I won't keep you. I just hated the idea of not hearing your voice on your birthday. I needed you to know how much I love you."

That was it.

Tears popped onto Sally's lashes before she could stop them. Her lips began to tremble, and she couldn't hold back a pitiful sniff and whimper.

"Sally? What's the matter, babe?"

"I'm not with Nate."

"What?"

"He's not here," Sally wailed.

"Wait, what? Has something bad happened to him?"

"No, of course not!"

Annabelle went silent for a minute. When she spoke next, her voice had dropped low and was practically vibrating with anger. "Are you telling me he's at freaking work? On your birthday!"

Sally sniffed and slashed a tear off her cheek.

This was the point where she'd usually stand up for him.

It's an important case.

You know how dedicated he is.

I'm proud he's got such a great work ethic.

He's the best detective in Aspen Falls for a reason.

But she couldn't bring herself to say any of it.

"Okay, you know what?" Annabelle spat. "That's enough, Sally. You can't keep putting up with this shit! He promised you a special night. You forfeited all of Mom's amazing plans for a party in order to be with him, and he's not even there!"

Sally winced.

"I am so pissed off right now, I could kill him!"

"Don't talk that way, Bells."

"How much longer are you going to put up with this crap? You are a good person. You deserve someone who cares about you."

"Nate does care, he just gets caught up—"

"Don't start making excuses for him," Annabelle growled. "We all know the story. We've been listening to it for the last three years. Mom warned you about getting involved with him."

"Don't." Sally shook her head.

"No. I'm not shutting up this time. Nate has an obsessive nature. We all see it. You deserve better than this. You have to end this, Sally. You've wasted nearly three years of your life with this guy. Do you honestly think he's going to change?"

"He has his reasons for being the way he is," Sally murmured, Nate's husky voice infiltrating her mind. The way it shook slightly as he opened up about his nightmare and watching his mother die. His handsome face on the pillow, his tender fingers combing the hair back from her face.

Her insides squeezed with longing. "He's a good man."

"Yes, he's a good, brave detective. No one can ever criticize him on that score. But he's a shit boyfriend. You deserve to be someone's top priority, sis, and I know you don't want to hear this, but it's obvious you're never going to be his. The longer you leave it, the worse it's going to get. You're still young. You have your whole life ahead of you. Get out now, or you'll lose another three years without even realizing it."

Annabelle's sharp words were like gunfire. Sally's chest caved, her voice growing weak. "But I love him."

"I know you do." Her sister's voice suddenly softened, a soothing edge leaking into her words. "I know it hurts. But you have the biggest heart of anyone I know, and one day you'll fall in love with someone who puts you first. That's what you want, right? A family man. Someone you can have kids with and know he's going to be around to help you raise them."

Sally sucked in a breath that made her entire body shudder.

"I know you, sis. I know that's what you want. And you need to ask yourself, are you going to get that with Nate?"

Licking a tear off the edge of her mouth, Sally sniffed again.

"Breaking up with him will hurt like a sledge-hammer, I'm not denying that, but you won't get what you want by staying with him, and once the pain heals, you can move on and be happy. I just want you to be happy, babe."

"I know," she squeaked. "Thanks."

"Do you need me to come over?"

Sally shook her head. "No, it's okay. I've got Rusty."

She ran her fingers through the dog's sandy-colored fur. He looked up at her with his adoring brown eyes, and her heart squeezed in her chest.

"A dog's not going to cut it. You need wine and a fierce hug right now."

"I'm okay, Bells. Really."

"Are you sure?"

"Yeah." Sally cleared her throat.

"What are you going to do?"

"Think. I'm gonna think about what you said, and then I'm going to make a decision."

"I can be there in ten minutes."

"No, really. I… please, just let me do this on my own."

Annabelle sighed. "Okay. Just promise me you won't bend as soon as his sexy ass walks through that door. You have to be strong to get the things you need, Sal. Can you be strong?"

Sally clenched her jaw, seriously doubting it, until Annabelle's deafening words echoed through her mind: *"Are you going to get that with Nate?"*

The family. The husband who put work aside to be there for his wife and children.

Would she get that with Nate?

No.

Because he couldn't let go.

He couldn't turn his back on injustice.

He couldn't let someone else do the job.

Sally closed her eyes and set new tears free. They trickled down her face, and this time she didn't bother brushing them away.

She hated that her sister was right.

Hated what it meant.

Life without Nate sounded hideous. She was his, and he was hers.

But she wasn't.

Not really.

He hadn't proposed, even though she'd been hinting for months.

They were making no steps forward, and if she didn't do something to break the grind, she would lose another three years without even realizing it.

"I love you, sis," Annabelle said.

"Love you too," Sally whispered before hanging up the phone and sobbing into her hand.

8

Friday, April 27th
8:45pm

Kelly had arrived with her forensic gear just after Jarrett. Alaina snagged the reporter as soon as he stepped onto her property, which gave Kelly room to check out the scene un-badgered. She took one look at the skeleton, gulped, and immediately called the pathologist, Chad, who no doubt gulped as well and said he'd hunt down a forensic anthropologist. She then got to work—methodically, meticulously… slowly. She never wanted to miss a thing, and Nate appreciated that about her. She wouldn't even touch the remains until she'd photographed the scene from every angle possible, hunting for clues as she went.

Time was working against her. They had no idea how long the body had been there, and any fresh evidence had no doubt been lost years ago…maybe even decades.

"So, how's it going?"

Nate turned at the sound of Jarrett's voice and gave the guy he usually considered a friend a tight smile. "Hey, Jarrett."

The reporter from Aspen Falls' paper strained up to his tiptoes, trying to look past Nate and get an eye on what Kelly was doing.

"Back off." Nate flicked his finger at the door and started walking until Jarrett was forced to retreat into the backyard.

Lucas and Alaina were huddled together on the lawn, talking quietly while Alaina shot daggers at the back of Jarrett's head.

Nate smirked and quietly muttered, "How'd you get on with Little Miss Spitfire?

Jarrett's eyes rounded with amusement. "I told her I wouldn't agree to jack shit until I talked to you first."

"Okay." Nate nodded.

"So what can you give me?"

"Not much." Nate shrugged. "Human remains found in the back shed of the farmhouse on Fraser Road. Kelly is currently examining the scene. We won't have any more details until the skeleton has been analyzed by a forensic anthropologist that Chad is calling in from Hamline University."

Jarrett had his trusty pad of paper out, jotting notes and nodding. "And what else?"

"Nothin'." Nate shrugged.

"Nothing?" Jarrett gave him a skeptical frown. "Gimme a break, man. You've got to know something more. This could be really big."

"Well, it isn't right now," Nate told him. "I need you to keep this low-key."

"What?" Jarrett was incredulous.

"Don't be poking your nose in and trying to make it something bigger than it is. Not until we have more to go on."

"You can't ask me to do that." Jarrett was shaking his head. "Not with a story like this."

"I *can* ask you, and I will. Jarrett, you've got to give us some room here. I'll feed you information as I get it, but please don't jump the gun. And don't get in the way."

Jarrett's expression darkened, so Nate gave him a friendly pat on the shoulder. "I'll owe you lunch."

"Lunch?" Jarrett scoffed. "Try plural meals. And drinks. And maybe your firstborn." He wrinkled his nose. "Actually, scratch that last one."

Nate grinned. "I swear I'm good for it."

With a resigned sigh, Jarrett shoved his pen in his pocket and gave a reluctant nod. "Fine. I'll report bare minimum for now, but I'm expecting something pretty damn decent when you know more."

"You'll be the first to hear it."

"I want the exclusive." Jarrett gave him a pointed look.

"You got it." Nate held out his hand and they shook on it. "Now get out of here and let me get back to work."

Jarrett wouldn't comply—Nate knew well enough that he wasn't going anywhere—but he did at least turn and head back to Lucas and Alaina.

Nate stepped back into the workshop to check on Kelly's progress.

She was just placing her camera down, which meant she'd finished thoroughly recording the scene. Kneeling beside the skeleton, she started a close-up analysis just as Chad arrived to help her. Nate stepped aside to give him some room. The guy didn't usually come out to the field, but this was a special case and he wanted to ensure the remains were moved as he'd been instructed by the forensic anthropologist, who was making arrangements to come down that week and examine the body.

Nate stayed for the entire process, asking questions and building as much of a story as he could.

When Cam arrived, he went through the details with her, the evening disappearing as they discussed theories that couldn't yet be confirmed.

While they were working the case, he felt like he was on fire—his brain alert and focused, his pulse upbeat and thrumming through his veins.

It wasn't until the property had been cleared for the night and he finally dropped the car back at the station and collected his bike that everything came crashing down around him. Glancing at his watch, he noted the time—11:35pm—and felt like someone had just smashed him in the chest with a mallet.

"Shit." He closed his eyes, bowing his head and squeezing his knee.

Sally.

He'd forgotten about Sally.

Reaching into his jacket pocket, he felt her gift and knew that trying to give it to her when he got home was potentially a wasted moment.

He'd screwed up big-time.

So much for a special night.

"Dammit," he muttered, shoving the key in the ignition and gunning it home.

He didn't want to waste time with a call or a text. He just needed to get in that door, apologize, and spend the night making it up to her.

Sally was a forgiving, patient angel. She understood that cases popped up. She understood that he had a job to do.

Clenching his jaw, he sped his way home and was relieved to see the lights on when he pulled into the driveway. She'd waited up for him.

As he hopped off his bike, the thought hit him that she'd waited up to yell at him. But that wasn't Sally. She wasn't a yeller. She went quiet.

Thankfully, he knew all the right moves to coax a smile out of her. She never stayed mad for long.

He stopped outside the front door and pulled in a slow breath before unlocking it. All the right words were drumming through his mind, but they were cut short when he nearly tripped over a suitcase by the door.

He frowned at it before glancing up at the sound of Sally's footsteps.

She appeared in the room with Rusty by her side. She was wearing her favorite pair of blue sweats, her tattered college hoodie and a pair of scuffed white Converses. Nate focused on those, needing a minute before reaching her face.

Rusty glanced across the room at Nate and kind of whined, but he knew better than to leave his favorite girl. He gazed up at her and Nate followed his line of sight, landing on Sally's face.

It tore him to shreds.

Her cheeks were pale and blotchy, her eyes

rimmed red. She'd obviously washed her makeup off, but he could detect the faint mascara tears that must've been running down her cheeks throughout the evening.

He winced, his expression creasing with remorse. "Baby, I am so sorry."

He went to move into her space, but she held up her hand and scuttled back so far she banged into the wall. She'd never reacted like that before and he stopped, fear clipping the edge of his stomach.

Glancing over his shoulder, he looked at the suitcase again and dread rushed through him. Icy blood turned his body cold.

When he looked back, she started to make his nightmare a reality.

"You forgot about me." Her voice quavered like she was fighting for control.

"I..." He sighed, knowing she was right. "It's a new case. That's—"

"I don't want to hear about your new case. I don't care about your new case!" she spat. "Tonight was supposed to be about me. And I know that may sound selfish and immature, but I don't give a shit. I could've been with my family and friends, but I gave that up for you." She pointed an accusing finger at him, then spread her arms wide. "And big surprise, something more important came up."

"I can't predict when a new case will—"

"You don't always have to be the first one there! There are other people at the AFPD! But you just can't let these things go, can you? You are addicted to your work, and I am tired of always coming second to that. I want to matter."

"You do matter."

"Well it doesn't feel like it!" She stamped her foot, her expression tortured. "I just… I don't know if I can do this anymore."

"What?"

"I…" She sucked in a shaky breath, then pressed her lips together and started blinking like she was fighting tears.

Nate's air supply was being cut off as invisible fingers squeezed his throat. "Are you…saying you want to break up with me?"

She looked to the floor. "Maybe," she whispered.

"Maybe? Why haven't you talked to me about this?"

"I've tried. I just…" She shook her head and shrugged.

"You can't have tried that hard." Nate threw his keys onto the side table. "I thought you understood about my work. How important it is. Of course I care about you, but I'm a cop. I can't turn my back on a case because it's your birthday."

Admittedly his voice had turned snappy as he

argued with her, but the look on her face made him feel like he'd just been punched in the stomach.

He swallowed, instant regret flooding him.

The tears she'd been fighting trickled free. "Work will always come first, won't it? No matter what is happening in my life, a case will *always* come before me."

He couldn't speak past the ash in his mouth.

"I can't do this anymore, Nate."

He blinked and looked at her like she was crazy.

Her chin bunched, new tears brimming on her lashes. "I can't keep waiting around for you."

Fear clenched him, panic making him reach into his jacket pocket for the gift. "I'm here now. I'm—"

"No! I can't!" She held her hands. "I can't keep making excuses. I need a break."

No. No. She couldn't be saying that!

It was Sally.

She understood!

"We need some space." She shook her head and started crying.

"I don't need space," he argued. "I need you."

Her body trembled as she let out a broken laugh and slashed the tears off her cheeks. "No you don't. You need your work. That's all you need. And I thought I could do it, you know? But tonight gave me a chance to really think it through." She sniffled.

"I was imagining the future and what that might look like. You know, I've been hoping for months that you'd propose, but as I sat here, waiting for you yet again, I realized I don't want this life. I don't want a husband who is constantly late and always puts work before me. What if we had kids one day? They would never see their father. You would miss everything, and I'd be raising them alone. I can't do that."

He gripped the present in his pocket, struggling for the right words, but finding none.

"I can't do it, so what's the point of us being together? We have no future, Nate, so we may as well end it."

Letting the gift go, he pulled his hand out of his pocket and crossed his arms, an unexpected anger coursing through him.

She was giving up. Just like that.

Ending it. Just like that.

She wasn't even letting him have a say. It was like being blind-sided.

Running trembling fingers through her hair, she pulled herself tall and walked around him. He could've so easily caught her wrist and pulled her close. He'd hold her tight and whisper into her hair.

But this time, she wouldn't let him.

He could feel it.

She'd made up her mind, and nothing was going

to stop her from walking out that door. So instead he stood with his arms crossed, staring at the spot where she'd once stood. The pastel green wallpaper mocked him as the sound of Sally's footprints echoed on the hard wooden floor.

When the door creaked open, Rusty let out a confused bark. "It's okay, boy. Go to the car. We're going to see Yvie."

So she was high-tailing it to her parents' place.

Most women would be kicking him out. The house belonged to Sally; the mortgage was in her name, and Nate had no right to it.

"I know you weren't expecting this, so I'll stay at my parents' until…"

Nate filled the silence, his husky voice barely audible. "I'll be out before sunrise. This place isn't mine anyway."

He didn't glance over his shoulder to see her expression, but her soft whimper made him cringe. He closed his eyes and listened as the door shut behind him. He remained a statue until he heard her car pulling out of the driveway.

As the silence engulfed him, he shuffled to their room, staring down at the bed like a robot who'd just had its system wiped clean.

He had no idea how long he stood there, but eventually he sniffed and pulled the small black box from his jacket pocket.

Brushing his finger lightly over the red ribbon, he threw it onto the bed and then turned for the closet.

He said he'd be out before sunrise, and that was exactly what he intended to do.

9

Saturday, April 28th
1:25am

THE DUFFEL BAG on Nate's back weighed a thousand pounds, but he adjusted his shoulders and kept driving. He pulled up to Blaine's apartment block and locked up his Harley before taking the stairs two at a time.

He didn't care what the time was. He pounded on his brother's door until it finally jerked open.

"What! The hell! Is your problem?" Blaine gritted out, running his hands through hair that was already standing on end.

His chest was bare and he was wearing a pair of boxer shorts…back to front and inside out.

Nate frowned at him, then muttered, "I need a

place to stay."

The comment took his brother off guard.

Blaine paused for a second, blinking in confusion before the lights slowly came on. "What happened?"

"She's had enough."

Blaine's expression crumpled with sympathy, but there wasn't an inkling of surprise evident.

Nate's nostrils flared. "If you say 'I warned you,' I'm going to smash you in the face."

"Not saying it." Blaine shrugged, then glanced over his shoulder. "But you can't stay here."

"What? Why not?"

Blaine's cheeks flared red. "I'm kind of in the middle of something."

"The middle of…" Nate's question evaporated as he quickly figured it out. "Aw, gross."

"You don't want to be sleeping on my couch tonight. Go to Dad's."

"You asshole. You're gonna make me stay with Dad?"

Blaine snickered. "It won't kill you."

"Can't you just explain to Rosie that—"

"No!" Blaine cut him off. "I'm having a good time, and not to sound harsh, but I'm not giving it up to help your sorry ass. Not when there's a perfectly decent guest room waiting for you."

"I don't want to go home," Nate practically whined.

With a firm expression, Blaine pointed at his face. "You've barely been back there since you left for college. Now get over yourself and get out of here."

Blaine closed the door before Nate could form another argument. Instead, he kicked the door just to really drive home his annoyance.

Blaine ignored him, no doubt already whipping off his boxers and diving back into bed with Rosie.

Jealousy tore through Nate, hot and fierce. He should've been in bed with Sally right then, making love and celebrating her birthday. But instead he was standing alone in a dark corridor.

He could go sleep at the station.

"What a joke," Nate grumbled.

'Sleep' and 'station' were two words that did not go together. He'd end up in a fitful sleep that would no doubt be interrupted, and then he'd wake up with an aching back and sore neck.

There was a perfectly comfortable bed available at his father's house, but the idea of going there was like acid in his throat. It was the house his dad and Gillian had bought when they first got married. The house Silas had tortured him in. The house Blaine had been born into. He hated it there.

With a heavy sigh, Nate wiped his burning eyes and shuffled away from Blaine's door.

He needed sleep.

If he was going to do this new case any justice, he needed to come at it fresh in the morning.

Fresh was probably a big stretch, but if he was going to get anywhere near that, he had to swallow his angst and get over to the house on Chestnut Lane.

Nate grumbled his way down the stairs and gritted his teeth for the entire motorbike ride. Parking next to his father's Buick, he had to force himself to walk up the path and knock on the front door.

It was a half-hearted thump, but his dad still heard it.

The stairwell light shone through the cracks in the door, and a few moments later it inched open.

His father's brown eyes took a second to register who it was, and then his dark eyebrows shot up in surprise. "Nate?"

"Yeah, it's me. I need a place to stay."

"Wh… Is Sally okay?"

The old man loved Nate's girlfriend, probably more than he loved him, and it hurt to choke out the words "We broke up, and no, I don't want to talk about it."

Harry Hartford's head jerked back in surprise. He brushed a shaky hand over his beard before finally murmuring, "Okay. Okay. Uh…co-come in."

"Thank you." Nate's shoulders tensed as he

walked into the house, memories flooding him with each step. The fights at the dinner table, the unfair way Gillian yelled at him when Silas had been the one to break the vase, stain the carpet, or pull apart the radio. The dreaded silence that descended every time he was sent to his room and the way his shy, noncombative father never stood up for him. His mother would've whooped Gillian's ass.

He shut his eyes to ward off the emptiness that threatened to swallow him whole. Being reminded of that lost boy who was trying to survive without his mommy still hurt, and he wasn't sure he could stand it.

He nearly turned and fled, but then his father's hand landed on his shoulder and gave it a firm squeeze.

"I'll get some sheets. Do you want to sleep in your old room or…?"

"I can just take the couch."

"I'll make up the bed in the guest room." Harry gave him a half smile and shuffled off.

Nate's bag thumped onto the floor in the entrance and the silence settled around him like a thick, suffocating fog.

He didn't know how he was going to survive this.

Sally was his light, and without her the world seemed shrouded in a darkness that wanted to feast on his soul.

10

Monday, May 7th
6:20pm

It had been ten days.

Ten awful days filled with tears and regret and second-guessing.

Each emotion was countered by a different family member assuring Sally that she'd done the right thing.

She'd taken two days off work to hug her pillow and cry. Her father forced her back to the hospital, knowing it was what she needed.

It had been.

Lena listened to her during every break, again with the reassurances. She was surrounded by them. Yet it still hurt.

She missed Nate.

And even though he hadn't been around much, he'd still been hers. And now he wasn't.

And that hurt.

"To you, Sal!" Lena called, firing the soccer ball across the field.

Sally surged toward it but fumbled the move and ended up kicking the ball out of bounds.

"It's all good. It's all good." Lena clapped her hands as the team reset and got ready for the throw in. Sally tried to focus on the ball and get into it. The sky was blue, the sun was high. Spring was in the air, promising warmth and good times ahead. It was usually her favorite season as she shook off the winter blues. But not this year. This year she felt permanently stuck beneath a rain cloud.

She pumped her arms and ran down the field to get into a better position, or maybe farther away from the ball. Working up a sweat was good for her, which was why she'd been running so much with Rusty and playing soccer any chance she got. But she couldn't get into the game and was grateful it was nearly over. Social soccer was usually the highlight of her week, and she felt weird not wanting to play. She loved her team, time with friends, drinks afterward, but she'd be foregoing that.

All she wanted to do was go home and have a hot

bath, then hide in her room with a romantic novel that would make her heart cry.

She hadn't found the courage to move back to the little bungalow she'd lived in with Nate, so she was still staying with her parents in the room where she had whiled away her teenage years.

Lena dribbled the ball up the field, two players supporting her on either side. Sally halfheartedly ran in that direction but didn't commit. They scored without her, and five minutes later the game ended.

They'd won, but Sally could barely muster a smile.

Lena wouldn't let her get away with it and wrapped her in a tight hug. "If you think for one second that you're not celebrating this win with us, you're crazy."

"I'm just tired." Sally pulled away and tried again for a smile. It didn't really work. "I'm going to head home and—"

"No." Lena shook her head. "I've already called Chantel and Bridget. They're meeting us at Nightfall in an hour. You're coming home with me, and we're going to get you spruced up."

Sally was already shaking her head. "I really don't feel like doing that."

"I know, but you need to get out there and have some fun. You need alcohol, you need music, and you need some time with your *chicas*. We will make you smile again." Lena cupped her cheek. Her dark eyes warned that she wouldn't take no for an answer, and Sally reluctantly bobbed her head.

"Yes! *Es tiempo de festejar*!"

Sally wrinkled her nose. "What does that mean?"

"It's time to party, *novio*."

With a soft snort of compliance, Sally let Lena drag her off the field. They walked their sweaty butts back to Lena's place and got dolled up. She borrowed Lena's red, backless dress that tied around the neck, the long silk ribbons tickling her bare spine. She wasn't a 'dress up and hit the town' kind of girl—at least she hadn't been in the last three years—but as she gazed at her reflection in the mirror, she did have to admit that she felt pretty hot.

Her blonde curls rested against her naked shoulders, and the bright red lipstick Lena chose gave her a flirty charm that empowered her.

It was the first time she'd felt strong since walking away from Nate.

"Nate." She breathed out his name, her insides shuddering with uncertainty.

"If you even think about him tonight, I'm going to kick your ass. You are single, you are beautiful, and he is not to be a part of this. You understand me?" Lena's ruby red nail pointed at her.

"Yes, ma'am."

"That's *senorita*, thank you very much." Lena

winked and laughed, shaking her tight ass and letting out a shrill kind of war cry.

It made Sally grin, and she grabbed Lena's hand and followed her friend into the night.

They took an Uber so they didn't have to be restricted when it came to drinking. Lena had grand plans of getting Sally thoroughly wasted.

"I don't want to be hungover tomorrow. I'm working," Sally whined when Bridget laid a tray of tequila shots on the table.

"Sh-sh-sh." Chantel waved her hand as if she was shooing off a bee. "You can handle a few shots. Come on. We'll dance in between and eat some fries. It'll be fine."

Sally looked to the sky, giving up immediately. Her girls were taking charge, and she was pretty sure she'd have no say in the matter.

"Alright, alright." Lena clapped her hands and raised her shot glass. "To new beginnings."

Sally winced.

"To bravery." Bridget gave her a heart-warming smile.

Sally's eyes began to glisten.

"To hot guys on the dance floor." Chantel's tongue peeked out the side of her mouth as she wiggled her eyebrows.

Sally cracked up laughing and lifting her shot glass. "Cheers, you guys."

They all downed the burning alcohol together, then burst into laughter.

As the tequila filled their bodies, their limbs liquified and inhibitions were thrown to the wind. Sally was dragged onto the dance floor where she let loose, the music pumping through her in waves. She jumped, she swayed, she shimmied and eventually dragged her sweaty butt up to the bar for a glass of water.

Her head was still pretty level; she just had a warm buzz going on. It made her giggle as she leaned against the bar.

"You look like you're enjoying yourself."

The smooth British accent made her turn and gasp. "Oscar!" She threw her arms around him and giggled. "I didn't think this was your kind of place."

The man chuckled and held her steady. "It's usually not, but it's been a long day and I needed a drink." His smile was gentle and warm as he drew back and looked at her. "Wow. Sally Richmond, you look amazing." A warm tingle buzzed through her, and she couldn't help a blushing smile. "Can I buy you a drink?"

"Oh, um…I'm kind of here with my friends." Sally pointed at the dance floor.

Oscar followed her finger and grinned.

Sally glanced over her shoulder and saw Chantel jumping up and down, her blonde-streaked hair swaying to the beat. Lena and Bridget were waving and no doubt trying to figure out who the hottie at the bar was. They knew Oscar by name but had never officially met him.

"We've been besties since high school," Sally explained.

Oscar's face crested with an expression Sally couldn't decipher, and then his lips turned up in a handsome smile that took her breath away. Geez, she must've been more drunk than she thought. Sally blinked and reminded herself that Oscar had always been good-looking. He was smooth, stylish. He reminded her of her father, and there was a certain comfort in that.

"Why don't you let me buy a round for all four of you, then," he said.

"Oh, I couldn't ask that."

"You didn't ask. I offered." His eyes sparkled as he leaned close. His aftershave tickled her senses. "And it'd be my pleasure."

She couldn't do anything but stupidly bob her head.

And Oscar joined the party.

The girls adored him, and Sally could understand why. He was sweet, attentive, generous and charming. He danced. He bought them drinks. He laughed at Chantel's lame jokes—they grew worse with every new shot of alcohol—and he entertained them with stories of merry old England, not afraid to make fun of himself or his English quirks. He even listened when Lena went into a spiel that quickly turned into a mix of unintelligible English and Spanish.

It was after that when he wrapped things up. “Can I give you ladies a lift home?”

“Oh, we can just call an Uber.” Sally started hunting for her phone.

He stopped her with a gentle touch to the back of her hand. “No, I insist. I want to make sure you all get there safely.”

“*Perfecto*.” Lena gave Sally a pointed look, silent screaming, *This guy! Fall in love with this guy!*

Oscar? Was she kidding?

He was a family friend!

Sally looked away from her forceful Latina sister and caught Oscar’s smile. It was aimed right at her and filled with something that made her insides warm and mushy. She blushed and glanced down at the table, becoming even more aware of just how drunk she was.

Oscar’s smiles didn’t usually make her blush. In saying that, he’d never smiled at her like that before. He was obviously liking the red dress.

“Shall we?” He rose and they followed suit, Chantel slipping when she jumped down from the stool.

Oscar caught her easily and ended up supporting

her out of the bar. He chatted softly with her while Bridget and Lena flanked Sally.

“I may be slightly drunk…” Lena started.

“Or totally drunk.” Sally frowned at her.

“But he is hot, he’s sweet, he’s rich, and he’s obviously into you. You have to go for it.”

“Would you stop?” Sally gave her a firm nudge. “He’s Oscar, he’s not—”

“Lena’s so right,” Bridge interrupted. “He’s a sweetheart.”

They all stopped to watch Oscar gently guide Chantel into the back seat of his Mercedes.

“Enough, you two. You’re both drunk. I’m not going for it. Are you crazy? I only just broke up with Nate.”

“Rebound sex is not a bad thing.” Lena’s right eyebrow arched as she pointed a finger at Sally.

Sally pushed the finger out of her face. “I’m not talking to you anymore tonight. You just zip those lips, baby girl.”

Lena sloppily mimed zipping her lips before falling against Oscar’s car. Sally winced and mouthed an apology, which Oscar simply smiled at.

“Here we go.” He led her around the car and made sure all three girls were secured in the back before opening the passenger door for Sally. “My lady.”

Sally giggled and slipped into the plush car.

The ride home was quiet. Chantel fell asleep, so Sally took over directions to her place. Bridget woke her and then offered to stay the night. Chantel replied with a dreamy giggle, and Oscar ended up carrying her inside for Bridget.

Sally then led Oscar to Lena's place. When she tried to get out, her best friend wouldn't let her, insisting Oscar take Sally home.

"I'll bring your stuff to work tomorrow."

"No, Lena, let me out of the car. Let me—" Her whispers were ignored as Lena slammed the door in her face and wobbled to the front door.

Before Sally could say she'd go help her, Oscar took off.

She was stuck.

"You have wonderful friends." Oscar leaned forward and turned on the radio.

Soft jazz wafted into the car. It was a trumpet solo that oozed the cool charm Oscar seemed to perpetually embody.

"Yes." Sally smiled, resting her head back against the headrest. "Thank you for looking after us."

"It's really not a problem. I had a fantastic evening…thanks to you."

She swallowed, unsure what to say.

"I was simply going in for a drink after a long day's work, and to end up spending the night with four beautiful, intelligent women was an added bonus."

Sally's lips twitched and she quickly changed the subject before she started blushing. "How is work going?"

"It's exciting. Working with your father is such an honor. He knows everything about the construction industry and is teaching me so much."

"How about Xavier?"

Oscar hesitated, then bobbed his head. "He's good. Intelligent. I like his sense of humor."

"He's driving you crazy, isn't he?"

Oscar grinned but didn't say anything else. He didn't need to. Xavier could drive anyone crazy, but someone he didn't like? They were done for.

For some weird reason, he'd never really warmed to Oscar the way everyone else had. Sally figured he probably felt threatened by the guy. Being the youngest of four, Xavier had always had to compete for attention anyway. Oscar was just another thing to get in the way.

"He'll warm to me eventually. I'm trying to make sure your father gives him some responsibility too. I don't want him feeling like some unimportant assistant. I really want to make him part of the project."

Sally was touched by Oscar's perceptiveness.

"Thank you. He'll really appreciate that, even if he doesn't say it."

"I'm trying to be subtle about it, so it looks as though it's coming from your father."

Her heart expanded and she couldn't hold back her smile. That was so sweet.

She blinked and gazed out the window, suddenly aware that Oscar was taking her to her parents' place without her having to tell him.

"How do you know…?"

"Where you're currently living?" Oscar gave her a sheepish grin. "Your father told me about Nate. I'm really sorry."

With a deflating sigh, she shook her head. "It's fine."

"No, it's not. It must be awful."

"It was my choice." She shrugged. "I brought it on myself."

"I don't think your family sees it that way. And don't get me wrong, I like Nate. He's a really good guy, but…if he treated you badly—"

"He didn't treat me badly, he just…was never there."

"Okay, well, if Nate *had* been there, been what you needed, then you wouldn't have broken up with him. So in a way, you didn't bring it on yourself. He did."

Sally pressed her lips together, her nose starting to tingle with the onset of tears.

He shot a glance in her direction. "Sometimes you have to let go of the things most dear in order to make way for something even better."

"I thought he was the best," Sally whispered, mostly to herself.

But Oscar heard her because he said, "When you're that close to something, it's hard to get perspective. I think what you've done is extremely brave. And your strength and courage will be rewarded. You just wait and see. There's good things in your future, Sally Richmond. I believe that entirely."

She glanced at Oscar, warmed by his words and sweet smile.

He slowed to pass through the gates, and she couldn't take her eyes off him. Studying his chiseled profile, she couldn't help admiring the sharp point of his nose and the shape of his jawline. He had a different kind of strength than Nate that she'd never noticed before.

It was soft and elegant. But it was still strength.

Braking next to Xavier's car, Oscar jumped out and rushed around to open Sally's door before she could.

He held out his hand and helped her as if she

were stepping out of a carriage. She'd never felt more like a princess. "Thank you."

"You're most welcome."

Once again blushing, Sally looked to the ground and softly whispered a good night before heading for the door. She stepped into the entryway and firmly shut the door behind her. Her insides felt like a maze that she was lost inside of. She didn't know whether to smile, laugh, cry, or puke.

Splaying her hand over her torso, she shuffled to the stairwell just as her father walked out of his office. He pulled the glasses off the tip of his nose. "Are you drunk?"

"Just a little." She raised a limp hand. "The girls took me out."

"How'd you get home?" He peered out the window. "Please tell me you didn't drive."

"No, Daddy. Oscar drove me. We met at the bar and he helped us out."

Her father raised his eyebrows, his lips pulling into a grin. "I like that man."

"Yeah, he's sweet." Sally's right shoulder hitched.

"He's a good fit for this family. Giving him the chance to live here and work alongside me was the best decision I've made this year." Her father's complete lack of subtlety was not lost on her. She gave him a dry glare that made him chuckle. He pecked her on the cheek before silently walking her up the stairs.

As soon as her door was shut, she flopped onto the mattress and pulled her pillow against her. Rusty was snoring lightly in his doggy bed. He'd no doubt stir soon and come join her. It would be a great way to end what had turned out to be a good night. She loved her girls, and Oscar had been sweet.

But a part of her still missed Nate. The feel of his body next to hers, the subtle scent of his shampoo, the way his arm instinctively wrapped around her waist and pulled her against him, even when he was sleeping.

She missed the look in his eyes when he studied her from across the room, that little half smile that warmed her insides.

Would it always be like that?

Or would those sweet, aching memories eventually fade?

A small part of her hoped not.

11

Tuesday, May 8th
9:00am

THE SMELL of the forensics lab always made Nate's nose wrinkle. It was a sterile, unnatural odor that messed with his senses. Everything about the area was clean lines and aseptic edges. Whites and grays. Nothing warm and enticing. Just the study of death.

He hated going down there, and Cam would often go in for the oral reports, but Nate was invested in the Fraser Road farmhouse case and he wanted to be involved in every aspect of it.

It kept him constantly busy and meant he could avoid his father's place...and any unbidden thoughts of Sally.

He'd contacted her the day after they broke up with a very brief text.

I'm out. The house is yours.

She'd replied: *Thank you. I hope you're doing okay.*

He hadn't been able to respond.

Doing okay?

He felt like his heart had been torn out of his chest and used for soccer practice. When he lay awake at night, he could picture it being booted around the field with Sally and her friends as they laughed at what a useless boyfriend he'd been.

It made his insides raw. Their three-year relationship had been reduced to a two-sentence text message that he couldn't bring himself to reply to.

She'd asked for space anyway, so at least he was giving her that. Sometimes, in his weak moments, he wondered if she missed him. A small spark of hope would start to burn—maybe she'd come back. Maybe some time would help her realize how perfect they were for each other.

But then reality would kick his ass.

Why would she come back? According to her, there was no point in them being together.

Trying to live and breathe when he thought

about that was basically impossible, so every time the ugly nightmare tried to steal his attention, he'd bat it away and focus back on the case, or any other damn work that Cam or Kellan could provide him with.

It was making him a tired, miserable bastard, and people at the station were avoiding him whenever possible.

He was still pissed off with Blaine for making him move in with Dad, and every time his younger brother approached, he warned him off with a glare or a sharp "get lost."

Each time, Blaine would raise his hands and walk away, only to try again the next morning.

Nate could be stubborn when he wanted to be, but his ability to keep pushing Blaine away was waning and he could feel himself getting ready to break. Next time Blaine brought him a coffee, he'd probably take it, but that was all. He wasn't about to open up and talk feelings.

He just needed to focus on work. That'd get him through.

Waiting for results on the unidentified skeleton had felt like an eternity and only further darkened his mood. He'd spent hours up at the house, looking in every nook and cranny with Kelly to see if they could discover any hidden clues. But the old house had no stories to tell. The place had foreclosed years before and had been sitting empty, just waiting for someone like Alaina to see its potential and take a calculated risk.

The shed where the remains had been found didn't offer up much in the way of clues either. The only evidence they had to work with was the skeleton and the blanket it had been wrapped in.

Forensic testing proved that the blanket was 100 percent polyester, which probably meant it was the soft kind of blanket used on a bed or thrown over the back of a couch. Being an unnatural fiber, polyester took decades to decompose, so that didn't help much with establishing a timeline. It was a newer material, most likely post—World War II, but that didn't help too much. Nate hoped they could get more from the remains.

He gazed down at the dry bones, neatly laid out on the table. The victim had been respectfully examined, every inch of its skeleton scrutinized by both Aspen Fall's chief medical examiner, Chad Hickman, and the forensic anthropologist, Professor Nigel Renshaw, from Hamline University.

Chad had called that morning to say he was ready to report, and Nate had leaped out the door as fast as he could.

It meant going to the hospital, which Nate didn't love, but he made sure to avoid any entrances where he might bump into Sally. His method of survival was to cut her out completely. Once the pain had died down, he'd find the courage to check in and see how she was doing.

The way his heart hurt, he was guessing it would take some time. Sally had plenty of family support and three of the world's best friends to keep her busy and take her mind off things—if she was even thinking about him.

His jaw tensed. Part of him wanted her to be miserable, to be filled with regret, to ache the way he was aching. But when the anger subsided, however brief the respite might be, he knew he didn't really wish those things upon her. Yeah, she'd dumped him, and losing her was killing him, but his feelings for her were slow to die. He wondered if they ever would.

"Morning, Detective." Chad smiled as he walked out from his office.

Deep dimples scored the man's dark round face. He always had such a jolly look about him, like the guy didn't realize he worked with dead people for a living.

"Hey, Chad. What've you got for me?"

Chad stood over the remains and opened his file with an air of reverence. Pulling a pair of small reading glasses from his pocket, he scanned the contents before saying anything. That was always his way—slow and methodical.

Nate gritted his teeth and resisted the urge to hurry him along.

"Okay." Chad took off his glasses and looked at Nate. "So we've established that the victim was female, most likely of European ancestry, and her bone growth suggests she was a teenager."

Nate's eyebrows rose as he jotted down the notes. "Can you be more specific on the age?"

"Judging on the fusing of bones and dental development, we can place her in her late teens."

"Have you cross-referenced dental records?"

"Where would we start? There have been a lot of teenage girls in Aspen Falls over the years, Detective Hartford."

Nate hitched his shoulder to hide his embarrassment. Of course going through dental records would be like wading through an ocean. They needed to narrow things down much further before going there.

Chad put his glasses back on and nudged them up his nose with his knuckle. "Height is five-six and the bone structure is fine, which suggests she was probably not a large person, although I have no substantial proof of this. She may have been carrying excess weight. There's really no way to tell, although Professor Renshaw did note that there looked to be no strain on the bones or wearing down of the joints, which indicates that she was most likely not obese and that she had never been subjected to hard labor."

Nate nodded, trying to build a mental picture as he wrote. "Cause of death?"

Chad slapped his file closed and held up his finger. "Now this was interesting. Almost makes me want to check out forensic anthropology. Who knew studying bones could tell you so much?" He chuckled.

Nate pressed his lips together and looked down as Chad leaned over the bones and pointed at the rib cage. "You see this tiny nick on the bottom of her fourth right rib?"

Nate cautiously leaned over the body and squinted at the bone.

"Renshaw's confident that was caused by a bullet. If his calculated trajectory is correct, the bullet entered the right atrium of her heart and exited out the back. There's a very fine abrasion on the T5, which suggests the bullet grazed her spine before exiting the body." Chad looked up. "You and Kelly didn't find any shell casings or damaged bullets around?"

Nate shook his head, frustrated by the lack of evidence on the property.

"I guess she could've been shot somewhere else and moved to the property."

"It's a possibility." Nate clicked his pen and stared down at the bones. "Would she have died instantly?"

"That depends on a few factors." Chad stood tall and picked up his file again. "Caliber of the weapon, distance she was from the gun."

"Can you tell any of that from the skeleton?"

Chad shook his head.

"Okay." Nate nodded. "But we're pretty sure the cause of death is a gunshot wound to the chest?"

"Yes."

"Time since death?"

Chad puffed out his cheeks. "That's the tricky part. Our Jane Doe was wrapped in a polyester blanket, which alters the rate of decomposition. However, it is clear that the bones have been there for some time. The blanket she was wrapped in could help figure out the timeframe. If we can find the manufacturer, we can work out when that type of blanket was first made and narrow it down from there. Although that's most likely a very big window."

Nate frowned in thought, then muttered, "We'll probably have more luck working through the history of the house. I've already started going through the list of previous owners."

"You assuming the victim lived there?"

"It's one theory." Nate shrugged.

Chad nodded. "It's a good place to start, but

there's every chance that the body was wrapped in the blanket and moved there to be buried."

"It seems an odd place to bury someone, unless you already lived in the house."

"Fair point," Chad admitted. "Or maybe someone was trying to set up the owner. Or maybe after the house was abandoned, they figured it was a safe place to hide a body."

"Also fair points." Nate clicked his pen off and on again. "Touché."

Flipping his notebook shut, he slipped it back into his pocket, clicked off his pen and tucked it away. "Thanks for your good work, Chad."

"No problem. Call me if you have any other questions. I'll type up my report today and send it over when it's done."

"Thanks," Nate called over his shoulder, exiting the hospital and getting back to the precinct as fast as he could.

Bustling through the door, he hurried to Jessica's desk. "How are we doing with the previous homeowners?"

"Getting there." She smiled. "I've emailed you an initial report with all the information I have so far. I can definitely compile more, but I thought it'd be more time efficient to let you narrow it down further, and then I can go in-depth on whichever homeowners you think are likely possibilities." She swiveled her chair to face him. "What did Chad say about the body?"

Nate gave her a grim look. "We're dealing with a murder victim. Teenage girl."

Jessica's expression buckled with sadness, but she pulled it into line quickly. "Timeframe?"

"Not yet. That's what we need to work on. Did any of the previous homeowners have children?"

"Yeah, a few of them."

"We'll start there. Work out which families would've had teenage daughters at the time they lived in the house. Start looking into school records for me. Let's build profiles for these families and see if we can't find a Jane Doe candidate among them. We have to narrow down this field." He spun and headed for his office, forgetting to thank Jessica for her work.

His mind was humming with notions as he relived his meeting with Chad.

Was it a suicide? An accidental death? A crime of passion?

Had the victim tried to dump her unstable boyfriend?

Was she cheating on him?

Or was it something else entirely?

Nate's brain buzzed with questions as he scrambled to turn on his computer and start digging through the history of the old farm on Fraser Road.

"Are you blind yet?" Camila dumped a paper takeout bag on her desk and slumped into her seat.

Nate rubbed his eyes and groaned.

"Seriously, move away from the screen. Go have lunch already. Or breakfast, knowing you. You haven't eaten properly today, have you?"

He responded with a grunt that screamed, "Shut up, Mom!"

Cam snickered and pulled a paper-wrapped burger from the crumpled bag. She threw it at Nate and he caught it one-handed. The idea of eating wasn't very appealing, but his grumbling stomach told him he was full of it.

Unwrapping the burger, he bit into the juicy beef and mumbled a quick thank you.

"You're welcome." She grinned, popping a French fry into her mouth and licking the salt off her finger. "So, how many homeowners with teenage daughters did the farm have?"

"Five," Nate grumbled. "The place is a hundred years old and has had a steady stream of owners from about 1935 onward."

"You shouldn't be looking at anything earlier than when the blankets were made."

"I know that," he snapped, dropping his half-eaten burger on the wrapper and looking back at the screen. "But we still haven't found the manufacturer, and polyester was introduced to America in 1951. I'm just being thorough."

Cam raised her hands and backed off. "So, you got anything of interest, then?"

"The Millers owned the property from 1963 until 1978. According to town and school records, they had two sons and a daughter. Jess is looking into where the family is now. After that, the property went to the Bormans, who owned it until '91. They had a daughter, but she left home only a year after they moved in."

"How do you know that?"

"I found a picture of them in the *Aspen Falls Daily*. She was some genius kid who won a scholarship to Harvard."

"So where's she at now?" Cam propped her legs on the corner of the desk and crossed her ankles.

"I lost track of her after she graduated from Harvard. She's probably gotten married and changed her name. I'm looking into it," Nate gritted out.

"Okay. So if you can't find her, then it's a possibility."

Nate glanced over his shoulder. "She graduated from Harvard, which meant she would've been in her twenties. I'm ruling her out."

"Good point." Cam's lips smacked as she licked

more salt off her fingertips, then reached for another fry. "Anyone else you're looking into?"

Nate sighed and scrubbed a hand down his face. "Another option is the Schnyders. They took over the property in '93. It'd sat empty for two years, and they bought it for a song and operated the farm until 2007 when the bank foreclosed on them after they failed to make mortgage repayments. From there, the house was bought one other time by a single guy in his forties, Melvin Sims, but after only two years of owning the place, he declared bankruptcy. It's been sitting empty ever since."

"Where's this Sims guy now?"

Nate flicked through the myriad of open files on his computer desktop. "According to Jessica's report, the trail runs dry in 2012. He left Aspen Falls and hasn't been back since."

"He could be the killer."

"I'm aware of that," Nate huffed. "But we have to identify the body before we start jumping to conclusions."

"Yeah, yeah, I know." Cam's feet thumped on the floor as she swung her legs down. "Let's go back to the Schnyder family for a second. Any daughters?"

"Yeah, Jess thinks so. According to her report, there was a Mila Schnyder who attended Aspen Falls High from 2003 to 2006. I need to cross-reference the address, but it could be another possibility, although any teenage girl who has lived in Aspen Falls since 1958 would've attended Aspen Falls High. It's the only school to go to."

"Have you managed to find this Mila chick? Does she still live in Aspen Falls?"

Nate shook his head and scribbled another note on the chaotic sheet of paper beside him. "Don't think so. I'll follow it up, though."

"Where are the parents now?"

"I'm not that far along yet. I've only just started looking into them."

"You said they foreclosed?"

"Yeah."

"And so did that Sims guy?"

"Uh-huh." Nate squinted at the screen, adding more scribbled notes to his list of things to do as he skimmed Jessica's report on the Schnyders.

"Geez, it's like the property was cursed or something," Cam muttered. "Is there anything there on why the Schnyders couldn't meet payments? Had they been struggling for a while, or did they get stung by the recession?"

"I need to call the bank and find out, but I doubt they'll tell us that kind of stuff. We'd need a warrant to get personal banking details."

Cam made a face. It frustrated Nate too, but people had a right to privacy.

A short knock at the door made them both look up.

"Hey, guys," said Mick, holding up a slip of paper. "A Mrs. Turner just called in asking about the Fraser Road place. She saw the article in the paper and was curious."

Nate rolled his eyes and Cam snickered at his expression before asking, "So, what'd you tell her?"

"That I couldn't disclose information about an ongoing case. She then went on to tell me that she was friends with one of the previous owners." Mick glanced at the slip of paper. "Darlene Schnyder, and she wouldn't drop the call until I promised to pass the information along to you."

Nate and Cam shared a quick look. She wiggled her eyebrows and shot out of her seat. "Leave it with me. I'll take that one. You follow the Mila thread and see if the school can tell us anything." She grabbed the paper out of Mick's hands. "Thank you, Micky Boy."

"Don't…" He winced. "Micky Boy." His pained expression made Cam laugh as he slumped out of the room.

Nate grinned and turned back to his computer.

Thirty minutes later, he and Cam reconvened to share notes.

"What've you got?" Nate pointed his pen at Cam.

"Okay." She took a swig of Coke, then placed the can down on the corner of her desk. "Jean Turner knew Darlene Schnyder, but wasn't close friends with her or anything. She was good friends with Darlene's cousin, who—before you ask—no longer lives in the area."

Nate let out a frustrated grunt.

"So, according to Jean, who used to gossip with Darlene's cousin all the time, the Schnyders were doing just fine until the middle of 2006 when Vern Schnyder just up and left. Darlene couldn't run the farm on her own and in the end, the bank had to foreclose."

"I wonder why the husband took off."

"Jean's theory was that Darlene kicked him out after everything that went down with the daughter."

Nate sat forward. "Which was?"

Cam frowned. "Jean clammed up when I tried to press her, like she was suddenly realizing that she was crossing some kind of line. I told her it was important, and asked if she knew where Darlene Schnyder was so I could speak to her personally about it." Cam sighed. "Unfortunately, she's gone. Died of cancer about five years ago."

"Shit," Nate muttered.

"I know." Cam dropped her pad on the desk.

"So she didn't say anything else? No clues?"

"All I got was that Vern Schnyder left and Darlene was all alone. There's obviously some kind of rumor circulating about the daughter, but I don't know what."

"Darlene was all alone," Nate murmured. "Do you think the daughter went with him? Or he took the daughter or something?"

"That doesn't exactly go along with her kicking her husband out." Cam gave a thoughtful pout. "I might go visit Mrs. Turner in person tomorrow, see if I can't get more out of the woman." Grabbing her Coke can, she took another large gulp and wiped her glistening lips with the back of her hand. "So what'd you find out?"

"According to her track coach, Mila Schnyder dropped out less than two months before graduation."

"Why?"

"He doesn't know. She just stopped showing up for classes. When the school contacted the family about it, the father said she'd decided not to bother graduating, but wouldn't say more. Eddie was gutted. Apparently she was quite the runner."

"Eddie?" Cam's dark eyebrows shot up, proving she wasn't a true Aspen Falls local. Anyone who grew up in Aspen Falls knew Coach Eddie Carlton. He was a freaking institution at Aspen Falls High. He must've been working at the school for at least twenty-five years.

Nate grinned. "Coach Carlton's my contact at

Aspen Falls High. If I ever need gossip on what's going on around the school, he's my man. The guy doesn't give a shit about policy and procedure. If it's helping out a police officer, he'll tell you anything."

"Good to know." Cam smirked and leaned back in her chair. "So, Mila dropping out with no explanation is weird, right?"

"I know. Unless she thought she was going to flunk out anyway." Nate made a note to see if he could get a look at her academic records.

"Teenagers can be impulsive."

"True, but she was seventeen. They usually have a little more direction by then."

"Something must've motivated her." Cam's brown eyes narrowed. "I wonder what happened with the father? What did Jean not want to tell me?" She tapped her long finger against her chin and glanced at Cam. "Did the coach say anything about Mila's emotional state?"

Nate shook his head. "He didn't know too much. All he cared about was the fact that he'd lost one of his long-distance runners, but he's not the kind of guy to mess around with quitters. He probably wrote her off after two missed practices."

"So a hard-ass coach, then?"

Nate raised his eyebrows. "Oh yeah."

"Do you know if any of the other teachers in the

school might remember her? Maybe we can talk to one of them."

"Eddie rattled off a bunch of teachers who'd been there for a long time. One of them is bound to know Mila," Nate murmured, turning back to his computer. "I'll go through the website and check out the names, see if any of them would be willing to have a casual chat with me."

Cam winced. "Until we identify Mila as the victim, it's not exactly legal to be hunting around the school and talking to a bunch of teachers."

Nate shot her a quick grin. "That's why I said *casual* chat."

12

Tuesday, May 8th
2:05pm

SALLY HAD FELT sluggish all day. Alcohol, even in moderation, always gave her a headache, and dragging her butt out of bed had been hard work. The hospital's usual bustle and hive of activity snapped her out of her stupor…until she took a break. If she sat down for even a moment, she knew the effects of the previous night would swamp her.

"You look exhausted, girl." The head nurse, Trisha, checked her watch and then lightly tapped Sally's knee. "You go on and take a break now."

"If I take a break, I'll fall asleep and never wake up," Sally moaned, resting her forehead against the cool desk. "Am I too young to complain that I'm getting old?"

"Oh, stop." Trisha snorted. "You have definitely not earned the right to talk like that."

"But I feel like a dinosaur today."

"Your bones aren't even creaking. Now get, before you miss your break altogether." She flicked her hand, sending Sally off.

With a reluctant sigh, she stood on heavy legs and shuffled away from the nurses' station. She didn't even make it to the break room before she was stopped by an energetic Lena.

Her smile was bright sunshine and Sally frowned at her. "You are such a cow for not feeling like crap today."

"What can I say? I drink well." She winked. "You taking your break?"

"Yep. Trisha ordered me away."

"Good. Go sit in the sunshine. It'll make you feel better."

Sally narrowed her eyes. Something in Lena's smile told Sally there was more to it. "What?"

"Nothing." Her voice pitched as she raised her hands in the air.

"You are the worst liar."

"I know." She blew Sally a kiss and walked away.

Sally gazed down the corridor leading outside. Part of her was tempted to walk to the break room and ignore her friend, but she knew she'd never hear the end of it.

There was obviously something outside that Lena wanted her to see.

Was it Nate?

Was he leaning against his bike with a bouquet of flowers and the world's best apology?

Her heart quickened with hope until she realized what an absurd dream that was.

Like a wounded puppy, Nate had gone into hiding, and he wouldn't be coming anywhere near her for a long time. She knew him well enough to know he'd drown in police work before buying flowers and trying to promise her something he couldn't deliver.

She'd left him.

Hurt him.

He'd struggle to let go of that.

Her eyes burned as she remembered the look on his face when she told him they might as well end it.

But what was she supposed to do?

He'd backed her into a corner. Worn her down. He wasn't going to change.

Could she have done more, though? Said more? Tried to reach him in a different way?

By the time she reached the door, her shoulders were slumped forward. The urge to drop to her knees and curl into a ball was strong. A decent sob-fest wouldn't be hard to muster. But she wouldn't get the chance, because when she walked outside she was met with the last sight she expected to see.

Waiting in the sunshine was Oscar. He was holding a large bouquet of flowers—yellows, oranges, purples and reds. A cheerful selection that could make any girl smile.

Sally did.

They were beautiful.

"I hope you don't mind me showing up unannounced." He pointed to the hospital. "Lena said it would be okay."

Sally took the flowers and sniffed them before giving him a shy smile. "Thank you."

"I just wanted to see how you were doing and, uh…" He let out an embarrassed laugh and then admitted, "I wanted to tell you that I had a wonderful time last night. I can't stop thinking about it. About you."

Sally swallowed.

She wasn't used to this. She'd been in a relationship for so long it seemed weird to be pursued again…and by Oscar, of all people.

"I was wondering if I could take you out sometime. I mean, if it's not too soon after the breakup." He winced. "I know it's weird. Your family is like, well, family to me, but last night, I just…saw you differently." Oscar took off his shades and perched them on the top of his head. His brown eyes studied her, making her feel pretty. He grinned. "Maybe we could go out for dinner or just a drive somewhere. Whatever you'd like, really."

"I..." Sally forced a smile. "That's really sweet, but I..."

"I know. The whole Nate thing, right? I really am not trying to take advantage of the fact that you're probably still hurting, I swear. If anything, I want to make you feel better."

His accent was cute. It made each word sound so strong and purposeful. His elegance was hard to ignore. His smooth way. It'd be so easy to have a meal with him. She could spend the whole time just listening to him talk.

"I just..." His straight white teeth flashed. "I would hate myself if I walked away without at least trying. I know gold when I see it, and you've never been available before. But now you are, and it's all I can think about."

Brushing a wisp of hair off her face, Sally felt herself blush. She seemed to do that a lot around him. Probably because he kept complimenting her. Making her feel like she was something special.

"I won't pressure you." Reaching into his pocket, he pulled out a business card. "I'm in town for a good long while and I'm a patient man. You give me a call whenever you're ready."

Slipping the card into the top of the bouquet, he gave her another stunning smile before walking back to his car. Sally watched him the whole way, raising her hand when he spun to wave goodbye.

Her heart fluttered oddly in her chest.

It seemed too soon to move on.

Her heart wasn't ready for someone new.

It still beat for Nate.

Sniffing the flowers again, she gazed down at the gorgeous petals. Oscar had picked perfectly. All her favorite colors bundled together into something pretty.

"Aren't they beautiful? I nearly died when I saw them." Lena slipped out the door and wrapped her arm around Sally's shoulders. "At first I hoped they were for me, but he asked for you the second he saw me." She looked at Sally with a hopeful smile. "Did he ask you out?"

"Yes," Sally croaked. "But it's too soon."

Lena growled in her throat and squeezed Sally's shoulder. "Don't talk stupid. It's not too soon if it's right. Stop waiting around for what you want and go for it."

"I want Nate," Sally murmured.

"You say that, but do you really? If Nate was so perfect, then why did he never show up? You want Nate to be something he's not, which isn't fair to either of you. Think about all those times you were miserable, complaining about how you never saw him. How his mind was always on work. Oscar is here, now, and he wants to spend time with you. He wants to take you out and treat you like a lady. You deserve that, *mi hermana*."

Sally grinned at her friend. "You're sweet."

"I'm right. Just admit it. A little part of you wants to go out with Oscar and see what it's like."

"Maybe." Sally shrugged, pocketing the card before Lena could steal it and somehow force her into a date she wasn't ready for.

As she followed her friend inside and walked the flowers back to the station, she was met with various reactions. All of them were good, including the last, which was a doctor who murmured, "He must think you're something special."

The man winked before turning away, and Sally had to admit how special Oscar had made her feel.

And for the first time in over three years, her heart spared a beat for someone other than Nate.

13

Tuesday, May 8th
3:45pm

Nate's shoes echoed in the empty school corridors as he clipped his way down to Ms. Stewart's science lab. She was the only teacher at Aspen Falls High who had agreed to meet with him at such short notice. Out of the eight names Eddie had given him, only two had taught Mila and only one was available for comment.

Nate racked his brain to see if he could remember Ms. Stewart when he'd been at Aspen Falls High, but she'd never taught him. He couldn't remember Mila Schnyder either. She would've been a sophomore when he was a senior, and as hard as he studied her picture, he couldn't even conjure an image of passing her in the school corridor.

He'd stopped by home on his way to the school and dug out his yearbooks. He found a few images of Mila. One on the track team, another in the Science Club, and then her student photo in the sophomore section. That was the best one. Her smile was broad and toothy, her blonde curls carefully managed. She had a cheerful sparkle in her blue-gray eyes, which reminded Nate of Sally.

His gut pinched as he fought off images of his ex-girlfriend and focused back on the case. He paused outside the science lab and tapped his knuckle on the door that was just slightly ajar.

"Yes, come in," a woman with a featherlight voice called.

Nate had already seen the woman on the AF High website, and she looked exactly like her photo—middle-aged, short gray-speckled curls, creases around her eyes. She wore pastel colors and clothes that looked a decade or two old. She obviously didn't care too much about fashion, but it was clear she'd dedicated her life to teaching.

Her lab was spotless and tidy. The board was covered with formulas and annotations, and assignments were piled high on either side of her desk. She was scribbling a lengthy comment on one assignment with a bright red pen, not even looking up as Nate approached her.

"Good afternoon, Ms. Stewart. I'm Detective Hartford."

She finally glanced up and pulled the glasses off the end of her nose. "Oh hello, Detective."

"Thank you so much for agreeing to meet with me."

"It's not a problem." She capped her pen and indicated for Nate to take a seat at the lab table closest to hers. "Although I'm not sure how much help I'll be. It was a long time ago now. But you are the police, and it's my civic duty to assist as much as I'm able."

Nate gave her a tight smile, glad she didn't know that this casual chat was kind of bending the rules. He pulled out his notebook and perched on the stool. "So, Mila was in your Advanced Chemistry class in her senior year."

"Yes. I went through my computer and pulled up her records, trying to jog my memory. That was twelve years ago now, and I had to study her ID photo to even remember her, but I think I do. She was a straight-A student. Very motivated and alert. Somewhat intelligent, although I think her grades reflected her attitude toward learning and hard work more than her natural ability."

Nate's eyebrows lifted in surprise. "Yet she dropped out."

"Yes." The woman frowned. "Very surprising, although according to my records here, it did show her grades slipping in the last few months." The woman closed her eyes, her wrinkles highlighted as she scrunched up her face. "There were a few wayward girls that year. I'm just trying to think if they were friends with Mila or not. I can picture a little cluster of them." Her curls bobbed as she shook her head. "Not sure, but Mila's test scores show a sharp decline after spring break. I don't know what she got up to, but she came back very distracted. She didn't seem to care about schoolwork as much as she had before, and it reflected in her grades."

"Do you know why she was acting that way?"

The woman shook her head. "I'm here to teach, Detective, not be a counselor. I leave that job to the experts, which is why I suggested she spend some time with our guidance counselor. I made a note of that at the time." She pointed at her computer screen.

"And did she?"

"Not that I'm aware of. I couldn't force her to go, and from what I observed in class, she wasn't high or intoxicated. She just seemed distracted." The teacher squinted at her screen, putting her glasses back on before reading. "Mila is not herself, staring out the window with a dreamy smile. I've never seen her so unfocused. Have suggested she have a session with

Mrs. Griffin before her grades are affected too badly."

"A dreamy smile?" Nate repeated.

"Yes." The woman nodded, looking slightly mystified by why a motivated seventeen-year-old would suddenly become distracted this way.

A dreamy smile.

Didn't that say it all?

Nate checked the woman's hand and saw no rings on her fingers. He was tempted to ask if she was single and how long she'd been that way, but it was none of his business.

A dreamy smile.

Anyone who'd experienced a high school crush would understand.

"Ms. Stewart, do you know if Mila had a boyfriend? Did she maybe start dating someone during spring break?"

"Oh, I wouldn't know." The woman stiffened. "It's not my job to keep track of my students' love lives. The amount they switch and change partners these days is ridiculous."

"I was just wondering if Mila was distracted because she was in love."

"She was seventeen." The woman looked incredulous. "You can't fall in love at seventeen."

Nate had to bite back his snicker. "I'm sorry to disagree, ma'am, but I think teenagers fall in love all the time. Their emotions are often much stronger too. Dreamy smiles and distracted behavior indicates to me that Mila Schnyder may well have been in love."

The woman frowned and snatched her red pen off the table, fidgeting with it while she muttered, "Yes, well, I don't really know too much about that sort of thing."

"Right." Nate swallowed and changed tactics. It was becoming increasingly obvious that Ms. Stewart was passionate about teaching science… and only science. She wasn't one of those teachers to get to know her students on a personal level. "So, when Mila stopped attending classes, were you aware of any rumors circulating? Did you hear any other students talking about her?"

She popped the cap off her pen, then replaced it. "Such a long time ago now, it's hard to remember. Rumors circulate around my lab constantly, and I tend to ignore them and tell my students to get on with it. Although…" She started wagging her finger in the air. "I get confused with who got up to what. I've seen a lot of students in my extensive years of teaching, but was she the girl who got pregnant? Or did she run away?" The woman's shoulder hitched. "Something like that sounds familiar. There were a couple of things going on with that senior class that year, I just can't remember which crisis belonged to which student."

Nate scribbled down 'pregnant' and 'runaway.'

"Can you remember anything else?"

The woman shook her head. "I'm sorry I can't be more helpful, Detective. I really see so many students each year and I don't get to know them all. There are just too many."

Her tight smile indicated that she preferred to keep them at a professional distance. They were there to learn, not bond with her.

Nate stood, holding his sigh in check as he slipped his notebook and pen away. "Thank you so much for your time, Ms. Stewart."

"Of course." She nodded once more before she uncapped her pen and got back to work.

Nate walked away from the classroom, his brain buzzing as he strode to the car. Pregnant or runaway. Two great reasons to drop out of school.

Runaway.

Nate toyed with that scenario as he walked to his car. "I wonder if there'd be a police report about that."

Picking up his pace, Nate double-timed it back to the AFPD precinct.

It took Nate longer than he expected, and he was close to giving up when he discovered mention of a 911 call from the farmhouse on Fraser Road. Dispatch had been called at 3:45pm on May 22, 2006. It was like the information had been buried intentionally with the effort it took Nate to dig it up. After multiple failed searches, he'd ended up trawling through records from spring break of 2006 onward.

Cam and Jessica had already checked out for the night, but he'd stayed on, unable to rest until he'd found something on the Schnyder family. And his determination had paid off.

Mrs. Darlene Schnyder had called the police, claiming her daughter was missing. Unit 2579 was sent to follow up.

"Missing. Bingo." Nate's forehead wrinkled as the skeleton on Chad's table flashed through his mind. Puzzle pieces were slotting into place quickly, and he didn't like the picture they were creating.

"So, where's the police report?" Nate scrolled down the login page and found no follow-up information.

With a marked frown, he stood from his chair and headed for the back of the station.

The storage unit wouldn't be manned at this time of night, so he'd have to hunt down the information on his own, but it wasn't like he had anything better to do.

Sally's beautiful smile penetrated his brain, like a painful knife wound.

He paused against the wall and squeezed his eyes shut, rubbing his temples and wishing he could live without her. Why did she keep haunting him?

"You okay, Detective?"

Nate popped his eyes open and spotted the new rookie. He stood there nervous and unsure which way to look.

Clearing his throat, Nate gave him a short nod. "I'm fine." And walked around him.

He reached the storage room and swiped his keycard, letting himself in and starting up the computer. It whirred and groaned for what felt like an hour before finally beeping that it was ready. Typing in his password, then the date and time stamp of the dispatch call, Nate tapped his finger on the desk while he waited. Finally the screen lit up with the same information that he'd been looking at in his office, except this system had the added bonus of a log number.

He touched the screen and murmured, "Two-five-oh-six-Mar-Sch."

Taking the second aisle from the right, he ran his finger along the shelf until he reached drawer 25-06. It screeched when it opened and Nate winced. Shuffling through the files, he found Mar-Sch. He pulled it out and clicked on his flashlight—a force of habit. Even though the lights were on, he still scanned things by flashlight. It helped him hone in on details he might otherwise miss.

"Arrived at the house at 4:12pm. Darlene Schnyder hysterical—agitated and yelling. Vern Schnyder visibly upset, but calm." Nathan murmured the important details as he read them.

Officer Glenn Marshall had written the report, and it was brief.

Basically he and his partner turned up at the house and talked the mother into sitting down and explaining what had happened. She was convinced her seventeen-year-old daughter, Mila, had been taken, but the father had a different story. The mother had been away for two weeks visiting with her sister in Montana, and in that time Mila had run away with her boyfriend. The father had tried to stop her, but he couldn't force her to stay and was worried if he did that they'd lose her forever.

"Did he call to give his wife a heads-up?" Nate asked aloud. He frowned, kind of appalled that the mother had returned to find a very important member of her family missing.

"She'll come back to us. We just have to give her time." Nate's eyebrows rose as he read a direct quote from the father.

Darlene Schnyder was unconvinced and wanted to file a missing persons report.

Mother wants a missing persons report filed, but father says there is no point as he let the daughter go willingly. Regardless, a report will be filed.

Nate flipped up the page he was reading and noticed the missing persons report behind it. He quickly skimmed Mila's details and the comments below them.

Runaway is turning eighteen in less than three months. Will keep an eye out for her when on patrol. If runaway is found, police will issue her with a warning and strongly suggest she return home. Boyfriend is liable to be charged with contributing to the delinquency of a minor.

Vern Schnyder claims the boyfriend is a white male in his early twenties (speculation). Sandy-brown hair. Name: Jamie. Drove a black sedan. License plate unknown.

Nate clicked off his flashlight but kept staring at the file.

Black sedan. License plate unknown.

He hated those words. It made him think about the mysterious black car that killed his mother. All he'd been able to tell the police was that it was black, and he'd hated himself for it ever since.

He wondered if Vern Schnyder felt the same way.

Or if his story about the boyfriend was a big fat lie.

Why was the mother so convinced her daughter would never run away like that, enough to call the police, yet they did nothing?

How could a father let his daughter go off with a man in his twenties so easily while the mother was away?

The father obviously knew something he wasn't willing to say.

Nate's gut twisted.

Slapping the file closed, he shunted the drawer shut and headed out of the storage room. He signed out the report to study more carefully.

What he really needed to do was speak to Officer Glenn Marshall, but he hadn't heard of him, so he was guessing the guy had retired.

He stepped out of the room and ensured the door was locked properly before opening the file again. Scanning down to the bottom, he noted the name of Marshall's partner—Brent Higginson.

"Higgs." Nate smiled and tapped the officer's name.

Walking into the meeting room, he checked the duty roster and saw the guy was on for the next day.

First thing in the morning, he was tracking the guy down and having a chat.

Maybe he could help clear up a few of the unsettling mysteries swirling in Nate's gut.

14

Wednesday, May 9th
9:30am

THE MORNING SUN was almost milky behind a soft white haze of cloud. Sally sat against the window of Lulu's Cafe, playing eye tennis between the street traffic passing by and the person she was sharing breakfast with. Oscar was telling her about his education at an all-boys boarding school. She'd heard one of the stories before, but the one about sneaking a stray puppy into their dorm room was new. He was very entertaining and Sally smiled, enjoying his funny antics. It was all so British and foreign to her, but his smooth voice and charming accent held her attention.

She was glad she'd called him.

She'd opted for breakfast, feeling it was the safest meal. It felt less like a date and definitely less romantic than a candlelit dinner. She was sure Oscar would've arranged something like that if she'd let him, but shifting from family friend to an intimate date was a little like whiplash. He'd made the transition pretty easily, which made Sally wonder if he'd been secretly harboring feelings for her for a while.

"Anyway, enough about me." Oscar waved his hand in front of his face. "I want to know what you were like as a child. Your father always says how sweet and gentle you are. Were you always that way? I bet you were the kid everyone loved."

Sally chuckled and shook her head. "I may've been sweet, but I wasn't gentle. I was always too busy trying to keep up with my brother Emmett." She tipped her head back. "Oh, man, he was my superhero, and I must've been so annoying, constantly following him around. He was really good about it. Annabelle, she was the lady. She'd rather paint nails than play soccer."

"Yes, I definitely know that." Oscar grinned. "Although you still strike me as very elegant."

Sally blushed and shook her head. "You're too nice. I just get so sick of Mom and Annabelle harping on about the fact that I'm a grown woman now. I basically wear a little makeup and brush my hair just to keep them off my back."

Oscar laughed. "I love your family. You're all so involved in each other's lives."

"Yes, we're close. Some probably think we live too much in each other's pockets."

Nate always had.

"I think it's lovely. I come from a family where affection like that was never encouraged. My boarding school mates were more family than my own parents were."

"You don't have any siblings, do you?"

Oscar tipped his head, then gave an awkward shake. "Sadly, I'm all alone."

"Oh, that's right. The car accident. You lost your parents." Sally's heart pulsed with sympathy. "That must've been really hard."

"It was. Very sudden and traumatic. It took me a while to find my feet. Actually, that's one of the reasons I came to America. I just needed a change, to get away and start afresh. With my grand-mother being a Chicago native, I managed to secure a work visa. Things just sort of snowballed from there, and then I got that entry-level job at Richmond Construction." His lips twitched with pride.

"You've worked your way up the ranks pretty fast, but my dad adores you."

"He's an amazing man." Oscar's smile was broad and grateful.

Sally shrugged. "He knows quality when he sees it."

Oscar brushed her compliment away with a shy smile. "Your family has been so wonderful, welcoming me in the way you have."

His expression helped Sally understand why he was so drawn to her family. It was kind of sweet.

A figure paused by the table, her long fingers smoothing down her black apron as she asked, "Is everything good here? Can I get you more tea?"

Sally glanced up at Rosie and smiled. Blaine's girlfriend had really grown in confidence the last few months. It was so nice to see. She remembered her from high school. They'd run in very different circles and hadn't had anything to do with each other. But since dating Blaine, they'd shared a few meals, and Sally discovered that she really liked her.

"No, I'm good. Thanks, Rosie."

"I'll take a top up of tea, if that's alright." Oscar held up his cup and saucer.

"No problem." Rosie took it with a grin and walked away to refill it. She shared a quick glance with Sally that told her she thought his accent was cute or he was cute…or something to that effect.

He really was.

Leaning his elbows on the table, his sparkling brown eyes gave her his full attention. "So you were a bit of a tomboy, then, I take it?"

"Yeah, you could say that. I'm pretty sure my mother was close to giving up on making a lady out of me, but high school and crushes on boys helped bring out my feminine side."

Oscar laughed and clapped his hands together before asking her another question.

He really seemed interested in her, and she was struggling to adjust to being the center of someone's attention for such a length of time. Being one of four, she'd always been competing, and then with Nate and his work, she was used to being an afterthought. He was able to ask her about her day and focus for most of her report back, but within minutes his eyes would start to drift, and his mind was back on whatever case he was currently working.

Sally had learned to keep things short and simple, but Oscar just kept on asking for more details.

She was halfway through a story of a family trip to Hawaii where she'd been stung by a jellyfish when Oscar's phone rang. She stopped immediately and pointed to his ringing pocket. "I'll let you get that."

"It can wait." He tapped his pocket and let the phone ring.

She raised her eyebrows. "I really don't mind."

With a gentle smile, he reached across the table and took her hand, lightly running his thumb over her knuckles. "I'm in a very important meeting right now. Whoever's trying to call me can wait."

Her swallow was thick as she blinked and started tracing the grooves in the table with her free hand.

"So, that jellyfish…how mean was he?"

Sally blinked and struggled to smile. Oscar's warm fingers around hers felt foreign and out of place. She was used to Nate's slightly rough hands, the soft calluses and broad fingers. She could still remember the feel of them tracing every inch of her body. His tamed strength, his protective tenderness. Her body still yearned for those moments.

But they wouldn't come anymore, because she'd walked away.

"Sally?" Oscar lightly shook her hand.

She swallowed, forcing Nate from her mind. "That jelly was mean," she finally said. "Really mean, and then of course Emmett wanted to pee on me because apparently that takes the sting away. You can imagine my reaction to that."

Oscar chuckled. "I bet you screamed the beach down."

Sally grinned. An image of Nate's face flashed through her mind. When she'd told him the jellyfish story, he'd kissed her cheek and playfully whispered, "I would've peed on you, baby. Anything to make the pain stop."

She'd melted at those words, her breathy giggle

swallowed by his kiss. Nate had always affected her so strongly.

But Oscar was sweet too, just in a different way.

Besides, he was there. He was attentive. Those were all good things.

Nate wasn't part of her life anymore. Was she always going to pine for him?

She was aware the break up was still fresh and she shouldn't feel pressured to rush into something new, but the idea of missing him with such intensity was a heavy burden…especially when the chances of reality changing were slim. Nate was married to his work, which left no room for her.

Maybe moving on would help dampen the pain.

Would being with Oscar help her get the life she wanted?

Or would Nate always be with her, no matter what, haunting her moments and making it hard to breathe?

15

Wednesday, May 9th
10:30am

NATE WORKED SO LATE the night before that he overslept and ended up barreling into work over three hours late. He cursed himself the entire way to the station, but his anger dissipated the second he walked in and spotted Higgs.

"You're still here."

Higgs gave him a confused frown before taking a sip of coffee. "Just brought in a drunk for booking."

"You got a second?"

"I'm about to head back out on patrol." Higgs pointed over his shoulder. Mick was waiting behind him.

"I need to talk to you for a minute." Nate remained quietly insistent.

The younger officer read between the lines and excused himself. "I'll wait for you in the car, Higgs."

"Sounds good." Tucking his thumbs into his belt, he gave Nate a curious smile. "What's up?"

"It's this Jane Doe case. I've got a horrible feeling that I know who the victim might be, and I need your help to ID her."

"Me?" Higgs pointed at himself. "Why me?"

With a little flick of his fingers, he led Higgs into his office and opened up the file he'd been reading the night before. "Do you remember visiting the Schnyder family back in May 2006? Your name's on the report as the accompanying officer."

"That was twelve years ago." Higgs frowned for a minute and pulled the file toward him. After a brief scan, he bobbed his head. "Oh yeah. I think I do remember this. Mrs. Schnyder was hard work that day. She was adamant her baby girl wouldn't run away with that boy."

"And you didn't believe her?"

Higgs shrugged. "I was with Glenn. He was a veteran cop, you know. He knew how to read people and he believed Vern. They were friends, and Mrs. Schnyder was kind of hysterical."

"So it just sat okay with you?"

Higgs closed the file and gave Nate a wary look. “I take it it doesn’t sit okay with you?”

“Not when I’ve got a teenage female skeleton of European descent dug up on their property.”

Higgs’s thick eyebrows dipped together. “You think it’s the daughter?”

“It’s a damn good guess. She dropped out of school and went missing while the mother was away.”

Higgs’s face wrinkled with a frown. “You don’t think the father did it, do you?”

“Why do you look so surprised?”

“I don’t know, I just… I mean, he was a friend of Glenn’s, and the way he described him, I can’t imagine a man like that hurting his kid. From what Glenn said, he was a really dedicated family man, and he just thought that letting the daughter go was the right thing. He didn’t want to lose her and figured she’d come back.”

“But she never did.”

“Well, I don’t think so, but it was a while ago now. Have you spoken to the mother?”

“Darlene Schnyder died of cancer five years ago, and I have no idea where the father is. All I know is that he took off shortly after that incident, and that’s a red flag to me.”

Higgs made a face and took another sip of coffee, clearly avoiding Nate’s gaze.

"What?" Nate crossed his arms and drilled the older man with a reprimanding glare. "What are you not telling me?"

With a reluctant sigh, Higgs finally muttered, "Look, Glenn made me swear not to perpetuate this rumor."

"What rumor?"

Higgs sighed, throwing his Styrofoam cup in the closest trash can before quietly confessing. "Word got out that Vern was messing with his daughter." His face buckled with disgust. "Molesting her."

Nate's head jerked back. "That's not in the report."

"Of course it's not." Higgs shook his head. "It kind of came up after Mila ran away. People wanted an explanation and someone—we never found out who—suggested that she ran away because Vern was… well, anyway, it tore the poor guy apart. It didn't help that his wife bought into it too. After that, he couldn't stay. He couldn't bear the idea that someone thought he'd touched his daughter like that. He loved her." Higgs looked convinced as he caught Nate's eye. "He loved her the way a father should love a daughter. The way I love mine. Glenn never once believed any of that crap, and I was with him."

Nate uncrossed his arms and slid his hands into his pockets. "Okay, so if you don't think Vern

Schnyder was capable of abusing her, then there's no way he'd kill her."

"Right." Higgs pointed at him.

"So who did? And why the hell bury her on the property? Unless it was this mysterious boyfriend. But even then, the risk of getting caught... it's just stupid."

Higgs shrugged. "I don't know. Criminals can be idiots."

Nate made a face, showing Higgs that the excuse wasn't enough.

"Look, how sure are you that the skeleton is the girl from this report? What if it's someone else?"

Nate pinched the bridge of his nose. "It just seems to fit, and I want to follow through on this until I come up with a better theory."

"Have you looked for dental records?"

"Yeah, Jess is tracking down which dentist she went to in town. Hopefully we can get her records, and then Chad can see if it's a match."

"So that should give you a positive ID, then."

"Yeah, but that still doesn't get me any closer to the killer."

"Look, if the records match, and the bones belong to Mila, my first bet would be the boyfriend. Vern Schnyder painted a pretty clear picture of the guy the day we visited the house, enough to make me think it wasn't a figment of his imagination. No one had seen or heard of the guy, but Vern was clear. Maybe he came back to the house after it was abandoned and buried her there, figuring it was a safe place to hide her."

"I need to find the father and see what he can remember, but we have no idea where he is. His trail goes cold after he left town." Nate huffed.

Higgs gazed at him for a long beat, then quietly offered a solution. "You know, Glenn Marshall still lives nearby. He and his wife own one of those hobby farms about thirty minutes out of town. He was a friend of Vern's. He might still know where he is."

Nate worked his jaw to the side as he pulled out his phone. "You know the address?"

"No, but I'll look it up for you before I leave." He stepped out of the room before Nate could even thank him.

Dropping his phone onto the open file, Nate raked a hand through his hair and held back his groan of frustration. This was never going to be a simple open-and-shut case. He felt like he was trying to construct a jigsaw puzzle with pieces from three different boxes. Between rumors, sketchy memories, and imprecise police reports, Nate wasn't sure who to believe. He knew what made sense, but sometimes the most logical story wasn't the right one.

16

Wednesday, May 9th
11:00am

As soon as Oscar dropped her home, Sally raced inside and got changed.

She needed to run.

To be out in the fresh air.

To think.

Oscar had kissed her before he left. Just a very chaste brushing of the lips, but still, it unsettled her.

She hadn't kissed another man since Nate, and she couldn't get over the fact that it felt too soon. Too rushed.

Her heart still beat for that infuriating detective, and even though breakfast with Oscar had been lovely and entertaining, she was left crying on the inside.

She wanted lovely, entertaining meals with Nate.

She wanted to glance up and catch his blue gaze on her, be warmed by his little wink and the way his lips pulled up into that half smile.

When Nate was there and not hindered by a case, he was everything.

Why couldn't he want her as much as she wanted him?

Why couldn't he put her first?

"Come on, Rusty Boy, let's go." She clipped on his leash and took him out the door.

The sun had burned the clouds away and the air had a crisp, spring freshness to it. Sally relished the clear blue sky, pulling Rusty along at a fast clip until sweat began to drip down her belly and her lungs burned.

She didn't care. She kept pushing until she'd made it all the way to Bleaker Street.

Rusty, his long tongue hanging out of his mouth, took a seat beside her as she rested her hands on her knees to catch her breath.

This was her halfway point and for the sake of her dog, she knew she'd need to take it slow on the way back. She'd probably jog/walk home and arrive thoroughly saturated and smelly.

That made her smile.

If Xavier was working at the home office, she'd track him down and hug him. She laughed, but the sound was cut short when she spotted Nate cruising down the road. He was in one of the department vehicles—silver and innocuous. His jaw was set tight, his eyes glaring at the road ahead.

He didn't see her. Drove right past without a second glance.

Or had he seen her? Was he just keeping his eyes forward to avoid looking at her?

She wasn't sure.

But it almost didn't matter.

There was a really strong chance that even if they were still together, he wouldn't have given her a glance or a wave. He was busy working, and that was all that mattered.

"Come on, Rusty," Sally rasped. "Let's go home."

She tugged on his leash and strolled back toward the place she'd spent her teenage years. Her little bungalow on Kent Street was still unlivable. The second she walked in, she'd smell Nate and be flooded with memories of them together. She just couldn't bring herself to go there. Besides, it was nice being home again. Having her family around.

Taking her sweet time, because that was all her legs would let her do, Sally wandered home and eventually walked in the door to the sound of laughter from the kitchen.

She went there before heading up to a shower and saw her mom patting Emmett on the back, still laughing. He was due back to the base in the next few days, and they were all going to feel his departure. The house would be just a little quieter, a little less complete.

Sally wasn't in the mood to find out why they were laughing, so she didn't ask. Instead, she got some fresh water for Rusty, gave him a little pet, then turned to get a glass of water for herself.

"Good run, sweetie?" Her mom smiled at her.

"Yeah. It's a nice day. Rusty loved it."

"He looks ready to keel over." Emmett stared down at the dog he'd bought Sally for her twenty-first birthday.

"He's just fine, thank you very much. He'll have a nap and then be a ball of energy again."

Emmett winked at her and took her glass, putting it in the dishwasher so she didn't have to.

Leaning her elbows on the counter, she resisted the urge to ask what everyone was up to that afternoon. She didn't really feel like hanging out. A hot shower and reading a book in bed would be a good way to spend the rest of the day.

"So…how was breakfast?" Emmett nudged her elbow, wiggling his eyebrows like only an annoying older brother could.

She jerked up with surprise. "How did you —Mom!"

"What?" Her mother laughed, wiping down the counter and trying to look innocent. "He asked me where you were. Was I supposed to lie?"

Sally groaned and tipped her head back.

"Oh, stop," her mother chided. "I'm excited you went out with Oscar. He's such a gentleman. Really good quality. Of course I'm going to share that with your brother."

Sally bit her lips together, hoping they wouldn't bring up Nate and start some kind of comparison.

Emmett folded his large arms, accentuating his finely honed muscles. "What's the big deal, sis? It was just breakfast. I think it's cool. He's a good guy."

"Who's a good guy?" Xavier sauntered into the room, unbuttoning his shirtsleeves and rolling them up.

"You ready for lunch, baby?" their mother asked, turning for the fridge.

"Thanks, Mom." Xavier, unaware of how pampered he was, leaned his hip against the counter. "Who are we talking about?"

"Oscar." Emmett started helping his mother with lunch prep.

Xavier stuck out his tongue. "Ugh. Gag me."

"You know you sound like a girl when you say that, right?" Emmett shot his brother a pitying look.

Xavier plucked a grape from the fruit bowl and chucked it at him. Emmett opened his mouth and dipped, catching the grape before raising his hands in the air and cheering.

The youngest brother rolled his eyes and turned away from the brother he could never compete with.

"I don't like him," Xavier grumbled.

"Who? Emmett or Oscar?" Sally winked.

It brought a little smile to Xavier's face, but then he spun to face them all. "I don't know why you all think he's so freaking wonderful. Plenty of guys could do the job just as well as he could." Xavier glanced over his shoulder, his expression flashing with concern.

"Don't worry, Dad's not home." Sally popped a grape in her mouth and grinned while she chewed.

Xavier huffed and shook his head. "I get that he's a nice guy and everything. I know his parents died and he's got no one else, blah, blah, blah. But contrary to Dad's popular opinion, the sun doesn't actually shine out his ass!"

"Yikes." Emmett winced. "Jealousy looks really bad on you, bro."

Raising his middle finger, Xavier flipped his brother off until he was scolded by their mother.

Sally snorted as he huffed and walked out of the room.

"You shouldn't tease him, Emmett." Yvonne

flicked him with the dishtowel. "Your father picking Oscar over him was a hard pill to swallow."

"Why'd he do it, Mom?" Sally took another grape.

Her mother pulled in a breath and held it for a moment before answering. "Oscar was better suited for the position. He has been nothing but an exemplary employee since he started at the company. He's got brains, foresight, he doesn't miss a detail, plus he's really good at dealing with people. He's got that British charm working for him." She smiled, but it quickly dropped away. "Xavier still has some growing up to do. He'll be ready one day. Assisting on this project is only getting him closer to what he wants. If he can do this well, and prove to your father that he's a man, ready for more responsibility, it'll happen for him."

"A man, huh?" Sally stepped back from the counter with a grin.

"That's right." Her mother nodded, rinsing off the lettuce and shaking it dry.

Sally crossed her arms and cringed. "Maybe you need to stop making his lunch for him, then."

Her mother jerked still and looked down at the food on the counter before narrowing her eyes at Sally.

"I'm just sayin'." Sally raised her hands and walked out of the room with a giggle.

Her mother couldn't help herself. If she had her

way, all four of them would grow old together in this big house. She had yet to lose a child to marriage or migration. Emmett was the closest with his tours of duty and living on the base, but so far he'd always come home every time he had leave.

Even though Annabelle and Sally had both been in serious relationships, they'd always lived nearby and came back frequently. Her mother loved them coming over. Any time. Any day.

Walking into her room, Sally peeled the sweaty clothes off her body and dumped them into the laundry hamper, wondering how long she'd end up staying here being pampered by her mother and avoiding the reality of life without Nate.

17

Wednesday, May 9th
12:05pm

NATE NAVIGATED THE LONG, tree-lined driveway with care. Tall aspen trees stood guard, allowing dappled sunlight to dance across the hood of Nate's car until he breached the end and pulled into a wide-open space that looked like something out of a *Better Homes & Gardens* magazine.

The property was well maintained—the lawn neatly mown, the hedges clipped. The wood siding on the house was old but, Nate guessed, recently painted. The smooth, glossy coat seemed to gleam in the sunlight—snow white with royal blue trim.

The Marshalls obviously took great pride in their home.

Stepping out of the vehicle, Nate buttoned his jacket and pulled it straight.

Chickens clucked to each other in the near distance, and he spotted a swing set and slide in a patch of grass by the trampoline.

So they were grandparents.

He could imagine happy family gatherings with little ones running around while parents stood nearby catching up. It was a nice picture, and for a fleeting moment he was taken out by the immense loss he felt.

His mother.

His Sally.

They would never meet. His mom would never be able to hold his children.

Shit, he probably wouldn't even have children now that Sally was gone. He couldn't imagine loving anyone else. She'd been it. And he'd lost her.

Splaying his hand on his chest, he forced air into his lungs and pulled himself together before crunching over the white landscape rocks leading up to the front door.

He hadn't called ahead—didn't want to be given an excuse not to come.

If they weren't home, he'd just wait in the car.

Cam was back at the station, and Kellan knew where he was going. He'd take all freaking day if he had to. He wasn't leaving until he'd spoken to Glenn Marshall about his friend Vern.

He rang the doorbell and stepped back to wait, grateful when the door opened only a minute later.

"Hello." A woman with a head of gray curls gave him a cautious smile. She obviously wasn't used to people venturing down the long driveway without calling first.

"Good afternoon, ma'am. I'm Detective Nathan Hartford." He flipped open his ID. "Aspen Falls Police Department."

"Oh." Her pale eyebrows rose. "Are you here to see my Glenn?"

"Yes, ma'am. I was wondering if I could speak with him about an old case he worked back in 2006."

"Well, that was the year before he retired. Let's hope he can remember what you want to know." She winked and opened the door with a kind smile.

Leading him through to the living room, she offered him a cup of coffee. He accepted and sat down to wait for Glenn, skimming the room as he waited. Family photos dominated the walls and were neatly laid across the top of an upright piano against the wall. There was a big box of toys in the corner between the two comfy couches, and all things precious had been moved to higher planes. Their grandchildren were obviously still young.

Nate was just about to stand and inspect the

books on the shelf when a bald man wearing tartan slippers shuffled into the room with his hand outstretched. "Detective Hartford."

Nate stood to greet him. "Nice to meet you, sir."

"Oh please, call me Glenn." He waved his hand through the air before falling into his seat with a soft grunt. Stretching out his leg, he lightly tapped his heel on the ground and asked, "So, what brings you out here?"

Nate smoothed down his tie as he took a seat. "I just have a few questions about a visit you made to the Schnyder farm in May of 2006."

Glenn's smile disappeared as he shifted uncomfortably in his chair. "Awful business," he muttered.

"I take it you remember the incident?"

The man pulled in a breath through his nose and slowly nodded. "I do. Vern was really cut up about his daughter leaving them." He pressed his lips together like he was restraining himself.

Nate gave him a moment to elaborate, but when he didn't say more, he continued. "I see in the report that Mr. Schnyder claimed he let his daughter go, but his wife was convinced their daughter would never run away. Can you expand on that for me?"

The man cleared his throat and shuffled in his seat. "Vern had mentioned a boy that his Mila had met over spring break. They let her go away with some of her girlfriends because she was a bit older, and more responsible. I can't recall where they went, but she must've met this guy there. I can't remember his name."

"Jamie. That's what it says in your report."

Glenn clicked his fingers and agreed with a nod. "He was older. Vern didn't like him and Mila knew it. She never brought him home to meet the family or anything. Even her friends didn't know what he looked like. It was very clandestine. She'd always sneak off to see him."

"But it says in the report that Vern let her go because he didn't want to lose her. Why was she sneaking off to see this boyfriend?"

"Vern found out about the sneaking and tried to convince Mila to leave it alone. That guy was too old for her, and she needed to concentrate on school. He forbade her to see him and it caused a huge rift between them. She stopped speaking to him and Darlene. The tension in the house was bad."

"So, while Darlene was away, this Jamie guy showed up and Vern just let her go?"

Scrubbing a hand down his face, Glenn let out a heavy sigh. "It cut him up big-time, but she screamed that she was going either way. She didn't care what she had to do and he couldn't stop her. If he tried, she'd hate him forever and he'd never see her again." Glenn's expression reflected the deep sympathy he must have felt for his friend, and revealed just how much he cared for his own children. "It was his only child. What choice did the man have?"

Nate scratched the bottom of his chin, trying to figure out how to steer the conversation. "So, you believed him, then?"

Glenn gave him a sharp frown. "Well, of course I did. I'd been friends with Vern for years. I knew him. Watching her drive away was the hardest thing he'd ever had to do. He had tears in his eyes when he was telling me. It cut him deep."

"But Darlene—" Nate stopped.

Mrs. Marshall had returned, bringing in a tray with two coffees and some homemade baking.

Nate smiled at her. "Thank you so much."

"Milk or cream, dear?"

"No, I take it black." He took the mug from her and thanked her once more before she left.

Taking a sip, he swallowed down the slightly bitter brew before asking, "Darlene Schnyder seemed absolutely convinced that her daughter would never run away like that. Why were you content to believe Vern over her?"

Glenn's head shook as he answered. "Because she wasn't there when it happened. She didn't have to face the battle Vern did."

"Why didn't he call to warn her?"

"You don't pass on news like that over the

phone," Glenn said gruffly. "He needed to sit her down and explain calmly so she'd understand."

"Which she obviously didn't."

"She was prone to flying off the handle. A very emotional woman. Vern was the quiet, calm one. He had the better relationship with his daughter. He adored his baby girl and she adored him. You'd see them together and know how close they were."

Nate was loath to suggest it, but felt he had to unpack the rumors Higgs had mentioned. "So…you were sure their relationship was innocent?"

"Excuse me?" Coffee spilled out of Glenn's mug as he thumped it down on the side table next to him. "If you're suggesting that Vern was some sick child rapist, you can get the hell out of my house!"

Nate quickly raised his hand. "I'm sorry. I don't mean to offend. I'm just trying to get to the bottom of this. I know there were some rumors circulating, and I'm trying to figure out the true story."

"He didn't do that to his kid. I don't care what anyone else believed. It wasn't true."

"So, why'd he take off?"

"You try looking people in the face when they think you raped your child. You try looking the woman you love in the face when she's thinking those things about you. I didn't blame him for running. Not one bit. He'd just lost everything." Glenn's steely gaze hardened even more as his eyes narrowed. "Why? Why are you dredging this up now?"

Nate clenched his jaw and set his coffee down. Resting his elbows on his knees, he said, "The skeleton of a teenage girl was found beneath the floorboards of the workshop behind the Schnyders' old home. She was murdered."

The blood drained from Glenn's face. "Well, it can't be Mila. She ran away with that man. How many other families have owned that house?"

"I've looked through all the possibilities, and one of my officers is chasing down a few leads, but Mila's the closest bet. As soon as we secure her dental records, our forensic pathologist will see if they match. My guess is that it's her, so now I'm looking for the person who killed her. I figure Mr. Schnyder might be able to tell me a little more about this man she ran away with. Do you know where he is?"

Glenn didn't speak for a moment. He turned away from Nate and licked his lips before finally rasping, "That'll kill Vern for sure. Knowing his baby girl has died."

"I don't want to burden him any more than I have to, but I want to close this case. Any victim deserves justice, sir, even if the crime happened years ago."

Glenn rubbed his head, blinking rapidly as he fought what looked to be a wave of sadness. "Poor

Vern. It was such a mess. Darlene blamed him entirely. Accused him of all that nastiness when he was already mourning the loss of his baby girl. He was sure Mila would come back once she'd gotten over her first love, but Darlene just wouldn't forgive him." Glenn's eyes glassed over. "He couldn't stay after that. That woman's anger was toxic, and he just couldn't bear it."

Nate licked his lower lip and winced. "I hate to say it, but his sudden disappearance makes him look guilty. Surely as a former cop, you can see the way it looks."

"He was my friend!" Glenn pointed a quivering finger at Nate. "I believe in him. I understood." He sank back into his seat, his head shaking slowly back and forth. "He left without even saying goodbye. I don't know where he is, but Darlene cursed his name right up until the day she died. Their girl never came home. Darlene stayed in Aspen Falls waiting for her, even after the bank took the house. She stayed in a trailer nearby, walking past the house each day. Mila was never there. She never came back."

Probably because she was buried underneath the workshop. Nate kept the thought to himself.

"So, you have no idea where Vern went?"

Glenn shook his head. "I can't help you."

Nate stared at the man, looking for a lie, but he

couldn't see one. From what he could tell, Glenn Marshall believed one hundred percent that Vern was an innocent, broken man. And his leaving town had hurt Glenn too.

"Did you look for Mila? It says in your report that you were going to keep an eye out."

"I did." Glenn bobbed his head. "But I think we all knew, deep down, that she was long gone."

Nate swallowed, the sadness in the old man's voice affecting him too. "Well, I, um, appreciate your time today."

"I'm always happy to help the AFPD." Glenn struggled out of his chair to walk Nate to the door.

The news of the skeleton had clearly unsettled the older man. Nate could tell by the way his eyebrows dipped together, the look of sorrow etched onto his features.

"I'm sorry to be the bearer of bad news," Nate told him. "The remains might not be Mila Schnyder."

Glenn looked up with a sad smile. "But if they are, you need to find the truth. I don't know who could've possibly killed that beautiful girl, but she deserves justice."

"I won't stop working until I give it to her."

Glenn nodded and shook Nate's hand again before opening the door and watching him leave.

Nate waved one last time before hopping into his car. Driving back to Aspen Falls suddenly felt like a heavy burden. All that awaited him at the station were more questions...and what felt like an impossible search for a man who'd obviously wanted to leave Aspen Falls behind him.

But Nate had to find him, because his gut was screaming loud and clear that the bones on Chad's table belonged to Mila Schnyder and that girl's father knew something that could help the case.

18

Tuesday, May 22nd
10:25am

THE EMERGENCY ROOM had that chaotic buzz to it.

Doctors were shouting orders that nurses rushed to implement. Panicked people were pacing the waiting room while two children wailed and a distraught mother cried as they sat behind curtains, coping with the aftermath of a car accident.

So far there had been no fatalities, but the man who'd just been rushed into the OR was touch and go. Sally couldn't say anything to the family yet, so she remained with the man's son, who was in agony as he waited for his leg to be X-rayed. He had a nasty compound fracture that the doctor had already inspected and dressed. The kid screamed bloody murder while that was being done. The sight of bone sticking out through skin can freak anyone out.

She'd told him not to look down, but he couldn't help himself. Poor kid.

"I know it hurts, buddy. The pain relief will kick in soon. Once the X-rays are done, we're going to get you into surgery and the doctor will straighten your leg up for you."

"I'm scared." He hiccupped and shuddered beside her, tears and snot running down to his chin.

She snatched a tissue and mopped him up. "I know. It's really scary. But the doctors here are so good and before you know it, you'll be running around with your friends again. Plus, you get time off school. That's kind of cool, right?"

The boy's lips twitched slightly but didn't form a smile.

"Doc wants to know if he's had a recent tetanus." Lena stopped at the end of the bed with her pen and clipboard.

"Yes, I checked with the mother. He had one about six months ago when he needed stitches for a gash in his arm. Abbey's double-checking the records for me."

"Cool. I'll pass that on. Orderly should be here in about two minutes." Lena winked at the patient before turning to deal with the next in line.

The boy whimpered. "What's an orderly?"

"It's the very nice person who is going to wheel you down to X-ray."

"I want my dad."

"I know, but he's busy right now, getting all fixed up. We've called your mom and she should be here any minute. In the meantime you've got me, and Spencer will be arriving any second to take you to X-ray."

The boy's chin bunched, his lips trembling.

"You know what I love about Spencer?" Sally ran her hand down the boy's arm, tucking her fingers within his shaking digits. He took the comfort, squeezing hard while she tried to calm him. "Spencer's got this really funny laugh. It's like high and kind of squeaky. So if you have any good jokes up your sleeve, you have to try them out on him. It's so worth it." The boy looked at her like she was crazy, but she kept going. "You know any good jokes?"

"I've got a knock-knock one," he said quietly.

"Okay, well when you guys get to the elevator, I want you to use it."

Spencer arrived just as she was finishing her sentence. Letting go of the boy's hand, she walked around to Spencer and gave him the specifics. Just before he took the brake off the bed wheels, she leaned up and whispered in his ear. "Laugh at his knock-knock joke. And make it a really decent Spencer giggle, got it?"

The tall, gangly man gave her a sideways glare before giving in with a grin and a nod.

"Thank you," she mouthed before turning back to the child. "You take care of yourself, and I'll come visit you tomorrow, okay?"

"Okay." The boy still looked terrified and Sally worried how he'd cope, but as the bed started moving away from her, she heard him softly say, "Knock-knock."

Sally smiled and turned back to find out what she needed to do next.

Abbey ordered her down to the last curtain where she got busy dressing the minor wounds of the main culprit. From what she'd gathered, the man was speeding and ran a red light, plowing into two vehicles. Because he was in a big pickup truck, he'd come away relatively unscathed, unlike the two other families.

Sally couldn't help a touch of anger toward his reckless driving, but she kept her mouth shut and still treated him with tender care. There was always a backstory, and even if his was selfish, he still deserved proper treatment.

A rustle of the curtain made her glance over her shoulder.

She spotted Blaine and her chest instantly constricted.

It'd been nearly two weeks since she'd seen Nate driving by in his car. Since then life had been a busy rush of work, family, friends...and Oscar. He'd embedded himself into her life—picking her up after work, joining her for walks with Rusty and appearing at family dinners. He brought her flowers, took her to fancy restaurants, and basically treated her like a queen. It was hard not to enjoy it. She'd never been so pampered in her life.

But seeing Blaine made thoughts of Nate come crashing forward, and she realized that she wasn't anywhere close to getting over her ex-boyfriend.

"Hello, Officer Hartford." She cleared her throat and turned back to the patient. "I'm nearly done."

"I can wait." Blaine spoke softly like he always did, his deep voice calm and undemanding.

The man in the bed seemed twitchy, his agitation only growing when he spotted the police officer.

"I need you to relax," Sally said quietly.

The man grunted and turned his head. She could understand his struggle. The man had ruined lives today, and the road to recovery would be long and painful. The consequences of his recklessness were really going to hurt.

"All done." Sally stepped back, pulling off her

gloves and throwing them out as Blaine stepped into the room.

"Simon Danforth, I'm Officer Hartford. I'd like to ask you a few questions about the incident this afternoon."

Sally slid the curtain closed to give them some privacy. The man would no doubt be under arrest, but he couldn't be taken out of the hospital before the doctor had signed him off.

Washing her hands, Sally dried them thoroughly before grabbing a quick glass of water.

"Take ten, Sal." Abbey pointed to the door.

She obeyed immediately, knowing that Abbey would have things on a tight rotation. She needed to give her nurses quick bathroom breaks and snacks in order to keep them fresh for the long day ahead.

Sally's sneakers squeaked on the shiny floor as she headed for the bathroom. She relieved herself quickly and stepped into the break room to scarf down half a muffin before going back to work.

Brushing the crumbs off her face, she headed back down the corridor and bumped into Blaine.

"Hey." He smiled down at her.

She was forced to stop, even though her quaking innards were telling her to run before she felt too much. "How's it going?"

"Good." He bobbed his head. "I haven't seen you in a while. How are you doing?"

"Yeah, okay." She forced a bright smile. "I'm doing really well. Life's busy with work and family. You know how it is." She brushed her hand through the air. "How's your dad?"

"He's keeping well, although living with Nate is driving him a bit insane. The guy can be a slob."

"Oh, yeah, he can." Sally raised her eyebrows. Nate was always so distracted with work that picking up after himself was never high on his priority list. Sally hadn't minded so much. She wasn't a neat freak, and he made up for his messiness in other ways. Heat rose up her neck and she quickly blinked to clear her mind.

"We miss you," Blaine murmured.

She flinched and looked up at him, unsure what to say. Her nose tingled. Her eyes began to burn.

She didn't want to miss them too. She was trying to move on…away.

"Nate's miserable without you," Blaine kept going, making everything worse.

She closed her eyes and dipped her head. She didn't want to hear that! She was trying to move on!

Blaine couldn't hear her internal screaming so he kept torturing her. "I know why you broke up. I get it. And maybe deep down, Nate does too, but he's too pig-headed to admit it. He's hurting so he goes into defense mode, pushing everyone away."

"I can't fix him, Blaine."

"I'm not asking you to." His smile was kind when she opened her eyes and looked at him. "I guess I just wanted you to know that he's a grumpy bastard without you. You always knew how to bring out the best in him. Take it as a compliment, not pressure. I just thought you should…you know…know."

"Thanks," she croaked and started walking away before he could say any more. "Say hi to Rosie for me."

"Will do," he called after her.

She could feel his eyes following her all the way until she turned the corner.

Leaning against the wall, she clenched her jaw and blinked at her stinging eyes.

"Don't cry," she ordered herself. "It's not your problem."

Her heart said otherwise, knotting inside her chest as she pictured Nate miserably sitting at his desk, overworked and stressed. His hair would be standing on end, his blue eyes blurry. He'd be wearing that cute scowl that made his eyebrows dip together.

A small smile flitted over her lips as she pictured him…and all the ways she used to make him feel better. She'd always been able to unwind him, bring him out from under his clouds.

She just wished she'd been able to figure out a

way to keep him with her, away from the demons that drove and pestered him.

But he kept going back, because she hadn't been enough.

And she probably never would be.

19

Tuesday, May 22nd
11:45am

YOU OWE ME LUNCH. *I'll meet you at Lulu's in 15.*

Nate snickered at the message on his screen and shook his head. Jarrett had obviously gotten wind that the skeleton had been officially identified. Chad had called in the report on Friday. The dental records were a match for Mila Schnyder.

Nate didn't know how the hell Jarrett had found out, but he knew he owed the guy lunch and a little information.

With a reluctant sigh, he stood from his chair and grabbed his jacket. "I'm heading out to lunch. Be back in an hour or so."

Cam, her mouth full of muffin, gave him a thumbs-up.

Slipping his phone into his pocket, he made his way to the parking lot and decided it was a nice enough day to walk. The sun was shining bright and the sky was his favorite kind of blue—deep and endless.

He slipped on his shades and started the twenty minute walk to Lulu's, running over what he was going to say to Jarrett when he got there. The reporter would pepper him for all he had, and Nate needed to be careful what he disclosed about the case. He'd managed to blow his friend off for the last couple of weeks, but Jarrett's patience would only go so far. If Nate didn't give him something, Jarrett would break the deal and who knows what he'd print.

Nate didn't want to reinforce the nasty rumors about Vern Schnyder. They were too sensational not to print, and the poor man didn't need his name run through the mud over a decade later, especially when he wasn't around to defend himself.

After tracking down a few of Mila's friends at the time, Nate was convinced Vern never touched his daughter inappropriately. Mila's friends all assumed she'd run away with that guy she'd met over spring break. None of them knew much about him except the fact that he was this hot, older guy that Mila had fallen madly in love with. She was worried about losing him, so they met up in secret. He never hung out with them because Mila was too afraid of being seen in public with him. She knew her parents would never approve of her dating a man in his twenties, which was why she'd talked about running away with him. The sneaking around thing had gotten too hard.

"Did she seem like the kind of person to follow through with that claim?" Nate had asked Mila's closest friend from that year, while she distractedly watched her baby totter around the living room. The boy was obviously just learning to walk.

"Well, I would've said no, but she was pretty in love with the guy. I got the feeling she would've done anything for him, and he was really anxious for them to be together. Running away seemed like the only option."

"So you don't think it had anything to do with her father?"

The woman paled and stiffly shook her head. "That was so unfair what they said about him. Vern was the nicest man. We used to hang out at the farm sometimes and he was always really cool. Mila adored him…until she fell in love and got completely mind-warped by Mr. Smooth."

"How do you know he was smooth? You said you'd never met him."

"I never did, but he must've been something special if she was willing to quit on everything else in her life just to be with him." Her upper lip curled, giving away her aversion to the mystery boyfriend.

"Did you have a bad feeling about the guy?"

She rose from the couch and collected her little boy before he fell against the coffee table. "Come 'ere, you cheeky monkey." She picked him up and giggled when he gave her a drooling grin. Gazing down at her baby, she softly murmured, "Any guy who persuades a girl to run away from people who love her gives me a bad feeling. It was seriously like he'd cast a spell on her, the way she spoke about him. I get love at first sight and soul mates and all that stuff, I really do, but I've always thought the person you're meant to be with should bring out the best in you. Whoever that guy was, he wasn't bringing out the best in Mila, encouraging her to sneak away from her friends and lie to her family that way. And then she just disappeared without even saying goodbye. I guess I've always kind of resented her for that. I thought we were friends."

Nate didn't have the heart to tell her that Mila

was actually dead, shot through the heart by someone...quite possibly the guy she'd been in love with.

A sharp frown dented his forehead as he turned the corner and headed for Lulu's.

Vern Schnyder was the only person to have seen this guy with his own eyes. Nate needed to interview him and find out whatever he could. He needed to let him know that his beloved daughter was dead.

The thought sat heavy in his gut, but it was his job. Surely finding Mila's killer would comfort Vern in some way. Give him a sense of closure after years of wondering. Vern would probably be more than willing to help him...if he could just find the guy.

He reached Lulu's Coffee Shop and strode in, spotting Jarrett at a table in the corner. He raised his hand in greeting and headed to the counter.

"Hey, Nate." Rosie smiled. "I hear you're paying for Jarrett's lunch."

He gave her a wry smile. "I take it he's already ordered."

"Oh yeah." She raised her eyebrows, letting him know that the guy probably went overboard just to piss Nate off. "So, what'll it be for you?"

"I'll take a black coffee and..." He leaned down to look in the glass cabinet and pointed with his finger. "One of those raisin bran muffins."

"Oh, man," she giggled. "You and your brother

with your healthy eating. You know it's okay to treat yourself sometimes, right?"

He snickered and patted his belly. "I like the bran, thanks, Rosie."

She rolled her eyes and rang up the bill. Nate's eyes bulged at the amount.

"He's ordered a few things to-go."

"Asshole," Nate muttered, half-joking, half-not.

Rosie laughed and handed him his receipt. "I'll bring it over in a few."

Nate sauntered to the table and halfheartedly shook Jarrett's hand. "You're a pig. You know that, right?"

Jarrett shot him a winning smile. "You've made me wait three weeks, man. Be glad I didn't order even more."

Nate didn't respond, gazing around the coffee shop to see who else was around. He couldn't help scoping. It was ingrained. He rapidly took in the information—a young couple, college age, sharing a milkshake. An elderly lady near the window, shakily eating a blueberry muffin. A guy on his laptop, treating Lulu's like his personal office. A couple of businessmen, sitting at the table positioned under the giant photo of Audrey Hepburn.

Nate did a double take, his gut clenching when he noticed it was Xavier and Oscar. He shuffled in his seat, directing his body in the opposite direction. He hadn't seen any of the Richmonds since the breakup, and he wasn't too keen on hearing whatever they had to say about him.

"So, I heard you've got an ID. Who is it?" Jarrett had his phone unlocked, ready to take down notes.

Nate sighed and leaned his elbows on the table, delivering the speech he'd planned on his walk over. He told Jarrett what he could, making sure his friend understood that he was only to print the basics.

"I still need some more time to figure out who this mysterious boyfriend was," he told him. "If I can find Mila's father, then I'll have a better shot at identifying him."

Jarrett nodded. "I could print something that would encourage people to come forward with tips."

Nate shook his head. "Or you could send the killer into hiding."

"If he did happen to be an Aspen Falls resident, do you think he'd be stupid enough to stick around after the body was found? There's no way. By the sound of it, the guy wasn't a local. He probably killed Mila and took off for good."

Nate made a face, annoyed that he was right. He knew Jarrett liked his job, but damn, he would've made a good detective.

"What was his name again?" Jarrett glanced at him.

"We don't officially know. Mila's father thought it was—"

"Oh my goodness me!" an old lady exclaimed, a little too loudly.

Nate immediately noted the hearing aid in her ear and watched, fascinated, as the old woman shuffled toward Xavier's table.

"You're back. Is she with you?" She patted Oscar's shoulder and started looking around the café.

Oscar gave her a curious frown and pasted on a smile.

"I'm sorry?" he said, at an appropriate volume for a busy café.

"You used to wait outside my house. In your pale blue pickup truck. For her. You waited for her."

Oscar shared a quick look with Xavier, his face puckered with confusion. "I'm very sorry, ma'am, but I've never met you before."

"Well, of course you haven't." She giggled. "You didn't know I was watching."

Nate quickly deduced that the woman must've been suffering from some kind of dementia. Her giggle was too girly for an old woman, and there was something about the reckless movements of her shaking hands.

Oscar cleared his throat and stood. Obviously embarrassed, he rested his hand lightly on the woman's elbow and leaned in to speak softly in her ear.

She listened with a smile that started to waver. "Oh," she murmured. "Oh, yes, I see. Oh, I am so sorry. I must've made a mistake." She patted his cheek. "You sweet man. You just look like an older version of him, you do. I will never forget him. Always so nervous. Waiting. Waiting for the moment he could run to her."

"To who?" Oscar asked.

"His true love." The woman patted her chest with a dreamy smile floating across her face. "I wonder if they ran away together. Because both of them stopped coming."

Nate's ears started burning. Sitting up straight, he studied the woman more carefully.

With a kind smile, Oscar apologized once more for not being the man she thought he was.

"Oh don't you worry. My old brain plays tricks on me sometimes."

Oscar grinned. "Well, I'm glad, otherwise I never would've had the pleasure of talking to you."

The lady laughed and patted his cheek. "Oh, my boy. So handsome. Just like him. So handsome."

She shook her head, then turned and shuffled away with her cane as if she hadn't even started a conversation with Oscar. His confused gaze tracked her until it brushed past Nate. He kind of jerked and swallowed, giving Nate a nervous wave before plunking back down in his chair.

Xavier glanced over his shoulder and spotted Nate as well.

It was awkward.

All Nate could do was raise his chin in acknowledgement, then turn back to Jarrett.

"Was that weird?" Jarrett frowned. "I feel like that was weird."

Rosie approached the table with her ladened tray. "Here you go guys." She started unloading it, including *four* to-go bags.

Nate glared at Jarrett, who just winked at him before smiling up at Rosie. "Do you know the lady who just left?"

Rosie glanced at the door. "Oh, Ms. Parker? Yeah, she comes in here at least twice a week. She's a sweetheart."

"Is she, uh…" Nate tapped the side of his head. "All there?"

Rosie grinned and shook her head. "Not by a long shot. I mean, sometimes she is, but she's been known to come up to the counter a few times during a meal to order the same thing over again. She's harmless, though."

"Where does she live?" Nate frowned, worried that a woman like that wouldn't be able to find her way home.

"Just around the corner." Rosie hugged the empty tray to her chest. "Don't worry, she always finds her way home. Every store owner on this street knows her." Rosie lightly tapped Nate's shoulder. "I'm surprised you don't. Blaine's on a first-name basis with her. She adores him."

Nate shook his head, embarrassed that he didn't, but he wasn't a beat cop anymore and only dealt with the general public when he was investigating a case.

"Well, enjoy your food." Rosie grinned.

Nate thanked her and kept his gaze down as Oscar and Xavier walked past the table. Neither of them acknowledged him, and he was happy to keep it that way.

In fact, he didn't take his eyes off his muffin until Jarrett started kicking him under the table. "You need to talk to the guy Ms. Parker was just talking to."

Nate picked up his coffee and took a long sip. "And why would I do that?"

"Come on!" Jarrett looked incredulous. "She may be a dotty old lady, but she definitely recognized that guy."

"He said it wasn't him."

"He looked guilty." Jarrett planted his finger on the table. "He looked right over here and looked guilty. I'm telling you, that guy knows something."

Nate couldn't deny that Jarrett was right. Oscar had looked kind of guilty when he glanced their direction.

But Ms. Parker had agreed with him in the end that he wasn't the man she remembered.

"She said her brain plays tricks on her," Nate muttered.

"Even so, it's worth asking. Maybe the guy has a brother or cousin who looks just like him."

"I don't think so. The guy's from England."

"What, do you know him?" Jarrett spoke around his large mouthful of sandwich.

Nate silently cursed himself for saying anything, then reluctantly muttered, "He's friends with the Richmonds. Works for Michael."

"Perfect." Jarrett wiped the corner of his mouth with a napkin. "So just stop by and see what you can find out."

"What are you, a cop now?"

"I'm a reporter, and a damn good one. And if you don't want to do your job, then I can go talk to him myself." Nate shot him a look dark enough to make the guy swallow. "Okay, fine, you go talk to him, then." His lips pulled into a sad smile. "I was sorry to hear about you and Sal, by the way. It really sucks."

Nate clenched his jaw and looked away. Images of Sally attacked him from all sides—blonde hair and sparkling eyes. Suddenly Mila's face appeared beside Sally's.

They really did look alike.

Damn, if someone ever hurt Sally, took her, stole her away, Nate would move mountains to make sure she was safe.

Vern no doubt felt the same, but just hadn't been strong enough to do anything about it. He deserved justice for his daughter.

Nate had to give it to him. Whatever it took.

"Okay." He swallowed and leaned back in his chair. "You're right. Maybe Oscar does have some family here that I don't know about. It's worth talking to him."

"There you are." Jarrett winked at him before taking another monstrous bite of his sandwich.

Nate picked at his bran muffin, already trying to figure out what he was going to say to Oscar…and why the guy's face flashed with guilt when he looked across the coffeehouse at him.

20

Tuesday, May 22nd
4:05pm

NATE'S STOMACH was in knots as he parked outside the construction site. He felt ridiculous for being so nervous, but he just hoped like hell that Michael Richmond wasn't around to gloat.

Finally, his precious daughter was free of the annoying detective. Nate wasn't sure he could stomach even the smallest pleasantries with the guy.

Holding his breath, he walked over the loose gravel pathway and headed to the small office shed on the edge of the construction site. The door popped open just as Nate was buttoning his jacket, and he was relieved to see Oscar loping down the two wooden steps.

The Englishman looked up and spotted Nate, halting with surprise.

"Uh, hello, Nate. What brings you here?" His gaze was kind of twitchy and Nate immediately went into high alert mode.

Nate tried to hide his frown. Why did this guy look so nervous?

Forcing what he hoped was a casual smile, Nate extended his hand in greeting. "I hope you don't mind me just stopping by, but I'm here in an official capacity."

This seemed to relax Oscar. His shoulders dropped and he took Nate's hand with a smile. "What can I help you with?"

Nate's brows flickered with confusion and he licked the side of his mouth. "Actually, I just wanted to follow up on that conversation you had with Ms. Parker at Lulu's today."

"Ms. Parker?" Oscar tipped his head.

"The old lady who thought you were someone else."

"Oh." Oscar chuckled and shook his head. "Talk about confusing. She seriously thought she knew me."

"Why would she think that?" Nate asked, watching Oscar carefully.

The man shrugged. "I have no idea. I've never owned a blue pickup truck." He gazed into the distance for a second, then blinked and looked at Nate. "And I'd never set foot in Aspen Falls until I met Michael a couple of years ago. I don't know what she was talking about."

Nate rubbed his mouth and lightly kicked a loose stone with the toe of his shoes. "You don't happen to have any relatives who look like you? Siblings? Cousins? An uncle? Someone Ms. Parker might've mistaken for you?"

Oscar was shaking his head. "I wish I could help you, but it's honestly just me. I mean, my grandmother grew up in Chicago, so there's maybe a chance I have some distant relative I don't know about, but I can't say for certain."

Nate pulled out his notepad. "What was your grandmother's name?"

"I'm sorry?" Oscar leaned forward.

"Your grandmother's name," Nate repeated. "What was it?"

"Oh, uh, Jacqueline Plymouth, and actually that was her married name, so I'm not sure what her maiden name was. When she left Chicago for London, she really cut ties. I don't know the history. She didn't like to talk about it, but I've never met any of her immediate family. I don't even know where I'd find them."

Nate pressed his lips together and cleared his throat. It was an effort to hide his frustration. The talk with Oscar was achieving nothing. His best bet was still to find Vern, which was turning into an incredibly hard task.

"Okay." Nate bobbed his head. "Maybe I can try talking to Ms. Parker as well. She might be able to tell me more."

Oscar winced, like that would probably be a waste of time as well. "Good luck with that."

Nate agreed with an eyebrow raise, but then decided to give it one last shot before walking away.

"Well, if you could do me a favor and try to come up with your grandmother's maiden name, I'd really appreciate the help."

"Of course." Oscar shook his head while he was talking, telling Nate that he had absolutely no intention of wasting his time.

Clenching his jaw, Nate asked one last question before turning away.

"You know, when I was watching you in the café today, you suddenly looked kind of nervous. That's why I came out here to talk to you. I just wanted to check that you weren't lying to sweet Ms. Parker."

Oscar's head jerked back like he was offended, but Nate's unrelenting gaze made his expression buckle.

"I wasn't nervous because of that."

Nate frowned.

"Thing is, Nate, uh...well, Sally and I..."

Nate's stomach clenched.

"We've started seeing each other. I know you guys were together for a long time, and I just didn't know how you'd react."

Nate's mouth dried up, his tongue swelling with incompetence.

"I really care about her, very much. I know it may seem fast to you, but I've liked her for a long time. But she was always with you, see, and then after you broke up, she was so sad and I wanted to make her feel better…and, well, one thing has led to another. Quite quickly actually. It's kind of wonderful." A smile flitted over his lips and Nate's fingers bunched into a fist. He'd never wanted to punch someone more.

Oscar had moved in on Sally.

And things were going well.

Bile surged in Nate's gut, making it impossible to do anything but spin and walk away from him.

"I'm sorry, Nate," he called after him. "But I promise I'm taking really good care of her. I'll give her everything she wants and needs!"

It took everything in Nate not to cover his ears and run.

Oscar was taking care of Sally.

Nate's Sally.

The only woman he'd ever loved.

She'd moved on.

It hadn't been about space for her, it'd been about letting go so she could get the things she wanted. Things Oscar could provide.

Nate slammed into his car, puffing like a rhino before gripping the wheel and shouting, "SHIT!"

The agonized yell bounced off the windows and straight back at him.

Resting his head on the wheel, he could barely contain the emotions raging through him. They swirled around his body like a deadly tornado, hitting him with debris that bruised and wounded.

"I need a drink," he finally muttered. "I need a frickin' drink."

Screaming away from the curb, he double-timed it to Shorty's Tavern, where he spent the rest of his day and night huddled in a corner booth, nursing a bottle of Jack Daniel's.

21

Thursday, May 24th
5:45pm

Tap-tap-tap.

Tap-tap-tap.

Nate's pen was close to breaking as he tapped it on the desk, frustration making it move faster and faster.

"If you don't stop doing that, I'm going to smack you in the back of the head," Cam clipped.

A paper missile followed, and Nate flinched as it hit the back of his head.

With a huff, he slumped his shoulders. "Can't find this guy. Vern Schnyder has disappeared off the face of the earth!"

"So let it go! Move on, already. We've got other

things to keep us busy. Like this drug case I'm working solo."

He glanced over his shoulder and caught the tail end of her pointed look.

"You don't need me for that," he softly muttered, thinking immediately of Sally and her argument about how the AFPD had two detectives for a reason.

"You want in on this one, man. I promise you." Cam grinned. "If my source is right and surveillance checks out tomorrow, Kellan's going to authorize a big bust this weekend."

Pain seared the center of his chest as Sally continued to float through his mind—the feel of her blonde hair brushing against his chest as she fell asleep in his arms, the soft murmurs she made when she woke up, the sweet smile she gifted him whenever he appeared.

He rubbed at the ache and tried to push Sally from his mind. Missing her was torture, and picturing her with Oscar basically annihilated him, which was why he'd spent the last couple of days in a mildly drunken stupor. He was still hungover from his binge from the night before. His father had come home to find him passed out on the sofa, then forced some kind of hangover cocktail that tasted like cow piss down his throat that morning.

"I don't know what the hell you're going through

right now, but you are not turning into a drunken bum. You hear me? Get back to work and deal with your pain more constructively. Or better yet, talk to me about it so I can at least try to help you! Or even better still...go talk to Sally!"

Nate had clenched his jaw and turned away from his father, who huffed in frustration and stomped out of the room.

The old man had been right about one thing, though.

Liquor wouldn't fix Nate's heartache, which was why he'd hauled his ass into work and tried to focus back on the Schnyder case.

But no matter how hard he tried, he couldn't get the words "Go talk to Sally" out of his brain. In his weakest moments over the past few days, he'd contemplated showing up at her door and begging her to dump Oscar and take him back.

But how could he?

He wasn't about to give up work to keep her happy. He had a job to do. He had injustice to fight. People deserved closure.

Oscar didn't have to worry about any of that shit. He could give Sally everything she wanted. Everything she deserved.

Nate was a good detective. It was basically the only thing he *was* good at, and he needed to focus on that.

It may have happened twelve years ago, but Mila Schnyder's killer had to be held accountable for her death. Nate wouldn't rest again until he'd solved the case.

Talking with Oscar had yielded nothing. His additional conversation with Ms. Parker had been a total waste of time too. Her mercurial brain couldn't be trusted. He'd gone to visit her a few hours earlier and she'd had absolutely no recollection of talking to Oscar at Lulu's Coffee Shop. When Nate brought up the blue pickup truck, she simply repeated the information she'd told Oscar at the café, basically word for word. Nate had to wonder if it was simply a dream or teenage fantasy she'd once had. A handsome man secretly meeting up with his true love and running away together. It was kind of romantic. But totally unhelpful in tracking down Mila's killer.

So Nate was throwing all his energy into his hunt for Vern.

They'd managed to subpoena Vern's bank records and tax returns. Jessica was wading through them, looking for anything that might trigger his whereabouts. The guy seemed to have gone off-grid after being accused of molesting his daughter.

Driver's license databases had come up short. None of the Vern Schnyder hits they got were a match.

It'd been three weeks since talking to Glenn

Marshall, and then interviewing everyone in Aspen Falls who knew the Schnyder family. No one had any idea where Vern went. All they could talk about was how sad it all was—Mila running away and then the awful rumors.

"I never would've thought that about Vern Schnyder. He seemed like such a loving, family man." Almost everyone said that, which only made Nate's suspicions that much stronger.

The rumors were a big fat lie, and someone had spread them to cast suspicion on Vern so they could sneak away into the shadows. Nate had a theory that the killer had gotten the rumor going. And that only strengthened his gut feeling that the killer was the mysterious boyfriend, Jamie.

Standing up, he was about to find Jessica and ask for yet another update when he was stopped by Blaine, who barred the doorway.

"Hey, man."

"What's up?" Nate looked down, hoping his brother wasn't about to announce some irritating family dinner.

He was tired, and didn't mind the idea of heading home on time for once, but not if it meant having to hang out with his father and the two lovebirds.

"Where the hell have you been the last few days? I've been trying to catch you."

Nate hitched his shoulders. "You could have called me."

Blaine crossed his arms, his eyes narrowing in on his brother. "I kind of wanted to chat face-to-face."

"Well, you know where I'm living right now, so…" Nate flicked his arms up.

"When I stopped by last night, you were passed out on the sofa, you dumbass. Dad made me carry you up to your bed. You weigh a frickin' ton, by the way."

Nate flipped him off and Blaine couldn't resist a grin, which in turn made Nate's lips twitch.

"So, what do you want to see me about, little bro?"

"I had to go to the hospital earlier this week. Arrested a guy for reckless driving. Idiot mowed down two cars."

Nate grimaced, images of his mother's body flying through the area froze him for a second. He swallowed and tried to find his voice. "Any fatalities?"

"No, but one guy has a long road to recovery ahead of him."

"Ouch," Nate muttered as he buried memories of his mother's indented skull. Clearing his throat, he glanced back up, his gut twisting at the look on Blaine's face. He suddenly knew what his brother was going to say before the words even left his mouth.

"I saw Sal."

Nate's bones turned to rubber. Locking his jaw, he glanced over his shoulder and noticed Cam get up to leave the room. He should've told her to stay… because then his irritating brother wouldn't have the chance to get into a deep and meaningful conversation.

Part of him wanted to shrug and say, "So?" But he couldn't be that callous, because he was actually desperate for news. He'd only heard Oscar's side of the story, and a small, hopeful part wondered how truthful the guy had been. Had he embellished how good things were because he saw Nate as a potential threat?

Clearing his throat, he tried—and failed—to sound casual. "How is she?"

"Good. She says she's keeping busy with work and family."

Nate's throat thickened, his windpipe crushed beneath the weight of emotion. "Was she happy? I mean, how'd she look?"

"Beautiful, as always." Blaine grinned. "Why don't you just call and talk to her?"

"Because she doesn't want me. She made that clear." Nate sniffed, unwilling to admit that she more than didn't want him; she was actually moving on.

He busied himself shifting papers from one side of his desk to the other.

"It wasn't a case of not wanting you." Blaine leaned against the doorframe. "She broke up with you because you work too hard. You never put her first."

"It's my job, Blaine!" He threw his hands up before resting his fists on his desk. "I thought she understood that."

His brother's features dented with a sharp frown of annoyance. "You are a stubborn ass. No, actually, you're a coward." Blaine pointed at him. "I'm a cop too, you know. And I always manage to make time for Rosie."

"You're not a detective. It's not the same."

"You have a choice! You think you're the only detective in this country? All of them work hard, but they prioritize! Sally spent three years understanding and bending over backward to accommodate you because she loves you. And you totally took advantage of that."

Standing up against Blaine's verbal lashing was freaking hard work.

Nate glared at him, his nostrils flaring. "Get out of my office."

"I'm not trying to piss you off, okay? I just hate seeing you like this. She makes you better. She's good for you, and all you have to do is let go of this insane…whatever…that drives you to work like a demon. Other people can do some of this stuff. Delegate! Walk away from the job sometimes, or you're gonna lose everything."

"I already have," Nate croaked.

"Yeah, well it's not too late to get some of it back," Blaine spat, then walked away before Nate could argue with him.

Resting his hands on his hips, Nate stared down at his cluttered desk. The computer hummed, and it took every ounce of willpower he had not to smash his fist through the screen.

Cam clipped back into the room, clearing her throat like she hadn't just heard the entire exchange. She slapped a file on her desk and briskly announced, "I'm out. I've got a date." Pulling on her jacket, she grabbed her keys and walked to the door. "See you tomorrow."

"Yeah, I'll be here," he muttered.

Cam chuckled. "Of course you will be."

The comment riled him like it never had before. Shooting daggers at her back, he picked up his pen and hurled it across the room. It pinged off the whiteboard, then disappeared between the wall and Cam's desk.

Blaine's words were a bullwhip against his back, slashing and bruising.

Ever since he'd graduated high school, he'd

wanted to be in law enforcement. Becoming a detective had been the proudest day of his life. He could feel his mother smiling down from heaven, urging him on. He was going to find her killer and finally gift her the justice she deserved.

But he hadn't been able to.

And so he found other killers and criminals to take down, all the while trying to assuage the burning pain that had lived permanently in his chest.

Sally walking out on him had just lit the pain on fire all over again.

He couldn't imagine turning his back on a case.

Walk away sometimes?

That didn't even compute.

But life without Sally didn't compute either.

Her sweet face ran through his mind like a movie reel. Those times when work had been quiet and he'd been able to go home at the end of the day. Sure, he'd get bored and restless without a decent case to sink his teeth into, but it'd meant time with his woman.

They'd watch movies together, go running together, sit on the couch reading books. He taught her how to play chess, and she forced him into playing soccer in their little backyard. She'd kick his ass every time, but her triumphant laughter had been worth it.

He should've appreciated those moments more.

Cherished them.

His eyes glassed over and he quickly blinked, snatching his keys off the desk and checking his watch.

If Sally had been working today, her shift would just be ending. He was overtly aware that she was with Oscar now, but…how happy was she, really?

Nate had to know.

Sprinting out the door, he ran for his bike and zoomed away from the station, making it to the hospital in record time. His insides buzzed with nerves and excitement as he imagined seeing her again. Would she be happy? He had no idea what he was going to say to her. He just wanted to stand in her presence for a minute, soak her in. Hopefully his heart would take over and something intelligible would come out of his mouth.

Parking the bike, he was about to turn it off and dismount when he spotted Sally exiting the hospital.

He opened his mouth to call to her, but his words were cut short by a sight that felt like a thunder punch to the groin.

Sally was smiling…at another man.

Oscar.

The guy held out his hand to her and she took it. He pulled her close…and kissed her.

Bile surged up Nate's throat—a mixture of anger and grief.

Sally pulled away and he said something that made her laugh. Her distant giggle pierced him, and he felt like he'd been shot through the heart.

Oscar opened the door for Sally—always the gentleman—and then ran around to the driver's side. His flashy car started up and he reversed out of his parking spot, then drove to the opposite exit.

Before Nate could think better of it, he gunned the engine and followed them.

22

Thursday, May 24th
6:30pm

Oscar had been waiting for Sally outside the ER and as soon as she took his hand, he drew her close and kissed her.

She still wasn't entirely used to it.

His kisses didn't make her limbs burn the way Nate's did, but they weren't unpleasant and so she went with it.

Things with Oscar were easy.

Everybody loved him and they were all constantly encouraging her to go for it. They were happy that she was dating such a sweet, attentive man. Finally, after all her "suffering" she could move on and get all the things she wanted.

They were right, to some degree. Oscar was the type of man to give her the things she'd always dreamed of.

So why... She stopped the question in her head before it could fully form.

She had to stop asking why. She had to stop bemoaning the fact that her ultimate dream had Nate picking her up and taking her out to dinner.

Seeing Blaine earlier in the week had really messed with her head. She had to get over it.

"So, I've made reservations at Evana's." Oscar pulled out of the hospital parking lot and turned left.

"Wow. Fancy." Sally looked down at what she was wearing.

Evana's was the only gourmet restaurant in town. It was really expensive, and people only went there to celebrate special occasions. Sally wasn't sure if Bridget's floral spring dress would cut it.

"You look beautiful." Oscar took her hand and kissed the inside of her wrist. "And you deserve delicious food. Your mother told me you've had a tough week, and I want to treat you."

"A tough week?" Sally asked nervously, wondering just how much of her internal conflict she'd given away without realizing.

"Yeah. She told me about the big car accident a couple of days ago, and that your shifts have been really intense. I'm glad you have the next three days off."

Sally smiled with relief. "Me too. And you're sweet to take me out tonight."

"Someone has to look after you, right?" He winked and turned the corner.

Evana's appeared up ahead. It had a subtle entrance, wooden double doors indicating to passersby that you had to be something special to be allowed in. For some weird reason it had that allure that made you want to be special enough, like maybe you weren't quite until you'd dined there at least once.

Oscar stopped the car against the curb and threw his keys to the valet before opening the door for Sally. She took his hand and stepped onto the side-walk, still feeling underdressed.

"You look beautiful," Oscar reassured her again before kissing her lips and leading her inside.

They were seated at a table by the window. It would be an intimate dinner for two.

As Sally sat down, her stomach rumbled in antic-ipation. Thankfully Oscar was too busy ordering wine to notice. She hoped she could remember her mother's training and act like a lady rather than the complete pig she wanted to be.

Nothing would satisfy her more than a large bowl of curly fries, buffalo wings and a cold beer.

She and Nate used to order that at Shorty's Tavern. It was still one of her favorite places to eat.

Oscar's phone rang and he glanced at his Apple Watch to see who it was.

He winced and sighed. "I'm so sorry. I really must take this."

"Go for it." Sally smiled. "I don't mind."

And she really didn't. It would give her a second to breathe and prep herself for a romantic dinner. She was so tired, she wasn't really in the mood to talk. She'd like nothing better than a hot shower, pajamas, and to settle down and watch some superhero movie. Throw in a plate of fatty food and a tub of ice cream—heaven. However, that was not going to be, and she'd have to come up with something. Oscar had gone to far too much effort to be saddled with a grumpy, morose date.

The Englishman politely thanked her and stood from his chair, walking away for a little privacy.

Picking up the menu, Sally was about to scan it when she glanced out the window. She did a double take and gasped.

Nate.

He was sitting on his motorbike, his foot resting on the curb, staring at her with a look of complete heartache.

Sally's stomach convulsed, nerves instantly

buzzing over her entire body as she drank in his blue gaze.

She always thought she could drown in those blue eyes.

She probably already had—multiple times.

They called to her in a way that nothing else could, which was why she could do nothing but rise from her chair and walk outside.

Her strappy sandals scuffed the pavement as she approached him.

Damn, he was handsome. Pure rugged beauty that made her insides yearn.

She hated how easily her body could betray her. If his lips even thought about twitching with a smile or if he even uttered one syllable about missing her, she'd be putty in his hands.

She couldn't let that happen. This was the man who had caused her hours of frustration and heartache. She'd walked away for a reason.

Crossing her arms, she tried to quickly erect some defensive walls to safeguard her heart. "What are you doing here?"

He gazed at her, his expression a mixture of hurt and confusion. "You're with Oscar."

The bitter edge to his voice made her shoulders tense, yet still she whispered, "It's just a date."

Why did she say that?

Oscar was turning into more than just a date.

Was she afraid of Nate's reaction?

No.

She'd never been afraid of him.

So why did she feel so bad that he'd seen her with someone else?

It was as if Nate could read her mind, because he softened his tone. It dropped low with the sound of sad resignation. "He said you've been seeing each other. That things are going well."

Her eyebrows shot up in surprise. Oscar hadn't mentioned seeing Nate. "When did you talk to him?"

"The other day." He shrugged. "He seems really happy."

Sally swallowed, unsure what to say.

Nate looked up, capturing her with his intense gaze. "Are you?"

Oh man! His husky voice, that look on his face… how was she supposed to resist him?

Why was Nate's power over her always so strong? She didn't want to need him…want him…so badly.

It was a struggle to speak, but eventually Sally softly managed, "Yeah. He's taking good care of me."

A muscle in Nate's jaw worked as he gave her a jerky nod. She knew he was fighting for complete control, tucking all his vulnerable emotions behind that silent wall of his.

She wished he wouldn't. Part of her was

desperate to see him cry. To fall apart. Maybe then she could get a glimpse of how he really felt. What really drove him, and why she'd never been enough.

But there was no way he'd let her see that. It wasn't his style.

Nate cleared his voice then swallowed. "So, do you love him?"

"I don't know." Her response was quick and honest. "It's all kind of happened so fast."

Nate's expression crumpled and he turned to look out across the street. "We happened fast. It must be your style." The snarky edge to his voice made her want to snap back.

And she did. "You think I wanted it to work out this way? I gave you three years, Nate. Three!"

"And you asked for some space, which I gave you! But then you just move on?"

She scoffed before letting out a pitiful laugh. "What was I supposed to do? Wait around for you to come back and tell me that everything had changed? You weren't going to do that. I know you, Nate. And I haven't heard from you once since you moved out."

"You wanted space!" he shouted.

"No, I wanted you to let me in. To *see* me. To figure out that I somehow made your life better!"

Whipping back to face her, he killed her sparking fire with his blue eyes. They touched the center of her soul as he whispered, "I let you in."

Had he?

Really?

Her eyes started to glisten as she tipped her head and gave him a broken smile. "But I still wasn't enough for you, was I?"

Her statement confused him. "What's that supposed to—?"

And then his phone started ringing.

He didn't even hesitate, reaching for it and answering without a second thought. "Hartford."

Sally rolled her eyes and spun back for the door.

He'd never change.

Work could slice through the middle of anything...even a heart-to-heart that could've cleared up so much, and maybe even changed Sally's mind.

23

Thursday, May 24th
7:00pm

"HEY, it's Jess. I've just struck gold."

Nate straightened up, his heart accelerating in his chest. "Tell me good news."

"I found Vern Schnyder. At least I think I have."

"Where?"

"Ash Lake. It's this tiny blip of a place up north, just west of the Boundary Waters. Apparently an old guy matching Vern's description lives in this isolated cabin on the southwest side of the lake."

Nate was impressed. "How the hell did you find that?"

"There was a credit card transaction from July 2001, for Ash Lake Getaway Motel. Must've been a family holiday or something. Anyway, I called the owner and he doesn't remember that, but he did tell me about a hermit guy matching Vern's description. When I emailed him Vern's photo, he confirmed it for me. Apparently Vern drives past about once a month or so to get supplies, but other than that, he's never really seen."

"So, the motel owner was certain it was Vern?"

"He was 80 percent sure, which I think is worth a trip. I'm happy to drive out there tomorrow morning and check it out for you."

Nate was tempted to go that night.

"How far away is it?" he asked.

"Google Maps has it at a little over four hours by car."

He looked at his watch. By the time they got organized, they'd be showing up close to midnight. He winced, knowing the morning was better. Hating that it was.

"What do you want to do?" Jessica waited for his decision.

After an irritated huff, he muttered, "I'll go in the morning."

"Okay. Well, I'm going to knock off for the night, then."

"Thanks for your hard work," he said gruffly, still riled over fighting with Sally.

Jessica ignored his tone, answering in her usual,

upbeat way. "It's not a problem. As tedious as it's been, getting this breakthrough was like a rush, you know? It's a weird way to describe it. Putting the pieces together and watching them fall into place is such an adrenaline hit. I'm always happy to help you on cases, Nate. I really love it."

His lips twitched with a smile. "Good to know, Jess."

He understood her feelings completely. He'd been addicted to that sensation for a long time.

Totally addicted.

His smile faltered as a small part of him wanted to warn her against it. *Don't get sucked in. Don't make it your life.*

"Catch you tomorrow." Jessica ended the call.

As Nate hung up and slipped the phone back into his pocket, he glanced to the empty sidewalk and felt it all the way to his core. Sally was back inside, sipping wine and smiling at something Oscar was saying.

If she felt his gaze on her, she wasn't showing it.

Her focus was completely on Oscar, just like Oscar's was on her.

It should've been Nate in that restaurant, talking to her. Listening to her. Making her feel like she was the only thing in the world. But he'd forfeited that right.

He'd given it up for the thrill of the catch.

Was that what she'd meant when she said she wasn't enough?

The idea killed him.

Did she not know she'd been everything? That she did make his life better?

His chest deflated as he was forced to answer his own question. He'd done a pretty shitty job of proving it to her…or showing her just how much she meant to him.

The idea was a slap to the heart. All that time he'd been praising Sally for being so understanding, but maybe it'd just been an excuse to ignore that niggle of guilt—the fact that he wasn't being the boyfriend she deserved.

Oscar obviously was.

His throat burned with the idea. It made him want to storm into the restaurant and claim her back.

But he couldn't do that.

Because he had a long drive ahead of him, and he knew he wouldn't be able to turn his back on this case. Not even for Sally.

Starting up his motorbike, he gunned away from the curb and tried to conjure up the excitement of speaking to Vern Schnyder the next day.

But he couldn't picture it, no matter how hard he tried.

All he could do was lament the fact that Sally was moving on, and he'd probably never be able to.

24

Thursday, May 24th
7:15pm

THE RUMBLING of Nate's motorbike driving away made Sally flinch. She couldn't resist glancing out the window as he tore away from the curb. And her.

It hurt.

If seeing Blaine on Tuesday afternoon had unnerved her, talking to Nate had rattled her like tornado sirens going off in the middle of the night. Her insides were crumbling as she reached for her wineglass.

"Your hand is shaking." Oscar smoothed his fingers down her arm.

"Sorry." She put the glass back down, trying to

focus on the soothing piano music being piped through the restaurant.

"Hey," Oscar cooed. "You never have to apologize to me. You and Nate were together for a long time, and moving on is hard. He's obviously struggling." Oscar glanced out the window as if to make sure Nate was really gone.

"Yep." Sally nodded, tucking her hands under the table and gripping her napkin. "I guess I wasn't expecting to see him tonight."

"Neither was I," Oscar said dryly, a smirk flashing over his face before his gaze softened with tenderness. "Are you okay, though?"

Lifting her chin, Sally put on a brave smile. "I'll be fine."

"You don't have to be embarrassed or try to hold yourself together for my sake. If you need to cry into that wineglass, you go right ahead."

The thought made Sally giggle. It was a breathy wisp of sound that could've easily turned into a sob. She pressed her lips together, containing her emotions despite what Oscar had just said.

"Look, Nate hurt you. He let you down. And that's something I would never do." Oscar reached under the table for her hand and brought it back up to the surface. Threading their fingers together, he looked at her with his deep brown eyes. They were soft with affection, as was his voice. "Sally, you are so important to me. Nothing makes me happier than watching you smile, and treating you to all the things you deserve."

A nervous smile flittered over his face and he dipped his head for a moment.

Sally's stomach clenched.

"I know this might seem rushed, and you don't have to say anything in return, but..." He looked up and swallowed. "I love you. I love everything about you, and if you'll let me, I will look after you and give you everything you need...everything you desire. If I can make it happen, I will."

It was suddenly hard to breathe. Sally was sure it would hurt too much to inhale. So all she could muster was a surprised smile and lots of rapid blinking.

Oscar had just confessed his love to her. They'd been dating less than a month. It felt insane. Yet, she'd known she loved Nate by the end of date one. Was it that farfetched to fall so fast?

Could she fall in love with Oscar herself?

She wasn't sure. He was lovely, and kind, and would no doubt care for her and treat her to all sorts of surprises. She did love that about him. He was very romantic.

As the rumble of Nate's engine pulling away from her played through the back of her mind, she had to wonder if she should let Oscar try and do all the things he'd just promised.

Because after a month, she knew this much—Oscar Plymouth was a man of his word.

If he said he was going to be somewhere, he would be, and that scored him a hell of a lot of points in Sally's book.

25

Friday, May 25th
10:45am

NATE DECIDED to visit Vern alone. He felt a little bad leaving Jessica behind. But after a sleepless night, with thoughts of Sally and her new man pinging through his head along with images of what he'd encounter with Vern Schnyder, he'd ended up leaving Aspen Falls before dawn.

He'd pored over Google satellite images of the area and had circled three isolated cabins dotted around the lake. There were plenty more cabins than that, but he thought it best to start with the smallest, most remote ones first. If Vern was a hermit, then it was most likely a good starting point.

The trip was quiet and uneventful, much like the

town of Ash Lake. Gray clouds hung low in the sky, threatening rain. So much for summer. It was taking its sweet time to arrive.

Sipping on his second cup of gas station coffee, Nate turned off Highway 53 and onto Jacobs Road. He spotted the motel almost immediately and pulled in to have a quick word with the owner. His boots crunched on the gravel as he approached the old building. It looked a few decades old, but was obviously well kept. It was painted brown with forest green trim, echoing the colors of nature that surrounded it, and no doubt looked quite charming on a bright summer's day.

A bell above Nate's head rang when he pulled open the office door, and a man who looked about his father's age appeared from the back room.

"Hello there." The man finished wiping his mouth with a paper napkin and put on a business smile.

"Morning." Nate kept his tone easy and pulled out his ID. "Detective Hartford, Aspen Falls Police Department."

The man's graying eyebrows rose as he scrunched the napkin in his hand.

"A colleague of mine called here yesterday asking about a person of interest in a case we're investigating."

"Yeah, the old, weird guy." The motel owner was a mumbler, and Nate had to strain to hear what he was saying. "Haven't seen him in a while. Probably three weeks ago? Drove past in his old pickup."

"You know the license plate?" Nate went to pull out his notebook but stopped when the man shook his head.

"It's a fading yellow rust bucket. Think it's a Ford. Maybe an F100? Something like that, anyway." The man waved his wrinkled hand in the air.

Nate pulled up a mental image of Ford pickup trucks and nodded. "Do you know where he lives?"

"I'm pretty sure it's the house at the very end of the road. There's a fork and you take the left and head away from the lake. It's the only place not on the water's edge around here. Most people don't bother venturing up the hill. The driveway is steep, loose gravel. It's not an easy climb. And it's got a small switchback about halfway up, so you don't really know what you're getting yourself into since you can't see over the rise."

"You ever been up there?"

"Maybe twenty years ago." He chuckled. "There was just a small log cabin up there. Not much to look at." He scratched his freshly shaven chin. "Bet it's still not much to look at."

Nate tipped his head. "Why do you say that?"

"Oh, I don't know." The man shrugged. "If I'm right and the man who lives up there is the one I'm thinking of…he doesn't seem the type to take pride in his property. If his truck is anything to go by," he ended with a mutter.

Nate noted this, adding a sharpness to the mental picture he was creating.

"So, what's the case?" The man pressed his hands against the wooden countertop. "He being arrested for something?"

"Sorry. Can't disclose that information." Nate stood tall. "But I appreciate your help."

"Good luck, Detective."

Nate waved before heading out the door. He was glad he'd taken the time to stop by, and headed immediately to the end of the unsealed road, clouds of dust billowing up behind him. The car was going to be a different color by the time he got there, but maybe those rain clouds would open up and clean it off.

Nate drove fast and soon arrived at the fork. Taking the left, he slowed his pace and eased up the driveway. He could understand why people didn't bother with it. The tree-lined road was narrow and windy. The trees were dark, menacing centurions. Nate's skin prickled as he gripped the wheel and tried to deny the creepy vibe that he could feel but not explain.

Nate gritted his teeth as his back tire spun out but then found some grip. Two turns later and he was breaching the rise and staring at a small run-down cabin.

The yellow pickup truck was parked outside.

Nate parked next to it, then sat for a moment to study his surroundings.

It was quiet. There was no smoke coming out of the stone chimney—not that there would be at that time of year—but the curtains in the front room were drawn. Nate checked his watch. Seemed kind of late to not be up yet.

If it weren't for the truck, Nate would assume the cabin was empty.

It well could be.

Easing his door open, he checked out the rusted tin roof. Patches of metal had been secured over the holes but they were crooked and badly placed. The hack-job repairs on the cabin screamed of how little love and pride had been put into it. Nate couldn't help noticing a depressive gray cloud settling over him as he stepped onto the sagging porch. His mood was quickly matching the weather.

As if to prove his point, a light pattering of rain began to fall, pinging off the tin roof above him. He wrapped his knuckles on the edge of the screen door, noting the gaping hole in the mesh. The black fabric sagged over on itself, letting in any and all bugs.

Nate stepped back and lightly brushed his fingers

over his holster while he waited. It was a force of habit, checking his equipment to make sure he was ready for any threats or surprises.

Not that Vern was either of those things, but there was an element of the unknown. This was a man who'd run from nasty rumors and hidden himself away for over a decade. A situation like that could make anyone a little crazy. Nate hoped he'd be sane enough to answer a few questions and help Nate find Mila's elusive boyfriend.

It was taking a long time for anyone to come to the door. Nate was about to give up and check out the rest of the property when the front door clicked and then opened a fraction.

A tall man with weathered skin and sad brown eyes stared out at him.

"Vern Schnyder?" Nate reached for his ID. "I'm Detective Hartford from the Aspen Falls PD." He didn't even have a chance to finish his sentence before the man took off back into the house. He was stupid enough not to close the door behind him, so Nate bolted through it, chasing the guy down the narrow corridor and right out the back door.

"Hey! Stop!" Nate jumped down the back steps and pumped his arms, easily catching up to the lumbering man. He tackled him onto the wet grass and held him steady, blinking against the raindrops hitting his face.

The big guy was wheezing like a chain smoker, his arms slackening as Nate drew them behind his back. He couldn't feel any fight in the guy so chose to hold off cuffing him.

"You know running makes you look guilty, right? You don't even know what I'm here about."

"I didn't abuse my own daughter. She didn't run away because of me!" Vern wailed.

"Okay." Nate nodded and eased off a little.

"I'd never touch her that way. She was my baby girl. I love her. I respect her. I'd never..." The man's chest heaved. "I lost her. I lost her." He sounded broken and for a moment Nate thought the droplets streaking down his face might have been tears.

A sympathy Nate didn't understand tore through him. There was something so damaged about the guy.

"I believe you," he finally said. "Now, I want to be able to let you go and talk to you face-to-face. Are you going to let me do that?"

The man's large head shuffled on the ground as he nodded and Nate got to his feet, still ready to pounce if he had to. The large man pulled himself up on shaking legs and turned to face him. Wiping the wet hair off his forehead, he blinked at Nate and murmured, "Why are you here? After all this time, why do the police want to question me now?"

Taking a moment to study his reaction, Nate

slowly eased into the truth. "We've found your daughter's remains."

"Remains." The man shuddered, his legs buckling. Nate reached forward to steady him, dreading what he had to say next.

"They were discovered on your old farm in Aspen Falls. Dental records have confirmed it's her. And we have a few questions that need answering."

"Mila," he whispered, the man's shoulders beginning to shake. Bending forward with a broken wail, he braced his hands on his knees.

Nate gave him a minute then gently asked, "Would you be willing to help us?"

Vern didn't say anything. He just went still, sniffing occasionally before eventually swiping a finger under his nose. Nate was kind of surprised he wasn't cursing the boyfriend and wailing accusations into the rain, but he simply stayed silent.

"Come on, let's get out of this rain." Nate gently took Vern's arm and led him back toward the house. The man followed without a word, veering around to the front of the house when Nate tried to lead him to the back door.

"Hey." Nate chased after him and skidded to a surprised stop when he watched Vern walk around to the back of Nate's car. Opening the back door, he slipped inside and slammed it shut behind him.

Nate's eyebrows dipped together in confusion.

Running over to the car, he opened the back door and shielded his face from the increasing rain. "What are you doing?"

"I'm assuming you need to take me in." The man's voice was soft and hollow. "If that's my girl, I want to see her."

"I don't think you want to see her like this," Nate murmured.

The man blinked. "Take me in."

Nate frowned and glanced over his shoulder at the house. "Do you need any of your stuff?"

The man shook his head. "There's nothing of value in there."

Nate sighed, still confused by the man's bizarre behavior. "If you prefer, I can follow your truck down."

"That thing's not going to make it to Aspen Falls," the man scoffed. "Just drive. Just…drive." His voice broke on the final word, and Nate got into the car without argument.

He'd never had someone run in fear and then willingly get into his car.

As he started the ignition, his body was on full alert. He didn't know what the hell was going on with Vern Schnyder, but he wanted to be prepared for whatever the guy might come up with next.

26

Friday, May 25th
1:35pm

ANNABELLE CLIPPED up the front section of Sally's hair and combed out the back. Sally had arrived at her sister's salon about twenty minutes earlier to take advantage of the free cut her sister always offered. They'd booked it in the week before and Sally hadn't felt like going, but she knew Annabelle would ask why and then she'd have to come out with the whole story. It was easier just to go along, and Sally hoped it might relax her. She usually loved getting her hair cut.

Grabbing her scissors off the counter, Annabelle started to trim Sally's wet strands, taking off just half an inch as instructed.

Sally gazed at the mirror, studying the shape of her face and trying to avoid making eye contact with her reflection. She didn't want to see inside of herself, because she knew all she'd find was utter turmoil.

Oscar loved her. At least that's what he'd said, and she was struggling not to believe it. The look on his face had been so earnest and sweet.

"You seem quiet today," Annabelle said. "Everything okay?"

A hair dryer started up just behind them, and Sally waited for Chantel to finish styling her client's hair before softly answering her sister. She was grateful for the wait. She needed time to think of a good reason, but in the end she whispered the truth. "Oscar told me he loves me."

"What?" Annabelle's large eyes rounded, her smile radiant in the mirror.

Before Sally could tell her to calm down, Chantel came rushing over. "Don't start without me."

Hurrying her client to the counter, Chantel sped through the payment and led the lady out the door before running back to sit in the spare seat beside Sally. "Start from the beginning. What happened?"

Swallowing hard, Sally eased her eyes open, but kept them on her fidgeting fingers. "Oscar took me out for dinner last night…and told me that he loves me."

"Holy heck!" Chantel giggled. "That is so sweet." Her perfectly manicured hands curled around Sally's arm. "I'm so excited for you."

Sally managed a weak smile, but she couldn't speak.

"I guess the question is why aren't *you* more excited?" Annabelle raised her eyebrows before focusing back on Sally's hair.

For a moment, all that could be heard was the clean snip of scissors cutting hair and Chantel's barely veiled excitement as she kind of whined in her throat, desperate for more romantic news.

"You're killing me here," Chantel quickly snapped. "Would you hurry up and tell us why a gorgeous English guy confessing his love for you is a bad thing!"

"It's not a bad thing. It's just…" Sally sighed. "I saw Nate last night."

Chantel gasped and Annabelle went taut behind her.

Sally caught her sister's tight expression in the mirror and quickly glanced away. "He followed us to the restaurant…to…talk to me."

"About what?" Chantel squeezed her arm.

"He wanted to know if I was happy. He seemed kind of sad and upset that I'd moved on so fast."

Annabelle scoffed. "What was he expecting you

to do, wait around until he got his act together? Please."

Sally didn't respond, her heavy heart weighing more than it usually did.

Chantel gave her a sympathetic smile. "I know you still love him, and you probably always will a little bit. But he's never there, Sal. That's why you broke up with him. And unless he showed up last night to say sorry and tell you he's going to try, then you need to move on."

"Did he say that?" Annabelle's eyes rounded.

Sally shook her head. The lump in her throat hurt.

Deep down she knew Nate would never do that. Because he didn't get it. He didn't really understand why she'd left him.

Working too hard wasn't exactly a sin. He no doubt felt completely abandoned by Sally…and now she was moving on to someone else.

Annabelle sighed and rubbed her shoulder. "Look, Oscar is here and he loves you. Those are two really good things. Why not just enjoy the now?"

Sally nibbled her thumbnail, something she hadn't done in a long time. "Because I'm not sure."

Annabelle smacked her hand and mumbled, "Don't bite your nails." Coming around to Sally's left side, she let out one of the clips and began trimming that section of hair. "Oscar has been treating you like a queen, and I get that seeing Nate last night has thrown you, but come on, sis. It's Oscar. He's adorable."

Sally wrinkled her nose. "It just feels so fast. We've only been dating for a little while and he's already saying he loves me and inviting me to spend the weekend with him at the lake house."

"No way!" Chantel squealed. "I love that place. With just the two of you, it will be so romantic!"

"Yeah, Dad offered it to him and he really wants to go." Sally internally cringed. Dad had never once offered the lake house to Nate. It was reserved for family members and a select few only. She'd insisted Nate join them for a few family getaways, but they'd never had the lake house to themselves.

Her father obviously adored the idea of her and Oscar together. It should've made Sally happy, but it just felt like another weight bearing down on her.

"I think you should do it," Annabelle said.

Sally looked doubtfully into the mirror, suddenly wishing she hadn't said anything.

Her sister caught her expression and laughed. "Come on, it's a good idea. It'll give you an overnighter with Oscar to really see how you feel. You don't have to sleep with him or anything, just spend some uninterrupted time hanging out. If he drives you nuts by the time you come home, you can tell him that it's moving too fast."

"Or you can figure out that maybe Oscar is everything you've been waiting for." Chantel swooned. "Either way, it's not going to hurt."

Sally made a face. "It'll hurt him if we go away for a weekend and then I turn around and dump him."

"Who said anything about dumping?" Annabelle lightly slapped her shoulder. "I said slow things down. He seems like a reasonable guy. You can just say you need to cool off a little. He'll understand."

"I don't know, you guys." Sally's nose wrinkled.

"A weekend away at the lake house sounds delicious," Chantel said, jumping up from her seat and sweeping the floor in preparation for her next client. "You should do it just to get out of Aspen Falls for the night. You're not working, and you can't deny that being by the lake will be far more peaceful and enriching then curled up in your room lamenting the way things didn't work out with Nate."

Chantel was right. The lake house always restored her soul. The smell of the trees, the sun glistening off the water...

Her heart had already thrilled to the idea, even if it was just the lake house that made her feel that way and not the man who would be accompanying her.

Biting the edge of her lip, she mulled it over while Annabelle finished cutting her hair. Chantel's next client arrived, which gave Sally a little room to think.

Annabelle finished the cut, then blow-dried her hair. She always felt so beautiful when her sister was done.

"Thank you." She fingered the ends of her golden locks while Annabelle bent over her shoulder and caught her eye in the mirror. "The lake house is a good idea. You know that, right?"

"Yeah," Sally eventually whispered. "Yeah, I guess so."

Annabelle's smile was sunshine. Sally rolled her eyes and pulled out her phone before she changed her mind.

Oscar answered after the first ring. "Good afternoon, lovely lady."

Sally smiled. His voice was so sweet. "Hi, I, um… well, I was thinking about the lake house idea you mentioned last night."

"And?" His voice rose with obvious excitement.

"It's a really nice idea. We could drive up tomorrow and…spend the night." She swallowed and then quickly added, "There's plenty of rooms, so you can have a whole king bed to yourself."

She caught Annabelle's expression in the mirror and cringed.

Sally closed her eyes, hoping he wouldn't be offended, but she didn't want the pressure of sex. If one thing led to another, then that was fine, but she could do without the huge expectation.

"I can't think of a better way to spend my weekend." Oscar was smiling, Sally could tell by the lilt of his voice.

With a relieved breath, she opened her eyes. "Great. So, do you want to pick me up tomorrow morning, then?"

"Absolutely. I'll see you then, my love."

"Bye." She hung up and deflated in the chair.

"Wow, you're like the queen of romance." Annabelle's sarcastic quip made Sally raise her middle finger. Her sister laughed and kissed her cheek. "Just go be happy. Forget about Nate and enjoy Oscar."

Sally frowned at her sister's reflection. "Why have you always been so anti-Nate?"

Annabelle spun Sally's chair around and bent down to look her in the eyes. "I wasn't at first. I thought he was tall and gorgeous. A little closed-off and he never really smiled around us, but I was willing to try because you liked him so much." Annabelle's eyes dipped to Sally's lap, then she looked up with a sad smile. "But then you started to cry. He was never around, and I've spent too many hours watching you be miserable and listening to you miss him."

"You guys never even gave him a chance," Sally whispered.

"He didn't give us much of one either." Annabelle

looked a little offended before pasting on a confident smile and touching Sally's cheek. "Besides, you're our Sally. We have to protect you."

"From what? An amazing man?"

"He's not a god, sis," Annabelle scolded. "He's closed-off and addicted to work. I still don't understand why you stayed with him for so long."

Sally's voice dropped to a breathy murmur. "You didn't know him like I did. I saw who he could be, and it stole my heart."

With a little huff, Annabelle grabbed the broom and started sweeping up the floor. "Look, he may have stolen your heart, but he doesn't know how to look after it. Oscar does. I know you may not want to hear that, but sometimes things just don't work out the way we want them to. You can't force Nate to be something he's not. You need to let go of that pipe dream and move on with a reality that could be amazing."

Sally lifted her feet so Annabelle could sweep under her chair. Wrapping her arms around her knees, she stared at the floor until her vision blurred and her heart started to crack down the center.

27

Friday, May 25th
3:35pm

THE DRIVE back to Aspen Falls was uneventful. Vern didn't say a word. Nate stopped at a gas station halfway back and bought two bottles of water and a muffin for each of them. Vern took his without a word and left them on the seat beside him.

Nate nibbled at his food but wasn't hungry, so he ended up sipping on the water and stealing glances in the rearview mirror.

Vern remained expressionless the entire ride back to Aspen Falls and it was damn near painful.

Anxious to get on with it, Nate parked at the station and quickly led Vern to the interview room.

"Can I get you a water, or a soda? Coffee?"

The man shook his head, threading his fingers together and looking like his life was over.

"We'll do an interview first, and then I'll take you to see the remains...if you still want to."

The man gave a stiff nod, but wouldn't look at Nate.

"Let me set up the recording equipment."

Vern flinched, his expression grave.

Nate left the room, which locked automatically behind him, and hustled through the station to let Kellan know what was happening.

"He came back with you?" Kellan frowned and got out of his chair.

"He wants to see the remains."

Kellan nodded. "Fair enough."

Leaning on the doorframe, Nate sighed. "He's pretty cut up about it. I mean, he showed a little emotion when I first told him, but he hasn't said a word since. I thought I'd do the interview first. His emotions might rise to the surface when he sees the bones."

"He's finally getting closure," Kellan clipped, his expression tight as he no doubt thought about his own missing daughter. They'd never found her. "Everyone processes differently. Hopefully he'll want to help us find the killer. Do you want me to come watch?"

"Uh, yeah, actually, if you're free. Saves me hassling Cam."

"I'll be down in just a minute." Kellan's nod was a quiet dismissal and Nate quickly headed back to the interview room.

He went behind the glass first to check that the computer was correctly set up to record the interview and that the camera was positioned at the right angle.

"You all set?" Kellan slipped into the room and set up post behind the glass, studying the sad-looking man. "Geez, poor guy," he murmured.

"Yep." Nate brushed past him and walked around to the door, buzzing himself in.

He gave Vern a tight smile as he shrugged out of his slightly damp jacket. "So, Mr. Schnyder, thank you for your cooperation today." Hanging his jacket over the back of his chair, he smoothed down his tie and took a seat. "I know it's been a long time since you lost your daughter, but I'd like you to think back and tell me what you can about the night she ran away."

Vern's head bobbed like a jackhammer. Licking the edge of his mouth, he swallowed and let out an aching sigh. "What do you want to know?"

"Well, uh, according to the report I read, you claimed she ran away."

"Yeah," Vern rasped. "She, uh...she thought she

was in love with this boy…this man. They met over spring break and when she got back, she'd changed somehow. She wasn't the same girl. She kept sneaking out to see him. She told us she was meeting friends, but we quickly worked out that she'd been lying to us. She'd never lied to us before." The man blinked, his voice wavering over his words.

"Where was she for spring break?" Nate flipped open his notebook and clicked on his pen.

"Uh, one of her friends had an aunt in Nissawa. She owned a cabin up there, so they went away for a girls' trip. Three nights away to watch movies and paint each other's nails. That's how she sold it to us." Vern gave him a watery smile, which quickly disappeared. "She must've met him there."

Nate jotted that down. "And how did you find out she was lying?"

"Well one day she told me she was off to catch up with one of her girlfriends. I watched her drive off and then headed out myself. I was very surprised to spot her car parked by the train tracks, so I went to go check it out. I found her in an abandoned mill, practically naked with some man pawing her."

Nate swallowed. "That must've been a shock."

"I was horrified, and deeply disappointed. Mila was a good girl. She was such a good girl." Vern's voice broke and his lips formed a wonky line as he no doubt fought his roiling emotions.

"What did you do when you found them?" Nate asked, keeping his voice even and calm to counter the brewing storm.

Vern swallowed, running a shaking hand over his head before answering. "Well, I told her to get dressed and get back to her car. I'd follow her home and we'd talk about it then."

"What did her boyfriend do?"

"He grabbed his things and hightailed it like a coward. Mila was mortified and quite tearful, but when I asked her about the guy, she became very closed off. It was obvious she didn't want to tell me much. All she could admit was that she loved him. When I told her she was too young and that I didn't want her to see him again, she flipped. I'd never seen her like that before. She started screaming at me that I couldn't keep them apart. I didn't know what to do. My baby girl was turning into someone I didn't recognize…all because of that man," he ended darkly.

"You keep saying man. How old do you think he was?"

"I don't know." He shrugged. "Not high school. He looked to be in his early twenties, maybe. He had the body of a man. He was definitely too old for my Mila, so I forbade her to see him." His voice grew distant. "I tried to ground her, control her somehow, but she said I never could. She swore she'd never speak to me again and that she'd keep sneaking out. I warned her that I'd lock her in her room and bar the windows if I had to." His face bunched with regret. "I don't think she ever forgave me for threatening that." He sniffed and blinked at his tears. "She kept her word and stopped speaking to me. It was pure torture. But I knew I was doing the right thing, protecting her. I just had a bad feeling about that man from the start. What kind of person encourages someone to lie to her parents, to sneak out of the house? He didn't have the balls to come and introduce himself to me. He was trying to have sex with my baby girl, I knew it, and I didn't want him near her." His chin bunched suddenly. "I would've done anything to stop him."

"Do you know his name?"

"Jamie," he croaked. "At least I think that's what it was."

"Last name?"

Vern shook his head.

"Do you think you'd be able to describe him to a sketch artist?"

"Yeah." Vern's face took on a hard edge. "I can picture him alright."

"Good." Nate nodded. "I'll arrange for that after the interview."

Vern shuffled in his chair, looking on edge as he asked, "Can I see my daughter now?"

"Not just yet." Nate gave him a tight smile. "I need you to tell me about the night she ran away. Your wife was out of town, correct?"

Vern shifted in his chair again, scratching the side of his face with shaky fingers. "She went to visit her sister. She was gone for two weeks. I told her it was a bad time to leave, but her sister was sick and she trusted Mila to fall into line. We'd never had any problems with her before, and Darlene was convinced that everything would be fine. It'd be fine." A lone tear slipped from Vern's right eye, trailing down the side of his face. "I think Mila had just been waiting for her to go, because she tried to leave the night after Darlene did."

"And what happened?"

"I caught her sneaking out her window…with a bag, like she was going to leave us."

"So what'd you do?" For some reason Nate's heart rate had picked up. He swallowed and smoothed down his tie as Vern continued his story.

"Well, I chased her down. I wasn't about to let him steal her away for good. She was only seventeen. She hadn't even graduated high school," he spat. "And he was going to drive off with her and we'd never see her again." He thumped the table. "He was stealing her!"

Nate held up his hand to calm the man down. "It's okay, Mr. Schnyder."

The man let out a ragged sob. "He killed my baby."

Sitting to attention, Nate leaned his elbows on the table. "Did you see it happen? Did you see this Jamie person kill your daughter?"

"I just wanted to scare him away." Vern's face bunched. "But then Mila went ballistic. She was so scared and she came toward me screaming like a banshee. 'Don't kill him. Don't you dare.'" A sob punched out of Vern and he crumpled forward, holding his stomach like it hurt. "She tried to grab my gun, and I don't know how it happened. But if he hadn't been there, if he'd just left us alone, it never would've happened!"

For a second Nate couldn't speak, his brain scrambling to process the unexpected confession.

"Mr. Schnyder, are you saying… Sir, did you… Did you shoot your daughter?"

"It was an accident," he whispered. "She was wrestling for the gun and he was yelling at her to get it. 'Get the gun. Get the gun.' He had some kind of hold on her and she didn't see me anymore. I wasn't her daddy anymore; I was just the man stopping her. I told her to calm down and let go, but she just wouldn't listen. And then her body just… She fell. And the blood."

Nate was dumbfounded. It was the last thing he'd been expecting. He blinked and tried to find his voice, his lips opening and closing like a goldfish.

A sharp tap on the glass brought him to attention and he cleared his throat.

"Um…Vern Schnyder, you're under arrest for the murder of Mila Schnyder. You have the right to remain silent," Nate said, his mind still spinning. "Anything you say can and will be used against you in a court of law. You have the right to speak to an attorney, and to have an attorney present during any questioning." His voice sounded wooden as he read the man his rights.

Vern slumped forward, pitiful whimpers spurting out of him. Nate's eyes began to burn as Vern fell apart in the interview room. The whimpers grew to sobs that racked his body, punching out of his chest in heavily weighted moans.

Nate was usually so good at hardening himself against that kind of behavior. Cutting off the emotion. But this one was hitting him right in the core.

"He took off after that," Vern wailed. "Drove into the night and I was left holding my girl. She was gone. She was…gone."

Nate knew he should've asked why he didn't call the police, but he couldn't speak.

The man was still bent over, his sobs ebbing to a quiet weeping that broke Nate's heart. "I killed my own child and I was so ashamed. How was I supposed to tell Darlene? I'd only been trying to protect our girl!" He looked up, desperate for Nate to understand. "So I hid her under my workshop, and I tried to give her the dream she wanted. I told everyone that she'd been taken away by a man who loved her. And I was a good father, and I let her go because I didn't want to lose her. That's all I could give her. That's all I could…" Vern's voice was lost to more gut-wrenching moans.

Nate couldn't swallow. The lump in his throat hurt. Gripping the edge of the desk, he watched this man…this criminal…who had only tried to do the right thing, completely screw himself over.

He couldn't even muster anger at the man's terrible decision-making, because all he felt was pity.

Vern Schnyder would be going to jail for this, but he'd incarcerated himself already. Living in isolated squalor, haunted daily by the demons of his mistake. The burden he'd been carrying for the last twelve years had eaten him alive and taken everything from him. His wife. His home. His entire life.

A knock at the door pulled Nate to attention. He glanced over his shoulder then turned back to Vern and managed, "I'm going to need a s-signed confession."

Vern nodded. "And then can I see my daughter?"

"I'll see what I can do." Stumbling out of the

interview room, Nate stepped into the hallway and shared a sad look with Kellan.

His boss nodded and patted his shoulder. "I... uh... Case closed, I guess."

Nate couldn't respond as Kellan started talking logistics. He felt hollow. Raw and reeling. He couldn't remember the last time he'd felt so devastated by a case.

28

Friday, May 25th
7:20pm

AFTER VERN SIGNED HIS CONFESSION, his case would be passed along to the DA. Nate had no idea what she was going to do with him, but he hoped she'd give the guy a break. Nate was sure Vern would never get over the torture of what he'd done, and that was a lifelong sentence in itself.

Because Nate never did anything by halves, he stuck around and made sure a few things were set in place before heading home. Vern got to see his daughter's remains. Nate stuck to the edge of the room while Vern sank to his knees and sobbed. He murmured apologies over and over until Nate could barely stand it.

Seeing the man's broken mess touched something in Nate's heart.

He understood the pain.

The loss.

Maybe even the guilt.

He hadn't killed his mother, but he'd let the culprit free. He hadn't remembered enough about the car. He hadn't done enough and so he'd pushed himself through life, determined to make amends for his mistake.

Rather than hiding the way Vern had, he'd acted like a bullet, firing through life with blinders on. Obsessed with catching bad guys and doing good.

But in that moment?

He didn't feel good.

As he drove Vern back from the hospital to the precinct, he was consumed by every past case he'd closed. Slides ran through his mind—one image after the next—and it struck him with painful clarity that none of them had lessened the pain of losing his mom. None of them had redeemed him or filled the gaping hole.

When they arrived at the station, Nate gently helped the big guy out of the car.

"Do you still want me to talk to that sketch artist?" Vern asked in a wooden voice. The tall man's aching expression was pitiful.

"Do you think he was a predator?" Nate asked as they walked inside.

Vern's eyebrows slowly lifted, his eyes filling with tears once more, and Nate understood that Vern needed him to be. He needed this Jamie man to be a criminal too, or the hurt would be unbearable.

Clearing his throat, Nate pulled out his phone. "The fact that he took off and never reported the accident sets off alarm bells in my head. I'll arrange for a sketch artist to come by tomorrow."

"Thank you," Vern croaked.

Nate led him back to the holding cell where the officer on duty would book him and then lock him up for the night. Nate stood in the doorway, watching Vern get photographed. Fingerprints would come next. With a sad sigh, Nate turned away and shuffled out to his bike.

He felt heavy.

Tired.

Depleted.

Slumping onto the seat, he leaned forward and gripped the handlebars. But he didn't start the engine. All he could do was stare into the black night sky. Emptiness consumed him until it hurt to breathe.

He didn't know when he started the engine or how he even made it back to his father's house.

Climbing the porch steps, he let himself in and

found his father at the dining table, finishing his dinner alone.

His dad took one look at him and quickly asked, "Tough day?"

Nate leaned against the doorframe. "I just had to arrest a guy who accidentally killed his daughter."

His father hissed, his face a picture of sympathy. "Not so satisfying, huh?"

Nate shook his head, his throat swelling with an emotion he didn't understand. "Why do I do this job, Dad?"

His father wiped his mouth with his napkin and sat back in his chair to gaze up at his eldest son. "Because you love it."

"Do I?"

His father sighed. "Because you're good at it. You've always been driven by justice. It's what makes you such a great detective."

Nate gave a thoughtful scowl and went to turn away.

"It doesn't make you happy, though," his father said. "Nothing's made you happy since your mother died…except maybe Sally."

Nate closed his eyes and leaned his head back against the wall.

"She was nothing but pure sunshine, that girl." His father rose from the table, his penetrating gaze trying to peel the layers off Nate's soul.

"She doesn't want me anymore. I...I wasn't enough."

"Well, that's bullshit," his father muttered.

Nate's head jerked up, his eyes popping open in surprise. His father never swore.

The older man let out a hard, barking laugh and took his plate into the kitchen.

Nate could do nothing but follow him. "She dumped me, remember?"

"Yeah, because you weren't around, not because she didn't love you anymore. Not because you weren't enough. You just weren't there!"

Nate opened his mouth to argue but nothing came out.

"Look, son, I know you're dedicated to your job. And so does Sally. That's why she stuck around for so long. But those demons that drive you? They're hard task masters, and they are stopping you from dealing with the truth."

Uncomfortable with such a rare, honest conversation with his father, Nate crossed his arms and scoffed. "And what truth is that?"

"That you're still a scared little boy who's afraid that if you stop working, someone's going to slip through the cracks and hurt the people you love." His father's voice was soft and steady, yet it felt like he'd just blasted that truth from the rooftop.

Nate's nostrils flared, his heart hammering an unsteady beat.

His father placed his dirty plate in the sink and turned to face him. "I'm sorry to tell you this, son, but we can't stop bad things from happening. You can't fight a natural disaster or stop someone from getting sick. Accidents will happen whether we want them to or not. Now, you're doing your damn best to keep the people of Aspen Falls safe and I admire that, I really do. But at what cost, Nate? No one's asked you to give your life for the force. You deserve happiness just as much as the next person."

Nate looked to the floor, unable to hold his father's steady gaze.

"Sally was your happiness. You need to get her back."

"She's moved on," Nate muttered bitterly. "She's with someone else."

"They married?"

Nate glanced up with an incredulous frown. "No."

"Huh." His father looked thoughtful, then turned to start rinsing his plate.

Nate rolled his eyes. "I just told you she doesn't want me anymore."

His father laughed again, tipping his head back. "You know, for a man who notices everything, you are one blind fool."

The laughter grated on Nate's tattered nerves and he nearly walked out on it.

"Sally Richmond has been in love with you for years. You stole her heart, and as far as I'm concerned, you haven't given it back. You would be a complete idiot to give up on that girl. Now you stop fighting your demons, Nathan." He glanced over his shoulder with a sharp look. "Stop wasting your time, and start fighting for the woman you love." His father slipped his plate into the dishwasher and walked out of the kitchen.

Nate stayed where he was, staring at the wooden floors until the cracks between the boards started to blur.

Very slowly he reached into his pocket and pulled up Sally's number on his phone. Her beautiful smile stared up at him from the screen and his heart squeezed with desire, affection…happiness.

It was only then that it hit him with a force he couldn't ignore.

Putting bad guys away would never fill the gaping hole in his chest.

But love would.

29

Saturday, May 26th
8:55am

SALLY HAD a restless sleep and woke up tired. She envied Rusty, who was still snoring beside her as she stirred.

With a groan, she reached for her phone to check the time and noticed a missed call notification.

From Nate.

She blinked to clear her vision. She rubbed her eyes and blinked again to make sure she was reading it correctly.

She was.

And her heart skipped out of rhythm.

Why was he calling her? What did he want to say?

Part of her was desperate to call back and find out, but her fragile heart was scared.

"Sally Richmond, you're not up yet?" Her mother breezed into the room and snapped open the curtains. "You better hurry. Oscar's due here in less than half an hour."

Sally swallowed, watching her mother pull a dress from the closet. "This is my favorite one of yours. It always has been. You look like such a dream in it. Oscar won't know what to do with himself." She laughed and Sally suddenly felt ill.

Oblivious to her doubts, her mother grabbed Sally's overnight bag and walked it to the door.

"I'll take this down for you. Hurry up and shower, get dressed and I'll make you a peach and blueberry smoothie. You can drink it on the drive over." Her smile was bright and sunny. "I'm so happy for you, baby girl. You deserve such a sweet, kind gentleman. And you're going to have a lovely weekend."

Her mother's wink stayed in her mind as Sally slipped out of bed and got ready. She didn't linger in the shower, and although she wasn't a huge fan of dresses, she didn't hesitate slipping into her mother's selection. It was just easier to go with the flow.

Her family was right.

Going away with Oscar for one night would be a

good test and would hopefully help her sort out her feelings.

She glanced at the phone on her rumpled bed, thoughts of Nate searing her.

"You okay, sis?" Xavier popped his head into her room. "You look worried."

Forcing a bright smile, she crossed her arms. "No, I'm fine."

His keen eyes narrowed in on her. "Not having second thoughts about going away with King Clump Nugget, are you?"

"Get out of my room." She picked a cushion off the floor and threw it at him.

He snickered and used the door as a shield, slamming it shut before the cushion could hit him.

It fell to the floor and Sally stared at the colorful design—bright and happy, just the way she usually felt.

Turning her back on it, she stared down at the phone and nibbled her thumbnail.

Rusty, woken by the door slam, greeted her with a little whine. She grinned at him and walked around the bed. Sitting on the edge, she petted him until his tail was going crazy.

"Everything's fine, right, boy?" His tail thumped on the bed. "It has to be. I mean, what choice do I have? Calling Nate back is a bad idea." At the sound of Nate's name, Rusty's tail picked up even more. He jumped to his paws and licked her face. She giggled and moved out of slobbering range. Standing tall, she held his face and reminded him, "I know you still love him. So do I. But calling would only open up a bunch of unwanted feelings. I mean, right? I'm trying to move on. That's…that's what I should do." Her voice trailed off as she gazed around her room, suddenly pining for a different bedroom in a little bungalow for two.

"Sweetie, Oscar's here!" her mother called from the entryway.

Sally could hear her mother's joy, her anticipation. She could picture the look that would cross her mother's face if she knew Nate had called.

Rubbing her forehead, Sally whined in her throat and gave Rusty a quick kiss before heading for the door.

She couldn't take Nate with her to the cabin. So she left her phone beside her bed and walked down the stairs.

Oscar was waiting for her in the doorway, a dreamy smile on his face.

"You look amazing." He pecked her cheek like a gentleman, then greeted Rusty. "Hello, boy. Mind if I borrow your mummy for the night?"

Rusty barked his protest, which made Oscar laugh and quickly lead Sally out the door.

Before she slipped into the passenger seat, her

mother passed her a purple smoothie and kissed her cheek. "You have fun, darling."

"Will do, Mom." She nodded, feeling like a ten-year-old being sent off to camp.

Oscar finished his brief chat with her father before sliding behind the wheel. "Ready to be my navigator?" He grinned.

Sally nodded and sipped her smoothie, licking the sweet milkiness off her top lip before looking straight ahead.

That was what she had to focus on.

Looking ahead.

Not behind.

30

Saturday, May 26th
9:45am

NATE GROANED AND ROLLED OVER, the dreamy haze in his head shuffling from one image to the next.

Vern Schnyder's sobbing echoed in the back of his mind. His daughter's skeleton danced in circles around images of Sally's sweet smile. And then a gunshot rang out and Sally slumped to the ground, turning into a puddle of muddy snow that started to melt. Vern's sobs became Nate's as he dropped to his knees and tried to gather up Sally's snow before it liquified.

His movements became frantic as he wept.

"No, no, please. No!"

Nate's eyes flew open and he swallowed down his gasp. His heart was thundering and it took him a moment to register the sunlight, Dad's guestroom, the soft pillow beneath his cheek.

He sat up, trying to swallow the boulder in his throat. His heart pounded, and a fine sheen of sweat covered his forehead.

Snatching his water bottle, he guzzled it down then checked his phone.

No reply from Sally.

And oh shit, look at the time.

Throwing back the covers, he swung his legs over the edge of the bed and tried to motivate himself to stand. His body was heavy with exhaustion, his insides a restless torrent.

He didn't know how he'd face the day.

For the first time since becoming a cop, he didn't want to go in. He didn't want to catch any bad guys.

He just wanted Sally.

His phone vibrated with a text.

He jumped at the sound and snatched it, hoping to see a message from Sally, but it was from Cam.

Where the hell are you? The raid starts in 15.

. . .

Nate frowned, trying to decipher the message.

"The raid?" he muttered under his breath, and then his eyebrows popped high. "Oh shit! The raid!"

She'd told him about it the night before, called him just before he fell asleep. They were busting into the warehouse she'd been surveying for the last few days. Her contact had come through and it was happening.

Nate said he'd be there.

"Shit." Grabbing a pair of jeans off the floor, he hopped around the room, shoving them on and grabbing a dirty T-shirt draped over the edge of the laundry basket. He smelled it, wrinkled his nose, but then threw it on anyway.

It was a raid. The smell would be hidden under his Kevlar jacket.

He yanked his leather jacket off the back of the chair and threw it on while he rushed down the stairs.

Checking the time, he muttered another curse while shoving the phone into his back pocket and jumping on the bike. His boots weren't even on properly, but he'd do them up once he got there.

Cam would be pissed.

Screaming out of his driveway, he tore through town and arrived with five minutes to spare.

He parked the bike away from the scene and

jogged two blocks down to the meeting point—a cruddy-looking warehouse with a rusted tin roof and cracks in the windows. It used to be a storage facility for some medical device manufacturer. They'd opened a new warehouse closer to the cities and this building had been abandoned ever since… until it had been turned into a drug lab. At least according to Cam. The raid would prove it.

Nate's boots crunched on the loose gravel as he snuck down the driveway next door.

Everyone was already there, suited up and checking their weapons.

"About damn time, Nate." Cam threw him a Kevlar jacket.

"Sorry," he mumbled, pulling off his jacket and putting on the Kevlar without any more explanation. He shoved his leather jacket back on and zipped it up.

"I'm sending Higgs and Jessica around to the northeast side of the building. Mick and the rookie will come in from the west, and I'll take the front." Cam pointed over her shoulder. "Holly and Stan are covering the south exit in case anyone tries to do a runner."

"And where do you want me?"

"Keep yourself available to run backup where needed."

He nodded as he pulled out his gun and checked the magazine. Thoughts of Sally rushed him. He was usually able to control that kind of thing at work, but after his dream she was all-consuming. Her sweet smile, her tears…the way she'd turned into a pile of dirty snow. The complete grief he felt at losing her.

Since breaking up, he hadn't let it take him. But time had obviously run out and he couldn't keep ignoring the pain radiating inside of him. It was hot and fierce.

He felt completely lost without her.

And doing this raid, catching these guys, wasn't going to make him feel better. It wouldn't satisfy. It wouldn't bring his mother back. Nothing ever would.

But he could do something about Sally.

He could get her back.

"I've gotta go." He clipped the magazine back in and shoved the gun into his holster.

"What?" Cam frowned at him.

"You don't need me. The entire building is covered with competent police officers. You don't need me for this raid."

"But…" Cam shook her head. "You always want in."

He cringed. "Yeah, I know. But I don't always need to be in."

Cam let out a confused scoff. “Have you got somewhere better to be?”

His lips twitched. “I gotta get Sally back.”

“Right now?”

“Yeah.” He nodded. “Right now.”

31

Saturday, May 26th
10:35am

HE DROVE like the devil was chasing him.

Any cop on patrol would've pulled him over, but he managed to avoid them and screeched to a stop outside Sally's house. He still thought of it as theirs, which was why he hadn't been able to drive past it since the night he moved out.

Leaping off his motorbike, he ran to the front door and pounded the wood.

"Sally, we've got to talk!"

It wasn't until his fist started hurting that he realized his approach was probably way off.

Turning up like an angry madman? Was he nuts?

He stepped back from the door with a heavy sigh, and croaked, "Sally, please…let me in."

Her reply was silence.

He squeezed the back of his neck and cursed under his breath.

She was ignoring him, because she didn't want to see him. She wouldn't give him a chance to make it right.

Dammit!

"Or maybe she's just not home, you idiot," Nate muttered.

As his frantic brain calmed, his logical senses kicked back in and he made a quick call to the hospital to find out if she was at work.

But Sally was off for the weekend.

So where the hell was she?

With an irritated huff, Nate walked around the property to double-check that the bungalow was empty. It actually had the feel that it'd been that way for a while. The back lawn was long and unkempt, and a peek through the window showed thick layers of dust on the furniture. And there were zero signs of Rusty's antics anywhere.

How long had they been gone?

Shuffling to his Harley, he sat on it for a few minutes before starting up the engine. His brain ticked through the places Sally could be living—her parents', her sister's, Lena's, Chantel's, Bridget's... Oscar's?

His stomach rebelled at the idea and he revved the engine, heading to her parents' place first.

They wouldn't welcome him, but he didn't give a shit.

He needed to talk to Sally.

He needed her to know that he'd finally figured it out.

As his Harley rumbled through the open gates, nerves attacked him. He'd been so set on seeing her that he hadn't come up with anything to say. What did he start with? Would she even listen?

Sally was the world's most patient, compassionate woman.

She'd listen. Of course she would. Which meant he had to express himself pretty damn perfectly in order for her to hear what his heart was so desperate to say.

"Sally, I love you," he whispered as he hopped off his bike and pocketed the keys. "I miss you. I'm lost without you."

It was all so generic and borderline cheesy. Like something out of the romance novels she loved to read.

He had to be better than that.

She needed honesty—raw and ugly...but real.

Swallowing down the last of his tattered pride, he

knocked on the door and stiffened the second it swung open.

"Nathan?" Michael Richmond's face puckered with annoyance before smoothing out with a professionally tight smile. "What are you doing here?"

"I need to see Sally."

"She's not here." The man gave him a polite nod and went to close the door.

Nate shot out his hand to stop him. "It's important, sir. When is she getting back?"

"Not today. She's away for the weekend." With a short huff, Michael gave up fighting Nate for control of the door. Nate was stronger and, in that particular moment, far more determined. Scratching his forehead, Michael let out a resigned sigh. "Look, Nathan, I really don't think it's a good idea, you trying to see her again. She's moving on and you need to let her do that. She wasted a lot of years on you, and I don't want you messing with her when she's close to being happy again."

The words were like poisonous darts, hitting Nate's chest in quick succession.

The venom soaked into his bloodstream, trying to numb his heart, warning him to give up.

She was happy again. With Oscar. Which meant she was happy without Nate.

Dipping his head, he gazed down at his boots and could barely muster a nod. "I just thought..."

"You had your chance and you blew it," Michael clipped. "If you love my daughter, leave her alone and give her the life she deserves."

Nate couldn't argue with that. He did love Sally and he desperately wanted to give her the life she deserved. But with him.

"Goodbye, Nathan." Mr. Richmond closed the heavy door with no more fight from Nate.

Clenching his jaw, Nate kept staring down at his boots. He watched them walk to the motorbike as if they were detached from his body. He'd been so certain the night before when he called Sally. So determined when he drove here to win her back.

But was that fair?

She hadn't returned his call.

She'd gone off for the weekend, no doubt with Oscar, and she didn't need him.

His stomach clenched like there was a fist inside of him, trying to squeeze him dry.

"Hey, asshole."

Nate closed his eyes, resisting the urge to look over his shoulder with a snarl. *Shut the hell up, Xavier.* The words were right on the tip of his tongue.

"She's gone down to the lake house with the douche nugget," Xavier told him.

Nate could barely swallow past the bile surging up his throat. He gripped his hands into fists and kept his back to Sally's younger brother.

"You know, it wouldn't hurt, man. The worst she can say is no, right?"

Nate blinked. It took him a second to register Xavier's words. Then he frowned and spun to face him. "What?"

Xavier grinned, sliding his hands into his pockets just the way his father did. "If you show up at the cabin, she can tell you to piss off or…you know… lovingly fall into your arms."

Nate scoffed and shook his head. "From what your dad just said, I doubt she's going to do that."

"Dad doesn't know shit. And if you're standing here believing what he just told you, then you're just as stupid as he is."

Nate worked his jaw to the side, anger bubbling inside of him.

"Listen to me, man." Xavier glanced over his shoulder as if he was about to share the world's greatest secret and didn't want to get caught. Stepping forward, he waited until Nate was looking him in the eye before emphatically stating, "You were all she ever wanted…when you showed up."

Nate grimaced, disgusted at himself for being so damn blind for so damn long.

"I wouldn't be out here talking to you if I didn't think you were meant to be together. My family may not love you, but Sally has always adored you. I don't know how the hell your grumpy ass does it, but her heart is yours."

Nate blinked in surprise, his lips parting. It was all he could manage with the emotions raging through him. Speech seemed impossible.

"Look, go to the lake house, apologize for being a selfish prick and tell her you love her." Xavier slapped him on the shoulder and gave it a firm squeeze. "Oscar will probably hate you for it, but we can deal with that shit later. Just don't screw this up, and you may graduate from asshole to dude."

Nate snickered at Xavier's wink and shot out his hand. "Thank you."

"I'm doing it for Sally, but you gotta promise me that if you get her back, you treat her like—"

"I will. I promise you." Nate's voice was husky with conviction as he squeezed Xavier's hand. He didn't know what his eyes were doing, but it made Xavier smile and nod.

"Go get her, asshole."

Nate didn't need to be told twice.

Throwing his leg over the bike, he started it up and tore away from the Richmonds' house. He didn't want to think about the fallout of Sally taking him back. All he could focus on was the idea of seeing his woman and telling her that she was everything, and he'd never fail to realize that again.

32

Saturday, May 26th
12:05pm

THE DRIVE to the lake house was quiet, but pleasant. They stopped at a grocery store on the way to get supplies, and Oscar had gone overboard with treats and delicacies—cheeses, crackers, wine, grapes... even caviar. Sally didn't have the heart to tell him she hated the stuff.

She didn't have the heart to tell him much, actually. She wasn't in a talking mood. So Oscar filled in most of the space, chatting between songs on the radio. When they lost reception, he plugged in his phone so the silence between them was veiled by the strains of upbeat music.

Sally watched the countryside flash by, a palette

of spring and summer greens. The calendar might not say it was summer quite yet, but Mother Nature did things on her own timetable, and the heat and warmth told Sally her favorite season was already here. She loved the feel of the hot sun kissing her skin, the fresh breeze in her face. She loved the shocking contrast of jumping into the lake and cooling off. Her mother would move into the lake house for at least a month every summer, and the family would join her for portions of it. They always ended with a full family weekend away before Sally's parents took off for a week of romance somewhere in the world.

They were aiming for Vienna this year. Her mother had the trip all planned.

Xavier was taking off to New Zealand, and Annabelle was putting Chantel in charge of the salon so she could flit off to the Bahamas with her summertime boyfriend, Pedro. The guy lived in Florida and if just one of them was willing to compromise, they could probably have a real relationship, but neither would move, so they had one week of romance a year and then behaved like singletons the rest of the time. Sally found it weird, but didn't say anything. It wasn't like she could talk.

Last summer, she'd stayed in Aspen Falls while her family jetted off.

It had been lonely and boring, except for the time

Nate had surprised her, whisking her away for forty-eight hours of bliss at a gorgeous bed-and-breakfast up north. They'd spent the whole time focused on each other. They'd hiked, played chess, and she'd taught him the names of each and every bone in his body—a fun, naked way to spend an afternoon.

It had been the perfect getaway.

When she had Nate—his full attention—Sally was the happiest version of herself.

It wasn't that she needed him all the time. But forty-eight hours every once in a while wasn't enough, either. She wished Nate could see that. He needed to balance his life and stop pushing family down his priority list. If only he could work it out.

Sally closed her eyes and held the heavy sigh building in her chest.

Oscar didn't need to know what she was thinking. He was taking her away so he could give her all the things she wanted in a relationship—time, attention, uninterrupted conversation.

Nerves scuttled through her.

Would he want more than conversation? Could she give that to him?

They'd made out since they'd started dating, but nothing hot and heavy. He didn't spark her desire the way Nate did. Maybe he would in time, but with Nate it was instinct. Her body craved him. Her heart and soul could never get enough.

Rubbing the ache between her breasts, she tried to push thoughts of Nate from her mind, but it was a struggle. The last time she'd come to the lake house had been with him. Sure, her family had been around too, but they'd snuck away the afternoon before he had to head back to work and made love in the woods. They'd felt like the only two people on earth, naked in nature. She'd never felt more whole and satisfied.

"Penny for your thoughts?" Oscar asked.

Sally jerked in her seat and turned to face him. A hot blush burned her cheeks and she stiffly shook her head.

He gave her a hopeful smile and she internally groaned. Did he think she was dreaming of being naked with him?

She cleared her throat and forced a giggle. "Sorry. My mind was just wandering to past summers. My family has had a lot of good times at the lake house." She looked down and prayed he couldn't smell lies.

"Well, I'm very much looking forward to seeing it. Your father obviously loves it. When he offered it to me for the weekend, I could tell by the way he spoke that it's a very special haven for your family."

"It is." She nodded. "This will make up for last summer when you couldn't join us. Daddy's been desperate for you to see his favorite place in the world."

Oscar smiled and reached across the car, taking her hand and threading his fingers between hers.

She didn't wiggle free of his grasp. If anything, she tried to accept it. Her father never offered the cabin to strangers. It was almost sacred to the Richmond clan. The fact that he'd suggested Oscar bring her here meant a lot. It'd be so much easier if she fell in love with him.

Easier.

Simpler.

But...

"Is this the one?" Oscar let go of her hand to point at the narrow driveway.

Sally nodded and a moment later, they breeched the trees and pulled up next to the beloved lake house. Her father had built it two years after he and Yvonne had gotten married. A two-story log cabin right on the edge of the water, with a balcony off the master bedroom and a wraparound deck on the bottom floor. In the summer, every window and door was thrown open, which made Sally feel like she was living both inside and out at the same time.

Sucking in a full breath, Sally got out of the car, hoping the familiar scent of pine and fresh air would enrich her soul. Gazing up at the surrounding trees before taking in the rustic cabin, she tried to feel the warmth and excitement she normally did. But it was a struggle.

"This is amazing." Oscar grinned at her. "What an honor to be here with you."

Sally smiled. "Come on, let me show you around."

She took her time with the tour, telling stories as she showed him each room. They paused on the top deck for a long time, leaning against the railing and staring out at the water. It was a stunning view, the beautiful lake bordered by towering trees. Sally glanced at the dock and pictured their boat. When the hot summer weather hit, the boat would be permanently moored there so it was ready to go whenever they arrived.

"Should we go for a ride?" Sally pointed at the boathouse. "We could get the boat out and I could take you to the other side of the lake. There's some great hiking trails over there."

Oscar glanced at his watch and then looked up to the blue sky. "I love the idea, but do you mind if we spend a little while here first? I'd love to open a bottle of wine." He slid his hand around her waist. "Relax a little. We could sit out here, soak up the sun." His eyes traveled to the double doors and the king bed behind them.

Sally swallowed and forced a smile when he turned back to face her. The hunger in his eyes was unmistakable, and when he leaned in to kiss her, Sally jerked tall before she could stop herself.

"Okay," she said, brightly. "I'll go get some wine and food, then."

"Sounds good." Oscar failed to hide his disappointment and got busy unbuttoning his shirtsleeves and rolling them up as she walked back into the house.

Squeezing her hands in and out of fists, she tried to calm her jitters. She took her sweet time preparing food for them, taking extra care with arranging the platter. Oscar had brought everything from dried fruits to imported grapes, four types of cheeses, deli meats, and an array of crackers. She felt like a master chef, fiddling with the plating until it looked restaurant worthy.

She didn't usually bother with that kind of thing, but she was nervous.

"Are you nearly ready?" Oscar called from upstairs.

"Al-almost," Sally stuttered. She grabbed a few extra crackers and laid them out, determined to not let the wine go to her head. She wasn't ready to sleep with Oscar and didn't want to let her guard down.

She stilled.

That was it.

That was why the nerves were attacking her.

She wasn't ready to sleep with Oscar. Because she wasn't in love with him.

Gripping the handles of the tray, she slowly

walked up the stairs and laid it down on the table between them.

"Looks amazing." Oscar ran his hand down her back, his smile warm with admiration.

Sally was once again struck by his beauty. He was handsome. Smooth and untainted, his sharp features that of a model's, yet her heart didn't flutter the way it did around Nate.

Dipping her head, she willed herself to relax. Oscar was sweet, kind, handsome. Why was she getting so worked up? If she told him outright that she wasn't ready for sex, he'd probably hide his disappointment and accept it like a gentleman.

She held on to that thought and forced herself to calm down as they sipped their wine and chatted.

They talked around the mundane—nursing, Rusty, the building project. Stories were told and the time passed easily enough. After two full glasses of red, Sally's limbs were beginning to liquify, and she rested her head back against the chair and closed her eyes.

"You really are the most beautiful creature." Oscar's fingers skimmed down her cheek.

She flinched and turned to look at him.

"I think I loved you the first moment I saw you." Oscar's voice was husky and warm. "I prayed that one day I could make you mine, never thinking I'd be heard. To have that wish become a reality is beyond my comprehension."

Sally swallowed.

"I know it probably feels lightning fast, but for me, it's been years in the making. I love you, Sally Richmond. And..." He licked his lips while reaching beneath the table, then pulled out a ring box.

Sally's heart dropped into her stomach, her mind numb when he flipped open the lid to reveal a sparkling engagement ring. The diamond was the size of a large pea and sat within rose gold claws. It glinted in the light and all Sally could do was blink at it.

"I asked your father's permission earlier this week and he gave it." Oscar grinned. "He knows it's fast, but he wants you to be happy, and Sally, I can make you so incredibly happy. I know I can." Getting out of his seat, he knelt before her with a hopeful smile on his face. "Sally Marie Richmond, will you marry me?"

The thunderstorm in her chest made it impossible to speak.

Her father had agreed to his proposal?

What the hell?

Sally blinked, struggling to form an expression, let alone an answer.

How could she say no? Everyone in her family wanted it. Oscar was a safe bet.

But…

She couldn't.

She couldn't do it.

Her lips trembled as she opened her mouth, dread pulsing through her in anxious waves. "Oscar, I…"

And then she heard it.

The sound that would ultimately save her.

Nate's Harley.

33

Saturday, May 26th
1:20pm

SALLY JERKED FROM HER SEAT, running to the edge of the deck to look down at the front of the house.

Nate atop his Harley popped into view mere seconds later and her heart catapulted up her body.

A mixture of relief, joy and confusion waded through her, but the second he took off his helmet and looked up, the hurricane of emotions settled to a low thrum—a longing so thick and strong she could've cried.

"What the hell is he doing here?" Oscar snapped over her shoulder.

"I-I'm not sure."

Nate still hadn't said anything. He just stood by

his bike, gazing up at her—that gruff, unreadable expression on his face so familiar. Very soon it would either break into a smile or crumple with sadness. She'd seen it so many times before.

"Can we talk?" he eventually called up. "It's important."

"Okay." She nodded rapidly. "I'll come down."

She took off at a pace that was no doubt offensive to Oscar, but she didn't care. Nate was there. He'd come to see her. And she was desperate to hear what he had to say.

Her mind was racing with possibilities. For a second she worried that someone in his family was injured or had died. Whether Nate wanted to admit it or not, he cared deeply for his family. He just didn't know how to show it. If something disastrous had happened, it made sense that he'd come for her. She had always been able to make him feel better.

Weaving around the sofa, Sally rushed outside, ready to listen, to comfort—a role that came so easily to her.

Sliding the door open, she stepped onto the lower deck and found Nate still hovering near his bike. Part of her wanted to run to him, but caution held her back. She paused at the top of the stairs and rested her hand on the decking post. "Are you okay? Is…is everything okay at home?"

Nate looked confused for a second, but then

blinked and nodded, "Oh, yeah. Everyone's fine. I'm fine. I mean…I'm not fine. They're fine. I'm not." He grimaced and raked a hand through his hair. "I'm sorry to just turn up like this, but you've got to know something. I need you to know…" His voice trailed off, his blue gaze unraveling her with its raw beauty. "I've been a selfish prick. You had every right to dump me. I was wrong. I thought work could make it better." He tapped the center of his chest so hard the zipper of his jacket banged up and down. "I've been chasing demons ever since my mom died, and I thought that if I just caught enough bad guys that one day, I'll…I don't know, start to accept it." He swallowed. "Like being a good detective made me worthy or something."

Sally's eyes glassed over, her breath evaporating. Nate never spoke so openly about his feelings. He was a locked box…always…but there he was, unleashing everything in a voice so shaky she barely recognized it as his.

She could hear footsteps pacing around inside the house and quickly glanced over her shoulder. She couldn't see Oscar, but he was no doubt going insane. He'd just proposed and Nate's timing couldn't have been worse. At least from Oscar's perspective.

Sally closed her eyes, sick with turmoil yet knowing deep down where her heart wanted to be.

Right where she was, listening to Nate's heart.

She turned back to face him.

"I'm sorry," Nate rasped. "I'm ruining your weekend, but I couldn't wait. I needed you to know that—"

His phone started ringing and he closed his eyes, obviously frustrated by the interruption.

Sally dipped her head, her heart sinking as she waited for him to answer it. He yanked it from his pocket with an irritated frown and quickly shut it off. Sally had to blink three times to make sure she hadn't just been seeing things.

Did Detective Nate Hartford just ignore a phone call?

Shoving his device away, he caught Sally's surprise and his expression buckled. "Shit, I didn't see you, Sal. You were always right there, patiently waiting for me, and I never appreciated you. I didn't... I don't deserve..." He pulled in a ragged breath. "I'd love to drop to my knees right here and beg you for a second chance, but I don't want to put that kind of pressure on you."

Sally wrapped her arms around her waist and held tight. The hope in her chest had suddenly burst to life and was fluttering around inside her ribcage. It tickled and overwhelmed, making her dizzy.

But then her head started demanding that she pay attention.

It didn't matter that Nate was finally saying everything she'd wanted him to. That was no guarantee. Nate wasn't a man of empty words or promises, but he was still Nate. Ignoring one phone call didn't mean the change was complete.

And what about Oscar?

Soft footsteps sounded on the porch, reminding her that she couldn't forget about the man who'd just proposed.

He stepped up beside her, silently staking his claim with an arm around her waist.

Nate saw it and gave her a resigned smile. "That was my plan as I was driving down here to find you. I'd fall to my knees and beg until you couldn't turn me away. But then I realized that if I truly love you, your happiness has to come first." His gaze softened with a smile that Sally could've drowned in. "The whole time we were together, you were my solid rock, holding me steady, being whatever I needed, and now it's your turn. You have to come first." He swallowed, obviously struggling to say what he had to. "If Oscar makes you happy, then you should be with him. I just needed you to know that I will always love you, no matter what. You're it for me, Sally. You always have been. My heart is yours...forever."

The tears she'd been fighting finally surfaced and spilled over her lashes. She couldn't contain her smile. It grew on her face like a flower desperate to unfold. It'd just been waiting for the right amount of sun. And there it was.

Nate's lips twitched, the gooey expression in his eyes no doubt matching hers.

She opened her mouth to tell him he was forgiven, that taking him back was the easiest thing in the world, but Oscar stopped her, his fingers digging into her waist as he pulled her against him.

"I just proposed to you," he whisper-barked in her ear. His tone was sharp, his voice trembling with emotion. "I told you I love you. I have the ring!"

She tried to ease out of his grasp but he only tightened his grip. Resting her hand on his chest, she attempted to soothe him with a kind smile. "Oscar, you have been nothing but amazing, but I can't—"

He cut her off, turning to glare at Nate. "You shouldn't be here." Oscar's tone was only getting sharper. "You had your chance, and you blew it!"

Nate's face flashed with remorse, but his voice remained firm. "I had to come. I know it's selfish on my part, and I'm sorry if it hurts you, but she has to know how I feel."

"Well you're too late." Oscar lifted his chin. "I've just asked Sally to marry me and she was about to say yes."

Sally stiffened, wrenching out of his grasp. "Actually, Oscar, I was about to say no. I can't marry you, because it wouldn't be fair. I love Nate." She turned to smile at the man who had just bared his heart to her. "I don't think I could stop even if I wanted to. You have my heart, always."

Nate closed his eyes, placing a hand over his chest as if the weight he'd been carrying for centuries was finally lifting free.

With a soft smile, he opened his eyes and took a step toward her, but then quickly jerked to a stop. His blue eyes flashed with surprise as he reached for his gun.

Why his gun? What was happen—?

A shot rang out beside Sally and she screamed.

"You're not screwing up my plans!" Oscar shouted.

Nate's body jerked backward as the bullet hit his chest.

"Nate!" The word tore out of her soul.

Horror froze her as Nate's head cracked against his bike, his body slumping to the dirt like a misused rag doll.

"No!" she hollered, rushing forward. Her steps faltered as Oscar jerked her back against him. "Let me go!" She fought hard to get free, desperate to reach Nate.

"Stop fighting me!" Oscar's voice pitched. "Or you'll regret it!"

Cool metal dug beneath her chin. Sally gasped

and looked at Oscar like he was a complete stranger. Because he suddenly was. His brown eyes, usually soft with affection, had become hard and dark. It was like the man had peeled off his Oscar skin to reveal his true self beneath. Sally's brain was struggling to process her shock.

"What is wrong with you?" she whispered. "WHAT THE HELL IS WRONG WITH YOU!"

Oscar shoved her back against the post, his eyes glinting. "I had it planned. Over two years of work, of brown-nosing your father, and it comes down to this! I am not wasting it!"

Sally had no idea what he was talking about, but one thing was clear. She wasn't talking to Oscar the English gentleman anymore. His accent had completely slipped, an American twang coming through loud and clear.

"Stupid frickin' cop!" Oscar muttered, dragging Sally down the stairs. "Come on." He tugged on her arm and she fought him, her eyes still glued to Nate's fallen body.

"Go screw yourself." The words punched out of her, breaking with emotion as reality hit her full force.

Nate was dead. Oscar had killed him.

A short, harsh laugh spurted out of Oscar's mouth as he dragged her off the last step. "We'll have time for screwing later, baby. Right now, I need you to get into my car."

She fought him, pulling back and trying to wrench free of his iron grasp.

"Now, now, don't fight." His voice hitched as she clipped his stomach with her fist. She nearly broke free of him, but her feisty move only empowered the man. With a feral look that terrified her, he swung the gun at her head, striking her temple and liquifying her muscles. She flopped and he caught her against him, roughly yanking her to his car.

"Stop." Her groggy head turned the words in her mouth to thick mud.

Pain was a vise around her temples, squeezing tighter and tighter, willing the blackness in.

Like a low-lying cloud, it rolled through her brain, taking out each sense until the darkness had completely claimed her.

34

Saturday, May 26th
1:55pm

NATE SQUEEZED HIS EYES TIGHT. The pain in his chest was competing with the roaring between his temples.

What'd just happened?

He swam through a dark abyss, stretching for the light. It was behind his lids; he could feel the heat on his face.

Memories flashed through him, sharp and erratic.

Sally's smile. Oscar behind her. The malice on his face. The gun. The bullet.

The bullet.

He'd been shot.

The realization made his eyes pop open. Light assaulted him. He squinted against it as he fought his zipper and tore open his jacket with trembling fingers.

Ripping Velcro came next as his panicked hands fought the Kevlar, desperate for proof.

Proof that he wasn't dead.

Patting his chest, he soon realized that it was intact. It still frickin' hurt, and he coughed as he forced his chest to expand and inflate. Tipping his head back, he winced as the tender spot on the back of his head reminded him that he'd hit his head and blacked out.

As that reality dawned, a new terror took him out.

He sat up with a jerk and noticed the bullet embedded in the gear that had saved his life.

The bullet that Oscar had tried to kill him with.

"Sally." Nate's voice was weak and raspy. He staggered to his feet and stumbled against his bike, frantically scanning the area for her. "SALLY!"

A flock of birds took flight when he roared her name.

The rest of nature stilled.

Oscar's car was gone.

The lake house door hung open, but Nate had a feeling the cabin was already empty.

Squinting against the pain in his skull, he yanked

out his phone and called the second person on his favorites list.

Blaine answered after two rings. "Did you honestly skip out on a raid today? I don't think I've ever been so proud."

"He's taken her," Nate puffed into the phone, ascending the stairs and carefully peering into the house.

Pulling out his 9mm Glock, he unlatched the safety.

"What are you talking about?" Blaine asked.

"That asshole Sally was dating. He just shot me and took her."

"You've been…what!" Whatever Blaine was doing had been abandoned. Nate could sense he had his brother's full attention. "Where are you?"

"The Richmonds' lake house. I need you to put out an APB on a navy blue Mercedes-Benz sedan. No idea on the plate number, but it's definitely an Illinois tag. Are you writing this down?"

"Yeah, keep going. What happened?"

Pressing the phone between his ear and shoulder, Nate cocked his gun and worked his way through the house, relaying all the details in a soft voice. As he told his story, he checked each room, following protocol and sweeping the downstairs before moving up. He left the master bedroom until last, finding it abandoned. The only remnant of a weekend getaway was the bag at the end of the bed.

Nate ripped open the zipper and finished up his story. "So, she was about to take me back when that asshole pulled out his gun and shot me. I need you to head to the Richmonds' and find out everything you can about Oscar Plymouth," Nate spat his name like it tasted vile. "I want *every* detail. I've scanned the house and it's empty. The only thing he's left behind is Sally's bag." Nate pulled out Sally's pale blue shirt, the one with the Nike tick in the top left corner. It was one of her favorites.

He held it to his nose, which was a big mistake.

Raw fear clawed up his throat, threatening to take him out as the tidal wave of emotion rounded over him.

"We've got to find her." His voice shook and he had to clear his throat twice before he could speak clearly again. "I'll stop in town on my way back and question who I can. Someone might have seen them pass through. Then I'll come find you."

"Are you sure you should be driving?" Blaine sounded worried. "You might be concussed."

Nate scoffed. "I'll be fine."

He had to be.

Closing his eyes against the burn of tears, he licked the edge of his mouth. "As soon as that bulletin is out, get to the Richmonds' house. We obviously know nothing about this psycho and have no idea what he's capable of." He glanced at his watch and struggled to make the simple calculations. "I think she was taken about thirty minutes ago. Find me something I can use, brother."

He hung up and slipped his phone away before holstering his weapon.

He couldn't think about what Oscar might be doing to Sally. He couldn't let his mind go there. He had to be calm and unemotional.

For her.

He had to be the best damn detective he'd ever been.

For her.

35

Saturday, May 26th
2:25pm

SALLY WHIMPERED, then jerked awake, struggling to figure out where she was.

The space was dark, cramped and hard, a rough ply carpet irritating her bare legs. She swiveled her head to try and make out more but it hurt to move. Her head was being split open. It felt like someone had taken an axe blade to her temple. She went to investigate the wound but found her hands tied behind her. Duct tape held her lips together, and her feet were bound as well.

Erratic breaths spurted from her nose as her brain registered each part of her body that was fettered.

She'd been kidnapped.

Fear pinched her insides as she tried to pull the murky pieces together. Blurred memories assaulted her, trying to help her out, but doing no good. The fluid around her brain was acting like sludge, making everything slow and incoherent.

Terror punched at her chest, and she heaved.

Nate.

He'd been there.

He was telling her something, and she'd felt warm and happy and then…

Gunshot.

She gasped, the image of Nate's body flying backward appearing with cruel clarity. She could suddenly see every detail. The sharp sound of the bullet exploding out of the gun. The shock of knowing it was Oscar.

He killed Nate.

Nate.

Her Nate.

Sally's heart began to cry, the agony rising within her, breaking from her mouth and then being blocked by the duct tape. The pitiful sound was further muffled by the small box she was in.

She couldn't work out what it was, but her legs were bent and cramping. She tried to stretch them but hit a solid barrier. Her shoulder and hip ached, which told her she'd been lying this way for a while.

Wriggling on her side, she blinked at her tears and slowly took in her surroundings.

As her eyes adjusted to the darkness, she was finally able to work out that she was in the trunk of a car.

Probably Oscar's Mercedes.

Frickin' Oscar.

A dark hatred she'd never felt before welled inside of her. She wasn't one for rage or anger, but she felt it in her core now. Her body practically vibrated with it. Nate's body lying limp on the ground only added fuel to the emotion.

Oscar killed Nate. He tore out her heart and stomped all over it.

The anger rose like a volcano but didn't have the energy to erupt as a counter wave of terror blasted through her.

He killed Nate…and he probably had every intention of killing her too.

Panic sizzled down her spine, enhanced further by a voice approaching the car.

"Look, I screwed up, okay? And you gotta help me! I have a plan that should work, but I need you. … Yes, I know you warned me to leave, but do you have any idea how much time I've spent on this? I had them all in the palm of my hand, and then he stuck his nose in and ruined everything!"

Oscar. American Oscar.

Evil Oscar.

Sally clenched her jaw and strained to hear the rest of his phone conversation.

He huffed and cursed again. "It was impulse. I thought he might've worked it out! I had to eliminate him." More huffing and cursing. "Yeah, yeah, I get it! But we can still make this work. We'll hold her for ransom and get the money that way. I'll split it with you fifty-fifty. … Trust? You're gonna lay that on me now when you didn't tell me a damn thing before? … I took the fall for you, man. Four years in that hellhole. You owe me! You *owe* me!"

There was a long pause while Oscar puffed and listened to whatever the caller was saying.

"That's better. Now, we just need a base. … Shit, I don't know, I floored it! Give me a place to meet you. Somewhere not too far; I've got to get off the road and underground as soon as possible. Where are you? … Well, any ideas? … Where? … Are you sure it's safe? … Okay, fine. I'll see you in a few hours. You better show, or I will hunt you down and make you pay."

Oscar thumped the trunk, making Sally flinch.

She stayed motionless as she listened to his footsteps race around the car. A second later, the engine roared to life and they were screaming down some unknown road to a mystery destination.

Sally's heart beat so hard it actually hurt.

How was anyone going to find her?

Oscar had mentioned something about ransom, and she knew her father would pay for any of his children without hesitation, but would that guarantee her life? She was a witness to Oscar's deception. No matter how this played out, she couldn't see a happy ending on the horizon.

If Nate were still alive, he'd do everything in his power to reach her.

But he wasn't.

And she'd never felt so alone in her entire life.

36

Saturday, May 26th
10:25pm

NATE LEANED against the wall on the edge of the Richmonds' living room.

He felt sick. Exhaustion and hunger were tugging at him, but there was no way in hell he could rest.

Sally had been taken.

The vibration of anxiety and disbelief in the air was suffocating, but Nate couldn't make himself leave the room.

He'd spent the afternoon questioning people in the small town by the lake house. One old guy had seen Oscar's car drive through. He didn't know which way it had headed after passing by, but he was pretty certain there was no woman with him. It had taken every ounce of self-control Nate possessed not to lose it on the spot.

If Sally hadn't been seen in the car, it meant a few things—either she was lying down in the back seat, tied up in the trunk, or abandoned somewhere, most likely the surrounding forest.

All three options would've been against her will, which meant Oscar had physically forced her into one of those scenarios. It meant he'd hurt her, and Nate wanted to kill him.

He'd driven back to the lake house and searched the area until darkness got the better of him. He was satisfied that Sally hadn't been left somewhere around the house, and then he'd gotten a call from Blaine, letting him know that the Richmonds had received a phone call.

The phone call.

Nate had actually cried with relief as Blaine relayed the details—Sally was alive and the kidnapper was demanding one million dollars for her return.

He'd balked at the number, but then Blaine had only enraged him more when he quietly mentioned, "The family thinks Oscar's being held hostage too."

"What?" Nate snapped.

"The kidnapper put him on the line. He was crying and wailing, begging them to pay the money."

"But…*he's* the kidnapper!"

Blaine had sighed. "The Richmonds don't think so."

Oscar the Freaking Fake had really twisted the knife blade with that one. Nate had charged to the Richmonds' house and, within minutes of walking in, managed to start a full-blown shouting match with Michael and Yvonne. They wouldn't believe Nate's story, even after he showed them the bullet embedded in his Kevlar.

"Oscar would never do a thing like that!" Michael bellowed. "It must've been someone else who shot you, from the roof or something, and they've stolen Sally and him away." His voice was raw and raspy. "I trust that man."

"Well, you shouldn't. He shot me in the chest and stole your daughter!" Nate raged.

"Why? Why would he do a thing like that? He loves her."

"He's a fake, Michael! Are you blind? He's been playing you all. None of us saw it coming." A lump formed in Nate's throat, guilt swamping him. He'd let her go. He'd let Sally kick him out of her life. He hadn't even put up a fight, and she'd fallen straight into the arms of a vulture.

Sweet, trusting Sally. She saw the best in everybody.

Nate wanted to double over and unleash a gut-wrenching moan, but he held himself together, eyeing Michael's pointer finger as it stabbed through the air at him.

"Oscar's just as much a victim here as she is. He has no family. No one else to look after him. We'll pay the money and get them both back. And this will all be over."

"You're delusional," Nate spat. "He's been lying to you this whole time. Why won't you believe me?"

"Why should I believe you!" he thundered. "You broke my daughter's heart! You're the criminal here!"

Nate stumbled back like he'd been slapped in the face. Breaths punched out of him as he fought to rein in his anger. Blaine snatched his arm when his fingers started to curl into fists, and Kellan stepped between them.

"This isn't helping anyone." Kellan doused the fight with his cool, calm voice. "We need to deal with the information we have and focus on getting Sally back."

Blaine led Nate to the edge of the room.

"You need food," Blaine murmured. "And how's your head?"

Nate gave it an absent-minded rub. "It's a little achy, but nothing I can't handle."

"I'm heading out to get you coffee. I'll be back as soon as I can, okay?"

Nate nodded while Blaine turned and asked if

anyone else needed anything. No one responded, so he slipped quietly out of the room. Kellan shifted into Blaine's spot and gave Nate the silent support he needed.

"You believe me, right?" Nate whispered.

"Hell yeah, I do." Kellan gave him a sideways glance. "I've got Jess and Higgs doing background work for me at the station. I found a picture of Oscar on the Richmond Construction website, and they're running it through every facial recognition database they can get their hands on. That's going to take some time, though."

Nate gritted his teeth, hating *time* with a passion. He needed results *now*.

Kellan's smile was pained. "I've been trying to get more out of Michael, but he's unapproachable right now. He's convinced his star employee is a victim here."

Nate's nostrils flared as he glared across the room at Sally's father.

"Give him a little leeway. His daughter's missing and he's only just holding it together," Kellan murmured. "Realistically, it doesn't matter if Oscar's yanking their chain. *We're* the ones who need to know the truth. It would help if they weren't delusional, but we can work around it. All that matters is getting Sally back."

Bile surged up Nate's throat. He closed his eyes and rubbed the sharp ache between his eyebrows.

Kellan squeezed his shoulder. "We'll get her back, Nate."

"In one piece?" he croaked.

Kellan blinked and looked away from him, his voice husky. "One way or another you'll be getting her back. Just focus on that."

People being taken was a touchy subject for Kellan. His daughter had disappeared years ago. There'd never been a ransom call or even a chance of her return. She'd disappeared without a trace, and it had haunted Kellan ever since.

Nate couldn't think of anything to say to comfort him. How could he?

He had a chance of restoring his heart. Kellan's had been ripped to shreds.

Leaning his head back against the wall, Nate stared up at the ceiling and kept playing the waiting game.

Another call would be coming soon. He wanted to be here for it. After that, he'd take off and get back to the station to help Higgs and Jessica.

The kidnapper had said he'd phone back with instructions for the drop. Michael had demanded proof of Sally's well-being; a muffled cry in the background of the first call was insufficient. He wanted to talk to her, hear her voice.

Kellan coached them through what they should say when the guy called back.

Nate clenched his jaw while he listened, internally cursing Oscar and imagining what he'd do to him when he got his hands on the guy.

Minutes ticked by with aching slowness. The silence in the room was heavy and depressing. Annabelle sat in the corner of the couch, sniffling quietly while shredding a tissue. Xavier's arm was around her. He was staring straight ahead, his expression switching between black rage and lost despair. Nate knew exactly how he felt.

Yvonne paced like a caged lioness, her long finger tapping against her elbow. It was a rhythmic movement that soon became an irritant.

Nate wasn't sure how much longer he could stand around not doing something.

And then Michael's phone dinged with a message.

Everyone jerked to attention, gaping at him as he read the screen.

"I have to check my email."

"Can you do that on your laptop, please?" Kellan said. "It's a bigger screen, and it'll be easier for us all to read the message that way.

Michael robotically put down the phone and moved to his computer.

Kellan snatched the phone off the table and read

the message, then moved behind the couch to gaze down at Michael's laptop.

Nate joined him, his stomach pooling with dread when Michael clicked on a link that went straight to a live video feed.

37

Saturday, May 26th
10:40pm

THE VIDEO CAMERA panned around Sally. She was wedged into a corner, her shoulders jammed between a damp, rotting wall and a rusted filing cabinet. Her ankles were still bound, but they'd untied her hands and re-secured them in front of her body.

Oscar pressed against her, putting on a show while a masked man shot the footage. Just before turning on the camera, he reminded Oscar that it'd be a live feed so he had to stay in character until he stopped recording.

He then attached the camera to the tripod, rotating and zooming in from there.

"Please," Oscar rasped at the camera, "you have to help us. They…they want a million in cash delivered to…" he wailed, feigning terror, "delivered…to…th—there'll be a car…a white van waiting by the tracks at Massey Road."

Sally knew the spot. It was an abandoned mill about twenty minutes south of Aspen Falls. Suspicious people thought it was haunted. Teenagers often dared each other to run the gauntlet through the darkened building.

"Eleven thirty tomorrow night. No police. Just you, Michael. You have to come alone with the money and they'll tell you where to get us. Please. Please do this, or they'll…" Oscar slowly turned to look at her.

With her mouth gagged, all she could manage was a molten glare, but it didn't have time to properly form before the cameraman roughly grabbed her bound wrists.

Fear punched through her as she instinctively curled her fingers into a fist. He painfully fought her, and she screamed as he straightened the pointer finger of her right hand and held a knife blade against the skin.

Tears blurred her vision as she struggled, and she started begging behind the gag. He wrenched her tethered arms, spinning his body so he could trap her wrists between his leg and the filing cabinet.

"No, stop, please!" Oscar wailed.

Sally could've killed him.

The knife blade caressed her skin, threatening pain and mutilation. Terror made her scream. Pain radiated down her arms as they were squeezed between the sharp edge of the cabinet and the man's muscly thigh.

"You have twenty-four hours or they're going to start sending her back piece by piece. Please, Michael! You have to save her!" Oscar's voice pitched.

The cameraman suddenly released Sally and spun to punch Oscar solidly in the face. He fell back dramatically while Sally cradled her arms to her chest and shook with intense fear. She'd never been so afraid in her life, and almost felt ashamed for falling to pieces instead of standing up to fight.

Nate would've fought.

Sally whimpered as she pictured his body limp in the dirt—dead, lifeless. Her soul mourned his loss, a deep pit of emptiness forming in her stomach as the cameraman clicked off the video recorder.

"That was good." Oscar stood, slapping the cameraman on the shoulder. "But you didn't have to punch me so hard." His cute British accent had evaporated again, replaced with an American twang that had never sounded so nasty and repulsive.

She still didn't know who the other man was.

Oscar had driven for what felt like forever before reaching an abandoned house in the middle of a forest. Sally had no idea where they were, or if they were even still in Minnesota. Oscar had roughly yanked her out of the car and thrown her over his shoulder. Shouldering his way into the house, he'd thumped across the creaking floorboards and dumped her in the corner of a cold, damp room.

It was a dark, dingy, soulless place that gave Sally the creeps.

"Stay!" Oscar had pointed at her like she was some naughty dog before hustling out of the room and slamming the door behind him.

Sally had been too scared to do anything but obey. Curling her legs to her chest, she'd rested her head against the peeling wallpaper and focused on breathing.

A while later, the sound of another car pulling up to the house had made Sally's head pop up. Oscar's accomplice must've arrived. She'd strained to hear conversation and figure out who he might be.

"I told you this was a mistake." The man's voice was slightly deeper than Oscar's, but had a softer tone. "If I'd known you were going there, I would've warned you against it."

"Yeah, well, it's not like we stay in touch, is it?"

That was Oscar. His tone was brittle and hard, shutting the other man up quickly. "Okay, so here's my plan. I'll act like I've been taken too. The only person who knows I'm not is dead, so everyone else should believe that I'm a victim. It'll take the heat off them looking into me and my past. We'll put on a show, demand the money, which Michael will definitely pay. He's a real family man and will do anything for his kids."

The man scoffed. "You sure know how to pick 'em."

"Hey, it wasn't my original plan. After Shelly got killed, I took the money and had to go way underground until it blew over."

"What'd you tell her family?"

"I was the grieving widow who needed to leave the country and find myself while traveling the world."

There was a long pause and then a soft question. "Did you arrange the accident?"

"What do you take me for?" Oscar snapped.

"Did you do it?"

Oscar huffed. "I married her for her money. My original plan was to set her up to cheat on me and then secure the money through the divorce, but then the accident happened and it worked out much better. I didn't kill my wife, if that's what you're asking."

"So what was the plan with this one?"

"Originally I just wanted to get in Richmond's good books. I took a legit job to establish my new persona and it was an easy fit. Michael noticed me, liked me, and I figured I could work my way up and start embezzling the company. I knew it would take time, but I was willing to put in the hours. I'd finally gotten that project management job and was set to start working the numbers, but then Sally became free and it was too good an opportunity to miss. Marrying her would've been like a freaking insurance policy. I would've gotten the money either way."

The other guy snickered. "You've got it all figured out, don't you, man?"

"Yeah, well I thought I did, until that asshole detective started asking questions. How could you not tell me?"

"You were in jail. You told me to stay away. So I did. I got as far out of Arizona as I could."

"You could've told me when I got out."

"I couldn't talk about it," the man gritted out. "Besides, we've barely seen each other since you were sent away. I didn't even know you were working this long-time gig until you called me a few days ago! Shit, man, I was doing okay, but you just had to drag me into your mess."

"Oh, don't you frickin' dare." Something slammed

as Oscar shouted. Sally flinched but kept listening. "I could've taken you down with me, but I let you run when those cops showed up. I didn't say a word. Twenty years old, man. And they treated me like a hardened criminal while you disappeared and got on with your life. So don't you dare stand there and try to make me feel bad."

"Okay, fine. Whatever. Can we just get on with this, please? Where is she?"

"In the back room, but we don't need her for this first call. Just do what I tell you, and we'll soon have our money and be running free."

Sally had stayed in the corner of the damp room, listening to them setting up the first call. She'd heard Oscar's voice switch accents and fought bile as he put on a show for her family, even throwing in a muffled feminine scream when he pretended to be her.

After the call, the door had suddenly burst open, scaring her senseless. Oscar approached her with languid steps that made her skin crawl. The arrogant smirk on his face was punchable, but fear had locked her muscles, making it hard to do anything but sit on the floor and fight for air.

He'd crouched down in front of her and wiggled his eyebrows like he'd just won a gold medal and couldn't help gloating at his brilliance. She'd glared back at him. "Oh, don't worry, honey. We'll get you home soon enough and you can forget this whole thing happened. As long as the family comes through with the goods, this will all just be a bad dream."

He'd winked and walked out of the room, calling to his accomplice. "Let's give them some time to sweat it out and then make the next one a video." His laughter became muffled behind the closed door. "Let's really scare the shit out of them."

They'd done a good job with that. Sally was still quivering when the cameraman crouched down in front of her and forced her head up. "Do you want a drink?"

She frowned.

"Of course you do." His breathy laughter was almost apologetic.

Gently peeling back the tape, he let her open her mouth a couple of times before feeding a straw between her lips. She took a small drink of water and gazed at him while he reattached the tape. Her tender lips protested, but she was too scared to put up a fight.

"It's okay. I wasn't really going to chop your finger off. I mean, I don't want to have to. You think your parents will be good for it?"

"Would you stop talking to her and double-check

that no one's found our feed or anything?" Oscar walked back into the room.

The masked man studied her for a long beat, his brown gaze almost dreamy as he ran his finger gently down her face. "She had golden hair just like yours," he whispered.

"Hey!" Oscar shouted. "Get on with it!"

With an irritated huff, the man tore off his mask and looked over his shoulder. "The feed's untraceable, I already told you that. They won't be able to find us."

Turning back, he gave Sally a soft smile before standing tall.

If she hadn't had tape across her mouth, her lips would've parted in surprise. The masked man looked just like Oscar.

Same brown eyes, dark eyebrows and chiseled features.

Brothers, possibly even twins.

Was he a con artist like Oscar? Did he marry for money only to steal it away?

Sally should've been grateful things hadn't gone so far with Oscar…or whatever the hell his name was.

His smooth charm hadn't worked so easily on her. Thanks to Nate.

Sally closed her eyes and rested her head against the cabinet.

Nate. His big apology had inadvertently saved her life.

If only he was still breathing. If he had been, Sally knew without a shadow of a doubt that he'd be doing everything in his power to find her before her parents had to give one dime to these bastards.

38

Saturday, May 26th
10:50pm

NATE'S HEART disintegrated as he listened to Sally's terrified screams. He could feel the ashy flakes falling through him, sizzling in his stomach acid and driving him to kill, to hurt, to do whatever was needed to bring her home.

When that guy yanked her hand and slid the blade across her finger, he'd wanted to punch Michael's computer screen.

"Oh God, Michael." Yvonne wept against her husband.

Sally's muffled begging drove a stake through Nate's stomach. Oscar was putting on a damn good show, which only fueled Nate's rage. When the kidnapper—accomplice!—punched him, Yvonne wailed again, but Nate just felt a sick sense of satisfaction. He hoped it frickin' hurt.

Sally shook in the corner, her arms curled against her chest, and Nate thought he might split in half. Desperation raked his insides raw. He had to get to her. To save her.

The screen went blank and Michael went into immediate action. "I'll call Jerry and explain the situation. He'll be able to help us."

"It's eleven o'clock at night, Michael. The bank can't help us right now." Yvonne's voice was deep and quaking, her tear-streaked face capturing their shared anxiety perfectly.

"I have Jerry's personal number. We can get the cash. It'll be okay." He rubbed his wife's shoulder and moved around the couch.

"Don't waste your time," Nate muttered. "We're not giving them that money."

"Excuse me?" Michael's eyebrows rose high, the fire in his eyes warning Nate not to mess with him.

Nate pointed at the computer, refusing to back down. "Those delivery instructions are bullshit. Leaving the money and they'll tell us where she is? No way! They'll take that money and run. And all we'll find is a dead body." Annabelle gasped and started crying. Nate refused to be affected by her tears. He had a job to do, the most important job he'd ever had. "The only way we're getting Sally back is if we find Oscar first. Now, you need to tell me everything you can about this guy."

"Are you insane?" Michael shouted. "Did you not see that footage? He's a victim too! We have no idea who that masked man is, and I won't risk my daughter's life just so you can play detective for a day. I don't give a shit about your career and trying to be the best."

"What?" Nate stepped forward, anger firing inside of him like hot lava. "You think I'm saying this for me? All that matters right now is Sally."

"All that's ever mattered is your job," Michael seethed. "And I won't let you use my daughter to get another credit to your name. We don't care that you're the best at what you do! All we ever wanted was for you to love her and look after her the way she deserved!"

The words were bullet wounds entering Nate's soul, sharp and hard. So that's what they thought of him. It was a defeating blow, but he couldn't let it beat him.

Sally.

He had to think of Sally.

Clenching his jaw, Nate gritted out, "Believe whatever the hell you want, Michael, but I am telling you that if you want to see her alive again, you need to let me do my job. I know you think I'm a waste of space in this family, but Oscar is a lying shit. He's played you all, and he is not going to let Sally live through this. He wants that money and that's it. He's not going to keep her alive as a witness against him. He thinks I'm dead, so she's his last loose end."

Michael was shaking his head, his nostrils flaring as Nate tried to get through to him. But the man was too blinded by emotion to think logically.

"Screw you, Michael! I know what I'm talking about!" Nate swept his arm through the air, clipping the vase on the table and not even caring as it hurtled through the air and smashed to the floor.

Yvonne screamed and covered her mouth with trembling fingers.

Nate ignored her, pointing a finger at Michael and shouting, "I love your daughter more than you will ever understand! And I want her back. Help me! Help me get her back!"

Yvonne's sobs punctured the air. They were in time with Annabelle's, who was now weeping against her brother.

"Get out of my house." Michael pointed to the door. "You are not welcome here. I can get her back without you."

Nate lunged forward, ready to grab Michael's shirt and shake some sense into him, but Kellan blocked his way.

He glared down at his boss and was quickly

calmed by the look on Kellan's face. "Get back to the station. We need to find her before the drop, and you've only got twenty-four hours. Don't waste it here."

Nate forced air through his nose and took a stiff step away from Sally's father.

"Go." Kellan pointed at the door. "Go work some magic. I'll see what I can do here."

Nate clenched his jaw. He gave a curt nod to the only man in the room who believed him before turning on his heel and sprinting for the door.

He hoped to God that Kellan could pry something out of the delusional Richmond family, because finding a con artist was damn hard work and they were running out of time.

39

Sunday, May 27th
5:55am

SALLY HAD no idea what time it was. She hadn't slept since waking up in the trunk, and even though her body begged for oblivion, she couldn't get there. Her mind was too wired, the fear too raw to let any muscles relax.

They were going to kill her.

She'd listened to enough of Nate's closed cases to understand the criminal mind.

If her father brought that money the way they wanted, they had no incentive to keep her alive. She was a liability. A risk.

Closing her eyes, her mind drifted to Nate. She couldn't help thinking about the afterlife and what that really meant. Would she find him there? Could they still be together even after death?

In a weird way, the idea was a comfort.

But then she thought of her family.

They'd be devastated by her murder. She could picture each family member, imagining how they'd cope with it. It was horrible and she didn't want them to suffer that way. She had to survive. Somehow, she had to make it.

"This is bullshit! I don't like it!"

Sally tensed as the shouting voices rose in the adjacent room.

"I don't give a shit what you like. We're in it now and we'll soon be driving away with a million dollars, so get the hell over yourself."

"We've never killed anyone before!"

"We easily could have. Where the hell is your spine? This, plus the money I already have, will set us up for years! We can disappear to wherever the hell we want! But not if we're left with a witness."

"I'm not comfortable with it. She's done nothing to hurt us."

"You are pathetic!" Oscar roared.

Sally could tell it was him. Although the voices were similar, she'd managed to pick them apart. Oscar was definitely the harsher of the two. He'd shed his British airs the second he shot Nate and since then, he'd been nothing but a hard ass. The other one seemed to at least have a soul.

She strained to hear the rest of the argument.

"What? What did you just say? She looks like her?" Oscar again, his voice sparked with disbelief. "How many years ago was that now? You lovesick fool. Get over it!"

"You are such a heartless prick!"

"You don't like it? Walk away. I'll take the money for myself, and you can get busted by the cops."

"Hey! I showed up because you needed me to! You're just gonna turn around and abandon me?"

"You abandoned me."

"You told me to! You think I haven't been haunted by the fact that you took the fall?

Sally held her breath as she waited for Oscar's reply. She wondered who she looked like. Oscar's brother must've loved someone in the past. Oscar, on the other hand, seemed to be fueled by a bitter rage that stopped him from feeling anything more than sick contempt and arrogant pride.

"Don't look at me like that," Oscar snapped. "I'll kill her. Okay? You don't even have to watch."

"When?" The other guy sounded nervous.

"As soon as you get the money, give me a call. I'll do it and dump her body in the woods. Then we'll meet up where you suggested and take off from there."

They'd stopped shouting at each other, but their voices grew louder as they left the room and stopped outside her door.

"I still don't like this," Oscar's brother said.

"Look, I know it's not perfect, but it was the best plan I had at the time and we have to go with it now. Harden up already. She's just a woman." The word was spat with pure contempt. "Think about the money."

The door clicked open and Oscar walked into the room.

Sally tensed, squishing herself against the wall until she realized that it wasn't Oscar. It was his double.

He crouched down in front of her with a soft smile. "Thought you might want another drink."

Gently peeling back the tape, he lifted the straw to her lips and let her have a few sips. She took advantage and sucked down as much as she could. It could mean she'd have to pee, which was a pretty disgusting thought, but dehydration would only make things worse. She needed to stay alert if she wanted any chance at all.

When he pulled the straw away, she licked her lips and decided to play on her strengths.

"Thank you." She smiled at him.

He paused, guilt flashing over his expression as he placed the water bottle down beside her.

Pressing his lips together, he reached for the duct tape.

"Actually, do you mind not…?" She winced. "My lips are really hurting from the tape. I promise I won't scream."

He looked uncertain and glanced over his shoulder.

"Please," Sally whispered. "Please, help me."

His head whipped back to look at her and she stared him in the eye, silently begging for a little humanity.

"I can't stop this now, but…" He yanked the rest of the tape off her face and scrunched it up in his hand. "It won't matter if you scream. No one lives around here. August just didn't want you saying anything on the video."

Sally nodded, tucking the name away for later.

So Oscar was August.

She wondered what this man's name was, but didn't get a chance to ask, because Oscar…August… appeared in the doorway.

"She's beautiful, I'll give you that much." He leaned against the doorframe, his arms crossed as he stared at her with those dark, heartless eyes. "Have her if you want to. We've got time."

Sally's insides pitched, revulsion spreading through her system like a virus.

Thankfully the man beside her let out a grunt of

disgust and walked away from Sally, stopping to eyeball his brother at the door. "You're sick. You know that?"

August smirked at his brother. "You can't tell me you don't enjoy a little ass every now and then."

"Only if they're willing," the man gritted out.

August snickered. "They're good for one thing, and one thing only, brother." He turned his dark gaze back onto Sally and licked his lips like a hungry crocodile.

Sally's insides curdled. Backing further up against the wall, she looked at the floor and prayed he'd walk away. The thought of that bastard touching her was too much to bear. She'd rather be shot in the head than have to endure that degradation.

Closing her eyes against the burn of tears, she kept her head down and wished for Nate. It was illogical. He wasn't even a possibility anymore, but maybe he could help her from beyond. Her family and the AFPD would no doubt be working overtime to bring her home, but it was Nate's arms she wanted to fall into. It was Nate's determined face she wanted to see charging through the door. He was her true home. He always had been.

40

Sunday, May 27th
7:20am

BLAINE PLACED another coffee within Nate's reach and moved around to the other side of the desk. They'd pulled an all-nighter, sifting through meager information, trying to find something on Oscar Plymouth while they waited for the photo recognition to come through. Problem was, if he wasn't a past offender, he wouldn't pop up on any law enforcement radar, so they had to work other angles while they waited.

The board on the wall was covered with notes, small pieces they were trying to merge into a trail.

Nate had printed out an image of Oscar from the Richmond Construction website.

It was cheesy and irritating, a spot for Nate to seethe at when his emotions got the better of him.

The fight to stay calm was growing with intensity.

Jessica, Higgs and Cam had gone out door-knocking through the early hours of the morning, waking disgruntled citizens to find out anything they could. They'd questioned workers on the apartment project, phoned any business Oscar may have had contact with, but many of them were still closed and they couldn't get access to the personal numbers they needed. Unless the business had a mobile number on the website, they were screwed.

Nate had called Kellan hourly since arriving at the station, but Michael Richmond was still convinced that Oscar was innocent, and he was working to pull the ransom money together. He asked to speak to each family member individually, but Yvonne was too emotional to talk, and Michael refused to let his family be harassed.

Nate's frustration worked against him every time he got off the phone, and eventually Blaine told him to quit it already. "Stop trying to fight a losing battle and focus on what we've got."

A new day had dawned, but Nate couldn't see any light through the dark storm clouds enveloping him.

He gazed down at his watch, having to blink twice before registering the time.

Fourteen hours left.

"Shit," he murmured. "We're running out of time."

He thumped the desk and sat back, fisting his hair and wanting to unleash a scream.

Cam walked into the room, distracting him with a slap to the shoulder. "Drink your coffee."

He jerked forward in his chair. "Anything new?"

"Not about Sally. Sorry." She gave him a sad smile and perched her butt on the edge of her desk. "I just got off the phone with the owner of Highland Timber. He said Oscar was a nice, polite guy who he'd only ever spoken to on the phone. Pretty much the same thing every other Aspen Falls contact has said. Because Richmond vouched for him, no one thought to look any deeper."

Nate let out a disgusted sigh. "Michael Richmond is an idiot."

Cam tipped her head, then slapped him with the manila folder in her hand. "Is that really the way you should be talking about your future father-in-law?"

Nate's expression buckled, desperation surging through him.

"We're going to get her back, Nate," Cam reassured him. "And then you're going to marry her and have lots of babies with her and the Richmonds will eventually see the truth."

Nate forced a calming breath, clasping his hands

together and squeezing tight. "What's that folder in your hand?"

"Oh, the sketch artist met with Vern Schnyder yesterday. He couriered it over this morning." Cam flicked the file open and glanced at the picture. "I know you don't have time to look at it right now, so I'll just..." Her voice trailed off, her wide lips parting as she stared at the sketch, then jerked her head to look at the board.

"What?" Nate stopped reaching for his coffee.

"Holy shit," she murmured, slapping down the open file in front of him and pointing at the board. "Look familiar?"

Nate gaped at the pencil sketch, his mind reeling as he compared the two images—the one in the folder and the one on the board. The pencil sketch was definitely a younger version of Oscar, with longer hair and a slightly rounder face, but the similarities couldn't be denied.

"What did Schnyder say the boyfriend's name was again?" Cam asked.

Nate clicked his finger, forcing his fuzzy brain to remember. "Ja... Jay... Jamie!" He slapped the table, jerking out of his seat and snatching his jacket off the back of the chair.

"Where are you going?"

"To talk to Schnyder."

"All he remembers is the guy's name." Cam made

a face. "He had one interaction with him. He can't tell you anything you don't already know."

Nate raised his hands in frustration. "Then what the hell do you propose I do?"

"Talk to me." A voice at the door made Nate spin. His head jerked back in surprise as he stared at the guy standing in his office doorway. "Hey, asshole."

41

Sunday, May 27th
7:35am

"SORRY I'M late to the party." Xavier raked a hand through his tousled hair. Nate wasn't used to seeing the guy so unkempt and frazzled. "Getting away from two hysterical women and a delusional father was harder than I thought it would be."

"What can you tell us?" Nate kicked out a nearby chair and pointed to it.

Xavier took a seat. "Look, I don't know if I'll have anything enlightening to share. I just want to help. I can't stand the thought of that asshole hurting Sally. I believe you, 100 percent. Tell me what you need from me."

Nate's chest nearly caved with relief. A small part

of him wanted to wrap Xavier in a hug, but he quickly resisted the urge.

Slumping into the seat opposite him, he said, "Anything you can tell us. You worked with the guy. Did you notice any red flags at all?"

"I got a hit!" Jessica raced into the office, waving a sheet of paper. "August Cotton. Oscar is August Cotton from Fountain Hills, Arizona. He was convicted and sentenced to five years in prison for armed robbery."

"When?" Nate snatched the information sheet.

"Fourteen years ago." Jessica's face was alight with triumph. "He was twenty years old and got out early for good behavior at the age of twenty-four."

"Then what?"

Jessica deflated a little. "After his parole he left the state. Higgs is running a license search for us, and I've left a message with the Fountain Hills PD. The officer I spoke to thinks their captain might remember the guy. He's going to call us as soon as he gets in."

"Okay." Nate started pacing, energized by the information. "So he was in prison twelve years ago, which means that he couldn't have been in Aspen Falls trying to convince Mila to run away."

"Which means he has a brother who looks a lot like him," Cam stated.

"Is it safe enough to assume that his brother might be his accomplice on this one?"

"It's worth following." Cam nodded, then turned to Jessica. "Get back on the phone or internet, whatever you have to. We need anything you can find us on the Cotton family from Fountain Hills, Arizona."

"Got it." Jessica rushed out of the room, and Nate stopped pacing to stare down at August's rap sheet.

"This still doesn't tell us where they have her."

Xavier's face scrunched and he let out a frustrated sigh. "They wouldn't have made it to Arizona. They must be close by. Maybe this brother is…" Xavier clicked his finger and pointed at Nate. "The old lady. From the other day. Ms. Parker. She thought she recognized Oscar, remember?"

"Holy shit." Nate raked a hand through his hair. "I even went and questioned him about it, but he looked so damn innocent. Like he seriously knew nothing about it!"

"I don't think he did." Xavier stood with him. "I caught him that afternoon on the phone. He was shouting at someone, and it was so unlike him. He was saying something about honesty and that the person he was speaking to should've told him."

Nate's eyebrows dipped together. "What else did he say?"

"Not much." Xavier sighed. "He turned around

and saw me watching him. He ended the call pretty quick and then distracted me with work stuff."

"Okay." Nate swallowed. "Okay, so we need to talk to Ms. Parker again."

"Are you sure?" Blaine cringed. "Rita's not the most reliable source in town. I mean, she's sweet and everything, but...her stories can change."

"When I interviewed her last time, her story was exactly the same. I just didn't think to probe any deeper because I thought it was a dead lead." Throwing his jacket on, he spotted the bullet hole and felt his chest constrict. He shouldn't have been so careless. Every lead was important. Every clue. Every detail.

His voice shook as he glanced at Cam. "Vern Schnyder mentioned catching his daughter with Jamie in an old mill or something. Can you go see him, find out exactly which mill it was? Maybe that's where they met up in secret."

Cam frowned. "Sure thing, but I doubt they'd be stupid enough to take her there. They're probably not even in Aspen Falls."

Nate closed his eyes, feeling sick. "Just...can you do it, please?"

"Of course." Cam nodded. "I'll contact you as soon as I'm done."

He turned and pointed at Xavier. "Let's go."

"Me?"

"You were there when she recognized Oscar. Let's give her memory as many triggers as we can." Nate turned to Blaine, who was already looking her up on the computer.

"119 Hickory Crescent."

Cam threw him the keys before he had to ask for them. Grabbing the edge of Xavier's jacket, he hauled the guy out of his office and headed for the parking lot.

Time urged him into a run. Xavier kept pace and they were soon heading for Hickory Crescent, the hope of answers burning bright. Nate had everyone he trusted working on different angles. Surely one of them would yield something useful.

Ms. Parker answered the door after the second round of knocking. Nate felt close to blowing a gasket as he impatiently paced the porch.

"Here she comes." Xavier pointed at the door when a shadowy shape appeared behind the frosted glass.

The door cracked open and a moment later, Ms. Parker stood there smiling at them. Her smile was sweet and her eyes were a vibrant blue to match the color of her bathrobe.

"Hello." Her voice was high and a little shaky.

"Good morning, Ms. Parker. I'm Detective Nathan Hartford." He flashed his ID, figuring she might not remember him. "This is my…associate, Xavier Richmond."

"Oh, hello." She smiled at Xavier, her eyes narrowing as she obviously tried to work out where she knew him from.

Xavier glanced at Nate, his expression hopeful. "I saw you just the other day at Lulu's Coffee Shop. You were talking to a colleague of mine. An Englishman named Oscar. You thought you recognized him."

She frowned and shook her head. "No, I don't think so."

"He had a pale blue pickup truck."

"Oh." She grinned. "The young man. I will never forget him. He and his lady love. They ran away together."

Nate quelled his frustration at hearing the same story yet again. The fact that she repeated it word for word made him wonder if it was true, but he had to try. "Ms. Parker, would it be okay if we came in and asked you a few questions about what you saw?"

"Well, of course." She pulled the door open wider. "I may be losing my mind, but some things stick, and a love story like that will last me a lifetime. At least I hope it will." Her expression flicked with sadness as she shakily sat in her seat. Her toes turned in as she rested her hands in her lap, making her look like a little girl with an old wrinkled face. "He would wait outside my house. He didn't know I was watching. I didn't want to pry, but he intrigued me. He always looked so sad and restless, and then he'd check his watch and smile, excited, and race up the hill."

"Where did you used to live, Ms. Parker?" Nate started with the same question he did last time, hoping to trigger something new.

"Richard and I owned a small farm about ten minutes out of town. The road leading north. It borders Finch's Forest. Do you know it?"

Nate nodded and forced a smile.

She smiled back and dipped her head. "We lived there for many years. So happy together. So happy." This was where he'd lost her last time. She'd started rattling on about marriage and happiness and Richard. He'd managed to steer her back to Jamie one more time but as she'd tired, her chatter become harder to understand and she ended up talking in repetitive circles.

Nate had to control the interview more tightly this time around. "So, Ms. Parker," he cut her off. "The blue pickup truck. The man. He'd check his watch and run up the hill?"

"Oh, yes. I could see him quite clearly through my binoculars. He didn't know I was watching. He always looked so sad."

Nate gritted his teeth as the old lady repeated herself, going over the same details in exactly the same order.

His phone vibrated and he jerked to pull it out of his back pocket. "Excuse me for a moment." He raised his finger and read Cam's text.

Got directions to the old mill. Checking it out now.

Nate's heart hitched, his stomach clenching as he suddenly wished he were with her. What if Sally was there?

Keep me posted.

He sent back the quick response and resisted the urge to get up and leave. Cam was probably right. Oscar…August…wouldn't be stupid enough to keep Sally in Aspen Falls. His best bet was probably what Jessica could find out back at the station.

So why was he wasting his time with a lady who was losing her mind?

"Are you okay, Detective?" Ms. Parker leaned forward in her seat. "You look worried, dear."

Nate swallowed and gave her a closed-mouth smile, then got hit with inspiration. He wasn't sure if it would work, but desperation was leading him on this one.

Forcing his posture to relax, he rested his elbows on his knees and played to Ms. Parker's romantic tendencies. "The woman I love is missing."

"Oh, dear." Ms. Parker touched her chest.

"I need to find her. I'd do anything to find her and bring her home safely."

"Well, of course you would." The woman's eyes glistened and she started blinking. "That's true love. Putting your woman and family before anything else." She bobbed her head. "True love."

Her soft words hurt as regrets tried to seize him. It took him a moment to find his voice again. His eyes were burning as he croaked, "Like the true love this man had."

"Yes." Ms. Parker let out a dreamy giggle. "She was beautiful. Blonde hair and sparkling blue eyes. So pretty."

Nate's stomach pinched. Mila Schnyder had blonde hair and sparkling blue eyes. She was pretty. She was in love. She was the girl this nervous man ran up the hill to see. That man was Jamie, and he was linked to Oscar. And somehow that connection had to help. Somehow that had to lead to Sally—to *his* love with blonde hair and sparkling eyes.

Oh God, please help us find a link, Nate silently begged.

And the second the prayer left his mind, a thought hit him like a lightning bolt.

"Wait. How do you know she had blonde hair? I thought you only saw *him.*" Nate rushed out the words. "Did she come down the hill one day? Did you see them together?"

"Well..." The lady blushed and tipped her head. "I really shouldn't say."

"Please, Ms. Parker, it could be very important." Nate strained to keep his tone calm and in check.

"I was with Nelly, and I shouldn't pry, but he intrigued me."

"Who's Nelly?" Xavier frowned.

"My horse." She grinned. "So I decided to follow him one day. He trekked for about twenty minutes, up the hill to an old cabin that had been abandoned. I didn't even know it was there."

Nate licked his lips, hungry for more of the story. "Go on."

"Well, I left Nelly by the tree, worried she'd make too much noise. I crept very quietly up to the house, and that's when I heard them speaking. He was saying how much he loved her and nothing could keep them apart. She had a sweet voice. She loved him too, but was crying. When I got to the window, I heard him say they should run away together. She agreed and then…" Ms. Parker's cheeks flushed pink. "Well, they…"

Nate's eyebrows rose. "They…?"

"They made love." She giggled and leaned forward to whisper. "They didn't know I was watching."

Xavier cleared his throat and shared a quick look with Nate.

Pressing his lips together, Nate blinked a couple of times and then asked, "Ms. Parker, do you know which direction the cabin was from your farm? Do you think you could tell us exactly where it is?"

"Oh." She gave him a pained frown and scratched the side of her head. "Well, I… Richard and I owned a small farm near Finch's Forest. Do you know it?"

Nate held in his sigh and quietly asked, "Was the cabin north? South? East? West of your house?"

"The cabin up the hill?" She blinked. "I went there one day. I didn't even know it was there. I was with Nelly."

Xavier shuffled on the seat beside him, and Nate could feel his mounting frustration.

"Up the hill," he said softly. "From your house."

"Yes. They were going to run away together, and they did because he stopped coming back."

"So the cabin is quite isolated, then?"

"I didn't even know it was there. Very old and creaky. Hadn't been lived in for years. A good place for secret lovers to meet." She smiled at both of them and giggled again. "They didn't know I was watching."

Nate looked to Xavier, swallowing thickly before wrapping up the conversation.

At least he'd learned something new. There was an isolated cabin in Finch's Forest, up the hill from Ms. Parker's old farm. No doubt another dead end.

As they walked back to the car, Nate got another text.

The old mill is clear. Sorry.

Nate cursed and smashed his fist on the roof of the car.

"What do you want to do now?" Xavier asked.

Sharp breaths spurted from Nate's nose before he roughly grumbled, "Head back to the station. See what Jess has found for us."

"You don't think it's worth checking out that cabin?" Xavier asked.

Nate paused and looked across the roof of the car, skeptical. "You do?"

"Well, maybe. I mean, it's worth a shot, isn't it? If this Jamie guy thought it was completely hidden, then he might still think it is." Xavier ran a hand through his hair and huffed. "Look, I know it's a long shot, but she's my sister. I'll follow any lead I have to, no matter how small."

Nate studied his expression, understanding exactly how he felt. With a heavy sigh, he pulled out his phone and called Cam.

"Yeah, hi," he replied to her greeting. "We might have a lead. You got Ollie and Blaine with you?"

"They're in the cruiser behind me. Where are we going?"

"We're looking for a cabin in Finch's Forest. I need to check satellite images to try and find it, but it could be a go."

"We'll head toward Finch's Forest and wait for you there."

42

Sunday, May 27th
10:50am

SALLY ACHED from temple to toes. Her skin was raw where she'd been cuffed. Her limbs were screaming for movement and circulation. About an hour ago, they'd re-tied her wrists behind her back and shoved her back to the floor. It was much more uncomfortable and her arms and shoulders hurt.

She'd been in the room for hours and hadn't even come close to escaping. The windows were bolted shut and the only other exit was the door, which she'd never be able to sneak through with two hyper-alert guards standing nearby. They could hear her every time she moved and always rushed in to make sure she wasn't trying anything.

Jamie—the nicer brother had finally told her his name—had carried her to the toilet an hour ago. That was the excuse she'd used to explain why she was standing by the window. It had been nothing but humiliating, but Sally was grateful it'd been him and not August.

The way August kept walking past the door and stopping to check on her gave her the creeps. She couldn't decide if he was trying to psych her out or if he was intending to eventually pounce. Trying to stay strong against that kind of mental torture was hard work and Sally could feel herself breaking.

She had no idea what the time was, but the curtains across the windows let in a bright enough light to assume that it was early morning or later.

It was Sunday. And a pretty shitty way to spend one of her rare weekends off.

Her mind wandered back to Aspen Falls—her family, her friends…Rusty. Nate.

Her heart ached for each of them. If she'd known she wouldn't be seeing them again, she would've taken more care—hugged a little harder, chatted a little longer. Tried to make things work before walking away.

She should've talked to Nate before the big breakup. She could've told him how she was feeling. She should've stood up for him when her family went to town, criticizing his work ethic and inability to open up. She shouldn't have shared so much with them. Complained so hard.

She'd made so many mistakes, and now it was too late.

Her chin bunched with the onset of tears. Hope of escape was waning. Although Jamie was nice, her comments and sweet pleas had yet to sway him.

Footsteps approached and Sally stiffened.

August appeared in the doorway again.

He stepped into the room. "It's turning into a long day. All that's left to do is wait, wait, wait." His husky voice sent shivers down her arms, and not the good shivers but the kind of goose pimples that made her want to claw her skin and scream.

The door creaked as he gently pushed it shut with his foot.

Sally squirmed, shuffling back as far as she could. The damn wall stopped her, the peeling wallpaper tickling the inside of her arms.

The smile on August's lips was menacing. She knew it was him and not Jamie because of the dark hunger in his gaze.

Crouching down in front of her, he trailed his finger down her cheek and swiped the tear forming in the corner of her eye. "Don't cry now. It's okay. I'll make it quick and painless." Her chest shook and heaved as his finger glided down her neck and dipped into the gap between her breasts. "By tonight,

I'll be rich and you won't be alive to even remember this. It'll all be over. Quick." He snapped his fingers. "Painless."

Sally closed her eyes, releasing another tear. It ambled down her cheek, unaware of her inner turmoil.

"You know my one regret in this whole thing, though"—his finger trailed over the curve of her breast—"is that we never took it to that next level."

"Get your hands off me," Sally managed through gritted teeth. If her hands had been available, she'd be slapping and clawing at him with everything she could. But her only weapon was a seething glare.

He ignored her and kept outlining her shape. "You just wouldn't let go of him, would you? Your sappy heart just kept holding on. Even though he didn't want you."

"He wanted me."

August laughed. "You honestly believed those lies he fed you at the lake house? Yeah, he wanted you back, but he wasn't about to change." August's voice hardened, along with his grasp. Sally winced as he squeezed her breast like it was a stress ball. "People don't change, and why should he have to? He's a man, and you're nothing more than a pitiful woman…only good for one thing."

He lunged at her mouth, his hot tongue smearing her lips as he tried to kiss her.

Sally clenched her jaw and squirmed away from him.

"Stop it!" she cried. Rough hands yanked her away from the wall, tugging at her clothing. "No!"

She wrestled as best she could, her tied hands and ankles making the fight an impossible one.

The door suddenly flew open.

"August!" His brother rushed toward them, grabbing the back of August's shirt and pulling him away. "Leave her alone!"

August fell back with a hard thud and glared at his brother. "Butt out."

Jamie planted his feet in front of Sally. "If I can't feed her a scrap of food, then you don't have the right to maul her. She doesn't deserve that shit. At least let her die with a little dignity."

"Always such a romantic!" August shot to his feet. "She's just a woman. A worthless piece of shit."

"She's not Mom! You don't have to hate on every woman out there just because she was a psycho bitch!" Jamie's voice shook. "They're not all worthless. Some of them are…perfect." Jamie dipped his head while August rolled his eyes and scoffed.

"Oh, for God's sake. You need to get over that chick!" August's eyes narrowed, his lips curving into a malicious smile. "What was her name again?"

"Mila," Jamie croaked.

"Mila." August mocked her name, making Jamie's

head jerk up. August sniggered, obviously taking great delight in torturing his brother. "Well, from what you've told me, if you hadn't shown up to take her away that night, she'd probably still be alive. You ever think about that?"

There was a sickening beat of silence, and then Jamie roared and lunged at his brother, clipping his chin while screaming expletives.

Sally inched away from the tussle, eyeing the open door behind them. Resting her elbow on the floor, she started an awkward sideways shuffle.

Hopefully the boys would fight long enough and hard enough that she could inch her way to freedom.

She felt like a snail, the door taking forever to get within reach. Her mind started playing tricks the nearer she got.

They're going to stop fighting soon and notice you.

Where the hell are you going to go once you get through the door?

Are you going to shuffle back to Aspen Falls? You don't even know where the hell you are!

Sally fought her doubts and kept moving until the sound of screeching brakes outside made her pause.

Jamie and August jerked away from each other.

"What was that?" Jamie's eyes rounded as he scrambled to the window and peeked outside. "Shit! It's the cops!"

August was already on his feet, snatching Sally and dragging her across the floor.

She opened her mouth to unleash a scream but was stopped by a knife blade pressing into her cheek. "I will slice you open right here."

Instinct made her clam up. She couldn't have released a squeak if she'd wanted to.

"Move." Jamie rushed toward them, snatching Sally's other arm and painfully dragging her to a dirty rug in the corner. "There's a cellar. We can get under the house." He kicked back the dusty rug to reveal a door in the floor. Throwing it open, August hauled her into the cramped space. Her cry of pain was muffled by his hand across her mouth.

Jamie struggled to pull the rug back into place, then closed the door above them and crouched down, helping August control her. She was wrestling as best she could.

The cops were here.

She couldn't let this opportunity pass her by.

"Stop moving." The knife was positioned against the pounding artery in her neck as August's panicked whisper punched into her ear. "You stay quiet and still."

43

Sunday, May 27th
11:10am

"You take the back," Nate mouthed while indicating with his fingers.

Blaine and Ollie nodded and headed around the back. Nate glanced over his shoulder and directed Cam with a flick of his head.

She took the other side of the house while he approached from the front. The old cabin oozed a creepy vibe that screamed anything but romance to him. It was a horrible place to meet up with a girl, and Nate would never entertain the thought of making love to Sally inside what he was sure was an insect-ridden cabin. The place reminded him of the hovel in Ash Lake that Vern Schnyder had sentenced himself to.

Nate wanted his weapon drawn and ready to go, but he couldn't be certain that Sally was even at the house. It was a miracle they'd even found it in the first place; it was well hidden among the trees, and spotting the edge of it in satellite images had been a lucky break.

He assessed the old, decrepit structure, taking mental notes as he walked. It looked and felt completely abandoned. Nate's hope was stretched so thin he wasn't sure he could cope if they came up empty-handed.

They had twelve hours left until the drop, and if this lead was a complete dead end, he'd be furious for wasting time on it. They didn't have the luxury of making mistakes. Sally could be dead in twelve hours if they didn't find her.

Nate snapped his eyes shut for a moment, reminding himself not to get too far ahead of himself.

One step at a time.

Jessica and Higgs were back at the station, still hunting down other leads. Even Lucas had shown up and was pitching in.

They'd find her.

They had to.

Nate clenched his jaw and rapped on the door. "Police! Is anyone home?"

He was met with silence.

Nate pounded a little harder and shouted once more, but the house gave back an empty reply. He glanced over his shoulder, desperation thrumming through him. Like hell he'd come this far only to walk away.

Gently extracting his gun, Nate checked the safety and then softly murmured, "If they're not going to answer, I should just let myself in."

Nate raised his leg and kicked the door. It took three attempts and his leg was frickin' sore by the time the front door swung open, but he didn't have time to think about that.

"Checking the house," he shouted to his team as he began a careful sweep.

The other officers swarmed in from the back, and the house was thoroughly checked.

"Clear!"

"Clear!"

"Clear!"

Each shout was a whiplash and Nate walked to the front door ten minutes later, despair heavy on his shoulders.

"I'm sorry, man." Blaine lightly patted his back. "We'll keep looking. We'll find her."

Nate thumped down the front steps, unable to

speak. As the three morose officers converged in front of the house, Nate readied himself for the next plan of attack.

And that's when he heard it.

A muffled screaming.

44

Sunday, May 27th
11:20am

SALLY LISTENED to the retreating feet, her heart screaming out a fervent 'NO' as they cleared each room and then walked away.

It couldn't happen like this.

She couldn't come this close only to fail.

The knife against her neck was a constant reminder of her pending death, but screw it! If she was dead anyway, she might as well take these assholes down with her.

Curling her bound hands into fists, she punched backward, catching August in the groin. It took him off guard, enough for his hand to slip from her mouth. She let out a piercing scream and kept going even as he regathered her and pressed the knife back against her neck.

"Shut up! Shut up!" he whisper-barked into her ear, but she wouldn't let up.

Squirming against his grasp, she ignored the point of the knife and kept screaming out behind his hand.

"Sally?" someone called.

She jerked still, her heart punching against her ribcage.

Had she just imagined that voice?

"Sally!"

August flinched, obviously as shocked as she was, and his grip around her mouth loosened for a moment.

"Nate," she whispered. "Nate! NATHAN!"

Her screaming jerked August out of his surprise, and she had to fight to free her face from his viselike grip.

"NATE!" she cried, but the sound was muffled.

August tried to shut her up, wrestling to control her thrashing head. As his fingers went to squeeze her mouth shut, she clamped down her teeth, unleashing a loud howl from August.

"Sally!" Nate called. "Where are you?"

Jamie started to panic. "Shit! Shit. We're done!"

"Shut up!" August raged, fisting Sally's hair as she tried to scramble away from him.

She cried out as she was jerked back against him. The knife sliced her shoulder when he tried to rein her in, but she kept fighting. "Down here!" she screamed.

Nate.

Nate was there. He was there. And she had to get to him.

Feet thundered into the room above.

Yes! Find me! Please!

"Where?"

"The rug! Check under the rug!" a female shouted.

Cam! Sally strained against her captor while Jamie rattled off more panicked curses.

The door above Sally flew open.

August wrenched her back against him, digging the knife beneath her chin and shouting, "Don't move or I'll kill her!"

Nate fell into the space, his gun aimed and ready.

He didn't hesitate.

Two shots and August's hold on Sally went slack. He dropped to the floor, blood soaking into the packed dirt around his head, and Sally's legs buckled.

Nate rushed forward, catching her and dropping to his knees so he could cradle her against him. "Are you okay? Are you alright?"

All she could do was whimper and bury her cheek into the crook of his neck. "You're alive."

Blaine and Cam dropped into the room behind Nate, ordering Jamie to his knees and then onto his stomach.

Nate grabbed the knife off the floor and quickly freed Sally of the ties. Her arms complained at being set free. It hurt to move them, but she ignored the agony, straddling Nate's thighs and throwing her arms around his neck.

"You're alive," she kept whispering. "Thank God you're alive."

He held her close, cradling the back of her head with shaking arms and not saying a word. She pressed her cheek against his and felt their tears blending together.

"Jamie Cotton, you're under arrest." Blaine softly read Jamie his rights while Cam cuffed him.

Nate and Sally stayed where they were, locked together in an embrace that couldn't be broken.

As Jamie was hauled back into the house, Sally leaned away from Nate, caressing his cheek and smiling down at him. His eyes glistened as he drank her in.

"I thought I'd lost you," she whispered. "I've never been so afraid in my life."

His face crumpled and he held her face, gently kissing her—confirmation that he was real.

He swiped his thumb under her lashes, clearing

the tears and melting her with those blue eyes of his. "I love you," he finally croaked. "I love you."

She let out a trembling laugh and lurched toward him. Their lips met in a deep, passionate embrace. They clung to one another, kissing like it was their last goodbye.

Nate's mouth was a warm comfort, his tongue a hot reminder that he was alive and real, and that Sally never wanted to let him slip through her fingers again.

45

Sunday, May 27th
11:35am

SALLY DRENCHED NATE WITH KISSES, her emotions shining through as she pecked his cheeks, brushed his tongue, and then clung to him with shaking limbs. Nate felt like his body hadn't stopped trembling since he caught her in his arms.

Seeing August holding a knife to her throat was a horrifying image he'd struggle to forget. He had no regrets about the way he'd handled the situation.

All that mattered was Sally's safety.

Her life.

Nate wasn't sure how he was supposed to let her go. Now that he had her again, he was pretty sure he'd never be able to stop touching her and reminding himself of what could have been. If he hadn't heard her scream. If they'd followed a different lead. If Xavier hadn't stepped up.

He closed his eyes, the what-if questions making him ill.

Focus on the now, man, he thought. *She's right here. Now. In your arms.*

The comfort of that reality helped his emotions to settle, and logical thought began to kick in.

Sally's shoulder was bleeding. Not much, but it still needed attending, plus he needed to move her away from the dead body behind them.

"Coroner's on his way." Cam's soft murmur urged him up.

Slowly rising to his feet, he brought Sally with him, hefting her into his arms and helping her back through the door.

He steadied her as they made their way down the hill, and didn't let go until they reached his car and a pacing Xavier. The second he saw his sister, Xavier's eyes welled with tears. Stumbling forward, he wrapped his arms gently around her and hung on like he never wanted to let go.

Nate stood nearby as they cried against each other, wanting to give them a minute, but also anxious to get Sally checked out. Finally Xavier let her go and quickly assessed her.

"You okay?" His voice hitched.

She glanced at Nate, her eyes sparkling. "Yeah, I'm more than okay."

Nate mirrored her smile as he gently tucked her into the back of his car. Peeling back the edge of her bloodied shirt, he inspected the wound on her shoulder.

"It's fine. It's just a scratch," she murmured. Nate wanted to insist they go to the hospital and get it checked out, but then her eyes glassed over like she could read his mind. "Please take me home. I need to go home."

"Xavier will call to let them know you're safe," he assured her.

"I know, but they need to see me. I need to…" Her voice petered out as tears got the better of her.

"Hey, it's okay." He kissed her forehead. "I'll get you home."

How could he refuse her?

Digging out the first aid kit from the trunk of the car, he cleaned the wound, satisfied that it wasn't as bad as he initially thought. By the time he was done, Xavier was waiting by the driver's door. "You think I'd be allowed to drive this bad boy?"

Nate grinned and thought, "Probably not, but I'm not gonna stop you."

Without a word, he walked around to the other side of the car and slipped in next to Sally. Her tired smile was beautiful. He matched it, resting his head against the seat and gazing at her. Xavier drove them back to Aspen Falls while Cam waited at the house. Blaine and Ollie already had Jamie on the way to the station. He'd give his statement and hopefully not bother hiding the truth.

Part of Nate wanted to be the one to question him.

But a bigger part wanted to stay with Sally.

He threaded his fingers between hers and brushed his thumb across the back of her hand.

They didn't say much on the journey home. He was too drained to ask Sally about her experience, and he didn't want her to relive it just yet. Sally would need to give her statement, but that could wait until the morning.

She needed to be cleaned up and tucked into a soft bed.

He wished it was theirs. He'd like nothing better than to lock them inside their bungalow and sleep, with her tucked up against him.

But she had a family to see.

They'd be desperate to hold her and make sure she was okay.

Xavier's call of reassurance wouldn't be enough.

As they neared the Richmonds' home, Nate instinctively stiffened, preparing himself for the icy tension and cold rebuttal. He forced Sally and her needs to the front of his mind. She had to come first, and if she needed her family, then that's where he'd take her. The raw emotion from the night before would no doubt still linger, but there was nothing he could do about it.

The car's wheels hadn't even stopped spinning when the front door burst open and Yvonne and Annabelle came running out of the house. They opened Sally's door and helped her out, enveloping her and weeping together.

Nate shared a look with Xavier, who gave him a thumbs-up. "You can do it, man. You brought her home. That's gonna have to count for something."

Raising his eyebrows, he forced a grin and slipped out of the car.

Michael Richmond brushed past him, rushing around the car to Sally. Xavier slipped out of the vehicle, flashing a sheepish look at Kellan before handing over the keys. "Drives like a dream." He patted the guy on the arm and pasted on a cheesy smile.

Kellan's sharp glare quickly dissolved and he gave in with a small half-smile. "I'll pretend I didn't see."

"Thanks." Xavier stepped away from him and glanced at Nate. They shared a quiet look of gratitude. Xavier had really stepped up, and if it hadn't been for his belief in Nate, they never would've found his sister. The nightmare of that reality rushed through Nate and he leaned against the car, suddenly weak.

A dull ache still pounded in the back of his head. There was no doubt he had a mild concussion, and once Sally was inside, Kellan would insist he get checked out at the hospital. But he wasn't going anywhere until he'd said goodbye to his woman and promised her that he'd be back.

"Come on, let's get you inside." With her arm wrapped securely around her daughter, Yvonne led Sally away from Nate.

His heart was aching as he watched her walk right past him.

"Wait." She stopped and turned to find him. "Are you coming?"

"Only if you want me to."

She hesitated and pointed at Kellan. "You don't have to…work?"

Nate winced, yet again reminded of how blind he'd been. Looking in her eyes, he shook his head and said with certainty, "Work can wait."

Her smile of relief was telling and heartbreaking at the same time. Shifting out of her mother's hold, she shuffled toward Nate and tucked herself against him. "I want you to come in."

"Sally…" Michael stepped forward. "You need your rest."

Looking up at her father, she squeezed Nate

around the middle and said, "I need Nate. I love him. I knew that before Oscar…August…even took me. I've always known, Daddy. Nate's my heart, and you need to accept him, not just because he saved my life today but because he's my choice." Nate's heart swelled at the conviction in her voice. "If you can't accept that…if you guys can't welcome him in, then I'm asking Kellan to take us back to our place. I can catch up with you guys another time."

Yvonne paled and she grabbed Michael's arm. He stared at Nate, obviously wrestling with his daughter's stance.

"Of course he's welcome," Yvonne whispered. "He can stay for as long as he likes." She beckoned them both with a wave of her hand. "Come in, both of you."

Nate said a quick goodbye to Kellan over his shoulder.

His boss smiled and mouthed, "Good luck."

He raised his eyebrows and walked Sally inside. As soon as the door was shut and their shoes were lined up by the door, Annabelle whisked Sally away to clean up. Nate watched her until she reached the top of the stairs.

"Come take a seat, man," Xavier called him into the living room with a flick of his head. "I'll get you a drink. What do you want?"

"I don't know." Nate shook his head and plunked

onto the couch. Exhaustion covered him like a thick blanket. The last twenty-four hours had been harrowing, and it was catching up to him like a bullet train.

Footsteps sounded behind him and he glanced back to see Michael walking into the room with two glasses of straight alcohol. He instinctively stiffened, preparing himself for battle.

"Relax," Michael muttered, "I'm not going to yell at you." Instead, he held out one of the glasses.

Nate hesitated, then took the tumbler and gave it a sniff.

"Whiskey. All the way from Scotland." Michael took a seat opposite him, sipping his drink and looking lost for words.

Nate had never seen him so vulnerable before. For the first time ever, he looked older than he was —tired, haggard…so un-Michael Richmond.

The older man started blinking, then sat forward in his seat. "I was wrong," he whispered. "I should've listened to you."

It took Nate a moment to register the apology. It was the last thing he expected and it moved him. His throat swelled with emotion and he had to swallow before he could respond. "I'm the guy who broke your daughter's heart, right?"

Michael tipped his head and let out a soft huff.

"My family is everything to me. I just want them to be happy. I want the best for them, always."

"I can understand that." Nate stared at him for a moment before taking a sip of his drink. The alcohol slid down his throat, hot and welcoming. Even so, he placed the glass on the table and rested his elbows on his knees. "Sir, I love your daughter. She's everything to me," he said, echoing the same words Michael had just used to describe his own feelings for his family. "I know I screwed up and forgot to show her that, but…I'll always love her. I just have to figure out how to balance my life. I don't want to lose her again."

"Family first," Michael murmured. "That's always been my motto."

"How? How'd you do it? You own a huge construction company."

The edge of Michael's mouth curled up and he raised his eyebrows. "It wasn't always easy. Walking away from work is really hard. I want to be involved with every aspect. It's my business. My baby. But in no way will it ever bring me as much joy as the kids and wife I have at home. So I set myself a leaving time and I walk away. I've learned to delegate, to fit work into moments that I'm not needed at home. Sure, there are busy patches, but I never let them take over. It takes strength, Nate. Sheer willpower." He pulled in a breath. "Plus, I've built a reliable team around me. People I can trust. I let them prove themselves to me, and it's paid off." His expression buckled. "At least most of the time it has." A look of self-loathing made his shoulders slump. It was obvious he was thinking about Oscar the Fake.

"Don't worry about it." Nate brushed his hand through the air. "He fooled us all."

Michael scrubbed a hand down his face. "I should've seen it. He was so damn charming all the time, and…believable. He was everything I was looking for."

"You know…" Nate cleared his throat and shuffled in his seat. "According to Sally, there's actually a man in this house who is everything you're looking for, if you'll just give him a chance to prove it."

Michael's eyebrows bunched with confusion and he pointed at Nate.

Nate snickered and shook his head. "I'm a cop through and through. Xavier, on the other hand…"

Michael sat back with a smirk. "You telling me how to run my business now?"

"No way." Nate's knee started to bob. "I am in no position to give any man advice. Although…I do appreciate yours." He glanced up and looked Michael in the eye. "Family first. It's a good motto." Nate tried to smile, but his tired face could only muster a half grin.

Michael's stare was intense and unrelenting. "I'm

sorry if I've been hard on you. I feel very protective of my sweet Sally. When you first came on the scene you were so quiet and guarded. It was hard to get to know you."

Nate gave him a tight smile, unable to voice how overwhelmed he'd felt when he first met the family. He'd come from a disjointed home where loud, happy, family discussions around the table were not a common thing. To enter the Richmond home had been an experience.

"And then you just weren't around. Sally tried to put on a brave face and stand up for you, but I could see it was hurting her. It made it hard to like you." His gaze darkened. "I don't want to see you break her heart again."

"I won't." Nate sat up straight, his gaze unflinching. "I mean, I'm not perfect, but I will never lose sight of what's important again. I can promise you that."

Michael's gaze softened with a smile, and then something over Nate's shoulder caught his attention and made the smile reach his mouth as well.

Nate spun, hoping to see Sally, but it was her mother instead.

Yvonne stood in the archway, her eyes shining with emotion. "I've put her to bed. She's exhausted. Rusty's with her, but..." She glanced at Nate. "She's asking for you. Go get some sleep, and then you can have a meal with us later."

Nate didn't need to be told twice. He stood before anyone could argue, brushing past Yvonne and taking the stairs two at a time.

He crept into Sally's room. Rusty's head shot off the bed and he let out a soft whine.

"Hey, boy." Nate patted his head, then lifted the covers and slipped in behind Sally. She was already curled up asleep, her even breathing a sonnet Nate would remember forever.

Gliding his arm around her waist, he pulled her against him, smelling her freshly washed hair and lightly kissing the bandage on her shoulder.

She let out a dreamy sigh and shifted back even farther, so they were glued together like two spoons in a cutlery drawer.

Nate had never felt such an overwhelming sense of peace.

It was over. Sally was safe. And this was the start of his second chance.

A soft smile tugged at his lips and his eyes drifted shut, his soul inhaling a full breath as he drifted off to sleep with Sally in his arms.

46

Wednesday, June 20th
7:00pm

SALLY'S HEELS clicked as she walked into Lulu's Coffee Shop. The place had already closed for the night, but Nate had something special planned. Sally smiled as she took in the tea candles flickering on every available flat surface. The darkened room was made magical in the candlelit glow.

It was a far cry from where she'd been just weeks ago, curled up in a damp room listening to the Cotton brothers fight. Jamie Cotton had been charged with kidnapping and was awaiting trial. If he was found guilty, he'd probably be put away for five to ten years. A small part of Sally hoped for a lighter sentence. She didn't fear him, because Jamie didn't seem to have a vindictive bone in his body. As scary as Sally's entire ordeal had been, August was the one who had petrified her. He'd had a darkness inside of him, no doubt born from a terrible upbringing.

Sally found out he and Jamie had been taken from their abusive mother when they were eleven years old and put into foster care. Nate couldn't give too many details, but he did say they ran away from foster care when they were fifteen and had been stealing to survive. Getting busted for armed robbery broke the brothers apart and for safety, they went their separate ways. Jamie fell in love with Mila, got his heart shattered by Vern, and had struggled to move on. According to his confession, he'd been a nomad ever since, but doing his best to live an honest life. He owed August for taking the fall, though, and couldn't turn his back on the debt.

Kellan had told Nate that Jamie fell apart in the interview room, weeping out his confession like a broken man. He'd never meant for August to end up so twisted. After leaving prison, August had remade himself, trying to hit the big-time by targeting rich women and taking on different personas to con what he could from them.

He'd done a damn good job with the Richmond

family. But he'd gone too far and would never hurt anyone again.

Sally shuddered and tried to shake the thought of his dead body from her mind. This was her special birthday dinner, Nate's chance to make up for the last one, and she didn't want the Cotton brothers spoiling it.

Laying her handbag on an empty table by the door, she walked forward to inspect the table for two.

Cutlery had been set out perfectly, and a large candle burned bright between the plates.

"Nate, this looks amazing," she called out, turning for the kitchen, expecting to find him.

Instead she found Blaine.

"Oh, hi."

"Hey." He gave her a sad smile. "Nate's been called away. He's really sorry. He wanted me to let you know that he'll be here as soon as he can."

"Oh." Sally nodded, disappointment searing her.

This was supposed to be her birthday make-up dinner. Nate had promised not to miss it, and the way he'd been acting since that harrowing incident, she didn't even think to doubt him.

He'd been sweet, attentive, leaving work when he was supposed to. He'd had one instance where he was on call and really had to go, but it was obvious how much of an effort he was making. They'd moved back in together and things were looking up. They had forward motion for the first time in a long time and Sally had never been happier.

She reminded herself of this as she cleared her throat and took a seat. "I'm sure he'll be here soon."

Blaine grinned and pulled a small present from his pocket. "He'd planned to give you this on your birthday, but then… well, you know."

She cringed.

"Anyway, he wants you to open it while you're waiting."

"Okay." She took the gift, figuring it was probably jewelry from the shape of the box. Maybe a pair of earrings. Nate had obviously tried to plan something special, but then that Schnyder case had reared its ugly head and he hadn't been able to turn away from it. She shuddered as she briefly relived their breakup fight. She never wanted to go through that again.

Blaine stepped out of the room, and she carefully untied the ribbon and opened the box. She tipped out the velvet box inside and popped the lid, her heart thrumming madly as she stared at the diamond ring inside.

An engagement ring.

Nate had intended to propose?

A soft gasp puffed between her lips and she glanced up to find Nate standing by the door, looking like a supermodel in a black tux. His polished shoes were the only sound in the room as he slowly walked toward her.

"You little liar," she teased him with a smile. "I thought you'd been called away."

He grinned and knelt down in front of her. "I'm not missing your special birthday dinner twice."

She tipped her head, fighting tears as she lifted the ring box. "You were going to propose that night?"

"Yeah, I thought that's what you wanted."

"I did," she whispered.

"But I wasn't ready. I needed to lose you to truly understand..." He brushed his fingers down the side of her face. "I'm ready now, though." Taking her hands, he gently squeezed them between his and smiled at her. "Sally, you know I love you. I haven't always been able to show it the way you deserve, but you're my heart and soul. I want to build my life with you—the good times, the bad times, all of it. I want to share everything with you, forever. So..." His lips twitched with a nervous grin. "Will you marry me?"

"Yes." She didn't even have to take a breath before the word slipped out of her mouth. The joy radiating through her was so intense she thought she might explode into a million starbursts.

Nate's smile was radiant as he slipped the ring on

her finger. She admired it for a moment before taking his face in her hands and giving him a watery smile. "I love you so much."

He cupped the back of her head and pulled her into a passionate kiss. And a loud cheer went up from the kitchen.

Jerking back in surprise, Sally looked up and laughed as her family and friends appeared in the room. Everyone was there, even Nate's father. She glanced down at her fiancé and mouthed, "Thank you," knowing how much of a sacrifice having everyone there would've been for him. He was the introvert who preferred things low-key and quiet, but he was turning their engagement into a party… for her. Wrapping her arms around his neck, she kissed him again and kept going, even when the cheers rose to a deafening volume.

Champagne flowed freely as Sally got her perfect birthday celebration with an extra cherry on top that she could only have dreamed of. She stayed by Nate's side most of the night. They danced, they ate, they celebrated.

Around midnight, Nate drove them home on his Harley. Sally's mind was already buzzing with wedding plans. She was going to have a ball arranging this thing. Knowing Nate, he'd let her have full say. All he cared about was making her his wife, and that meant more than anything.

As they slipped into their home and greeted Rusty, Nate's phone dinged with a text. He checked the call and frowned.

Sally's plans of finishing up the celebration naked in bed wilted, but she put on a brave smile anyway. She could ask Nate to re-prioritize his life, but she couldn't expect him to suddenly start compromising on his job.

"Work?" She kept her tone upbeat. Nate nodded, not looking up as he replied to the text. "Okay. Well, I guess I'll see you in the morning, then?"

He glanced her way and grinned just as his phone dinged again. Reading the text, his smile grew a little wider and he threw the phone onto the couch. "If you think I'm leaving my fiancée on the night I proposed, you're crazy."

Sally giggled and pointed at the phone. "But…"

Nate stepped into her space, sweeping her off her feet in one easy movement. "Cam's going to cover the scene right now, but she wanted to let me know that I have my work cut out for me in the morning."

Sally scrunched her nose. "You sure you don't want to go?"

"I'm sure I'd rather be here with you." He captured her mouth before she could say any more.

They kissed all the way to the bedroom and finished off their night just the way Sally wanted.

As she snuggled her naked body against Nate's and fell into a peaceful sleep, her heart was full.

Keep reading to find out about the next Aspen Falls Novel….

DEAR READER...

Dear reader,

Some characters affect me more than others. I loved Sally and Nate right from the inception of Aspen Falls and writing their story proved it even more. I felt every emotion when creating this book and I'm so glad they got the happy ending they deserved.

To me, they are the heartbeat of Aspen Falls and I'm sure they'll find a way of appearing in every Aspen Falls Novel. The next book delves into an intriguing mystery with Nate's friend, Jarrett—the tenacious reporter. He has a story to tell and Nate's favorite cop, Jessica, is going to help him.

Desperate to prove herself, Jessica will put everything on the line to help Jarrett find the truth. As the mystery unravels before them, they will soon realize that the fight is not just for themselves, but also for each other.

DIRE STRAITS is available on Amazon.

Happy reading!

xx

Melissa & Anna

www.melissapearlauthor.com